HOLLISTER

MATT BANNISTER WESTERN 16

KEN PRATT

Published in the United States by Wolfpack Publishing, Las Vegas

CKN Christian Publishing
An Imprint of Wolfpack Publishing
9850 S. Maryland Parkway, Suite A-5 #323
Las Vegas, Nevada 89183

cknchristianpublishing.com

Paperback ISBN: 978-1-63977-131-8
eBook ISBN: 978-1-63977-130-1
LCCN: 2023931504

HOLLISTER

Dedication

For my beautiful daughter, Chevelle.
I love you.

Chapter 1

The Big Z Cattle Ranch and Horse Company had made some changes in the past year that were too sudden for Charlie Ziegler's liking. He had retired for the most part and spent more time with his missus near the house rather than out doing the work. But occasionally, he saddled his gelding and rode out to help where he could and oversee the fields and herds.

Charlie had always kept the ranch small enough that he and his hired hands could do the work without being too overwhelmed and still make a decent profit. He wasn't one to spend his money foolishly and had saved enough to live comfortably in his and Mary's golden years while his interest and sole ownership of the Big Z Ranch was being turned over to his niece, Annie Lenning.

Annie's interest was not in the cattle but in horses. Annie and her brother, Adam, approached Charlie and Mary with the idea of combining the

Big Z with Adam's ranch to the north, doubling the size of the Big Z. It was now a ten-thousand-acre ranch with twice the amount of cattle and a horse company that was beginning to thrive. To meet the growing need for extra hands, they built a bunkhouse with a kitchen and hired a cook and seven cowboys to help with the two businesses. The main expense of the Big Z Ranch over the past year was invested in Annie's horse company and a large new stable across from the old original barn near the homestead. A series of corrals and chutes were built around the stable for multiple purposes, including breeding, training, and saddle breaking.

It wasn't a bad agreement between the two siblings, but the expansion of the ranch was too quick for Charlie's comfort. He had spent his life making the Big Z Ranch into what it was when he handed the ranch's management over to his nephew and niece. Now, the ranch was in debt to the bank for a sizable loan needed for the expansion that Charlie wasn't comfortable with, but so far, Annie and Adam were making the payments on time.

Charlie sat in the shade of his porch as he watched Marvin Aggler and two other cowboys return to the ranch. Adam had sent Marvin to transport a pair of bulls to the Helm's Dairy in Natoma to breed with some of their heifers. The deal put a little money in the Big Z bank account and perhaps would bring a few young steers next spring.

Marvin waved the two men towards their bunkhouse over a hill about a thousand yards away. There were too many people and buildings for

Charlie's liking, but if the bunkhouse, cookhouse, and additional barns had to be built, Charlie didn't want to see them from his porch or upstairs window. He wanted his privacy and didn't want to be bothered. He didn't mind Annie building her large stable across from Charlie's barn or the maze of chutes and corrals, as it allowed him to watch her from his porch. Many times, he had wandered over to critique her knowledge and offer suggestions while he proudly watched the nearest to a daughter he ever had.

Marvin Aggler rode past the barn and stable, past Annie's two-story house, and stopped in front of Charlie's porch. He was a rough-looking old man with a few days of whiskers on his weathered, triangular face. A wide scar deformed the left side of his upper lip and pulled it upwards, leaving him unable to close the left side of his lips. Deep wrinkles surrounded his expressive hazel eyes that revealed a friendliness and humor that didn't quite fit his rough exterior. "Charlie, do you want to ride out east with me to check the fence along the river? It's a nice day for a ride."

"Haven't you done enough riding lately?" Charlie asked while holding a glass of water.

Marvin gave a lopsided grin. "Ah, those are easy miles, and the saddle's a bit more comfortable than a rocking chair. I think you know that, though. Grab your rifle and maybe we'll find a big buck on the way."

"The fence should be fine. What else do you have in mind?"

Marvin grinned wider. "I told Adam I'd ride over and see if I can't track that wild longhorn bull he insisted on buying. You know, he spent all that money on it just to put the skull up on his house when the animal dies. I figure he just wants the horns to get bigger before he shoots it himself. It's on the other side of the fence, free ranging. It has a nasty temperament, though, so bring your rifle."

Charlie Ziegler had shaved a week's worth of whiskers that morning. His hair had turned silver over the years while his aging green eyes looked at the world with more appreciation and humor than they did when he was younger and more aggressive. He still looked meaner than a crotchety old woman with her foot caught in a wolf trap, but appearances could be deceiving.

Charlie gave a short chuckle. "At least it was his money and not the ranch's. Adam sometimes has some odd ideas, but they seem to work out for him. Yeah, Marvin, I'll ride with you. Let me tell Mary and grab my rifle. Maybe we should bring the skull back to Adam and have some steaks tonight to top it off. It might save us trouble later."

Marvin laughed. "Yeah, now you're thinking like me about that beast. These dang goats of Annie's need to be shot too, but you didn't hear me say that. I'll go saddle your horse."

***

They rode east across the ranch, enjoying the warm sunshine and the casual ride through some beautiful country. It wasn't too brushy nor had too many trees, but good grass with scattered groves of oak, alder, and a few willow trees along the creek beds, as well as some scattered pine with underbrush growing thick here and there. Rolling hills gently broke up the monotony of flat ground, and an occasional small creek watered the critters that fed on the grass. Portions of the Big Z Ranch property line were fenced with barbed wire to keep the free-roam beeves belonging to neighboring ranches from mixing in with the Big Z herd. Adam's longhorn bull had been bought from another rancher to the east, and Marvin figured that since Adam let the bull roam on free range during the spring, it would head back home forty miles away, and they wouldn't find it anywhere nearby.

"The way I see it, that debt will be paid off in full within a year or two, and then, between the horse company and ranch, this place will be prospering more than ever. Adam's got a good grasp of what he's doing and so does Annie. You've taught them both well," Marvin said after Charlie asked what Marvin thought of the business being in debt.

"I always bought cash outright and made do with what I had. I bought a new rail system for our barn last year and a hay rake. I thought that was enough, but now they got the new barns, bunkhouse, cookhouse, and wages to pay, along with a bank bill. I guess it just makes me nervous now that I'm not so involved in it. I don't want these kids to expand so fast that they can't keep up with the bills. Like anything, if you let things get too top-heavy, eventually the base can't support it."

"I understand. But it takes money to make money, and they'll be just fine. Heck, the Helms Dairy just paid a nicely inflated fee for breeding their heifers, and that could bring as many as five or six free steers."

"That's nickel and dimes compared to the twenty thousand they borrowed," Charlie answered with a hint of annoyance.

"They're expanding, Charlie. You have all this land, and now they're going to put it to use. You wanted to stay small; they have larger goals. That loan will be paid off soon enough."

A rifle shot sounded in the near distance. They stopped to listen, but nothing more was heard.

"One of the boys must've shot at something," Marvin said slowly.

"We'll find out soon enough. Are you liking the men in the bunkhouse?" Charlie asked. He had met them all but didn't take the time to get to know any of them. Marvin was the top ranch hand and approved or disapproved of any hiring. He was trusted as the top hand to control the cowboys and make sure they were doing their jobs and minding the ranch rules.

Marvin nodded. "They're a fine bunch. Tough, hardworking, and experienced cowboys, one and all."

"What about the three teenagers?"

Marvin chuckled. "Gabriel and Evan are both fine boys. Eli Barso is a bit lazy. I hear Matt almost shot him?"

Charlie nodded. "He was stupid enough to try to ambush Matt outside the McDermont Mercantile when Matt came home Christmas before last. He didn't get a chance to fire a shot, and Matt put the fear of the Lord into the boy. It wisened him up a lot, I think."

Marvin laughed with his twisted grin. "With Gabriel and Evan leaving today to go to Portland, Eli is cleaning stalls in all the barns and stables. It will keep him busy for a while."

They rode over a hill and saw Adam about fifty yards away skinning a coyote. Charlie stopped his horse and shook his head. "I've never skinned a coyote in my life, but my nephew would skin a rat if he caught one, I swear."

Adam's proud smile couldn't be unnoticed as they approached him. He offered proudly, "It was sprinting across the open here, and I hit him right in the heart from way over there, about a hundred yards or so. It was hunting a mouse when I spooked it."

"Good shot. I don't know why you're skinning it, though. You can't get much for a tick-ridden summer hide," Marvin observed.

Adam wasn't just tall, he was broad-shouldered and burly. He was a physically powerful man with large hands that worked skillfully as he skinned the coyote. His misshaped hat covered his unkempt bushy dark hair that fell below his ears while shading his brown eyes. Adam was in his early forties and had a bushy beard that was ungroomed about six inches long. He wiped a few beads of sweat from

7

his forehead. "I have a few hides to take to the tannery, but I'll make a little more with it than without it. Or Hazel might use it for something. But what I am going to do is this…" He picked up the severed head of the coyote and began skinning it carefully.

Charlie's brow lowered curiously. "What are you doing?"

"I'm going to pull the hide off the head here," Adam focused on what he was doing as he sliced the hide from the neck tissues to get a good grip on it.

Charlie said, "Just set the head on a fence post or bury it for a month if you want the skull."

"I have coyote skulls. Nope, this is for my daughter."

"Your daughter wants a skull?" Marvin asked. "They don't seem like the kind of girls that would be interested in that."

"They're not," Adam said, setting the knife down and pulling on the hide to pull it off the head. He didn't want to rip it, so he was careful to stop and use his knife when needed. "My daughter has discovered puppets since going to Lee's house. Lee's girls have puppets; my daughter uses my socks. All of my socks now have ink faces drawn on them. So, I'm going to try to make a puppet out of the coyote's face. I'm not quite sure how yet, but I'll figure it out."

Charlie grinned with a soft chuckle. "You could just buy her a puppet or two."

Marvin leaned over the saddle horn shaking his head in disbelief. "Charlie, did you hit him too hard on the head when he was young?"

8

Adam offered a quick smile at Marvin's words. "It will be better than a store-bought puppet. When it's been properly cleaned and tanned, she can hold it, cuddle, pet, and kiss it like a real dog. Better yet, it even has eye holes so she can put it over her head and wear it as a mask. And best of all, I'll be able to find my socks instead of searching in her room and around the house or outside for one."

Charlie's grin was broad. "I think we'll follow you home and see what Hazel says about that."

"I'm curious about that myself," Adam remarked as he carefully worked on cutting the hide around the nose and snout. When he finished, Adam placed the head's skin on the body's coat, rolled them up, and tied it on the saddle.

"That skin is just going to invite yellowjackets if you ride with us," Marvin stated.

"Where are you off to?" Adam asked.

"To find your longhorn. Charlie wanted steak tonight."

Adam noticed the rifle in Charlie's scabbard and did not doubt Charlie would shoot it if the ornery creature charged at him. He furrowed his brow. "I better ride with you two to keep my big fella safe. I saw bear tracks in the creek a ways back and thought I'd if I could track it. That led here."

"Not a grizzly, was it?" Marvin asked.

"No. A medium-sized black bear, I'm sure. Let's see if we can find that pretty bull of mine."

Chapter 2

They reached the Big Z Ranch property line, which was fenced off with two strands of barbed wire to keep other free-range animals off Big Z land. The fence they were checking stretched across two miles or so of rolling grassland ending at the Lower Flint River to the south, where a fifteen-foot vertical bank made it most unlikely for any critters to walk around it. The north end of the fence was built ten feet up a steep, nearly vertical hillside that rose another ninety feet. That hill stretched along the free-range land a mile or so before curling northward. It was the first of many foothills leading to the majestic Wallowa Mountains twenty miles away.

As they came to the fence line, a flock of vultures circling to the north caught their attention, and as they approached, a lone coyote trotted nervously away, and a dozen or more vultures flew into the air leaving four dead sheep that had gotten caught in the barbed wires in recent days. All four sheep were mostly eaten by predators and scavengers, leaving skeletal remains and bits of discolored wool. Another sheep, eaten to the bones, lay in the grass forty yards away on the other side of the fence.

"Sheep?" Charlie asked no one in particular. He wiped his nose as the smell of rotting flesh was so thick in the air that he could taste it. "Why are there sheep here?"

Adam also wiped his nose from the strong scent of rotting flesh. The buzzing from flies and yellow jackets swarming around the meat filled their ears. "Nathan told me a couple of weeks ago that he thought he saw a sheep to the north of here. It was just one that he got a glimpse of, so he figured it might have been a mountain goat, but it looked like a regular sheep, he said."

Charlie peered over the eastern horizon thoughtfully. "I heard there was a sheepman that moved to Hollister, but that's what…forty miles northeast of here as the crow flies?"

Adam nodded. "We better check our free-range land and make sure there aren't any more sheep." There was a wire gate they could pull open to cross in and out quickly enough. But it was much easier when herding cattle onto the free-range land to pull down and coil up the barbed wire on two separate spools and create a wide swath for the herd to cross onto the free-range grass in the late summer and fall. The herd was rounded up, brought back onto the Big Z for the winter, and kept there through calving season.

Marvin's nostrils flared. "If there are any sheep, I say we shoot every one of them. I hate sheep with a passion. I don't like goats either, but sheep, I'd like to kill every one of them."

They rode off the Big Z through the gate and watched for any signs of overgrazing. It was a known fact that sheep could kill the grass if they were allowed to graze too long on the same ground. The grass was thick and long for two miles when another flock of vultures caught their attention. They rode closer to investigate, and Adam's prized longhorn bull was rotting on the ground. Someone had killed it about a week before and left it for the scavengers. The only parts taken were the head with the horns, probably the heart, and by the knife cuts on the rotting hide, a chunk of meat from the rump just below the Big Z brand.

"Someone killed my longhorn and stole my horns," Adam complained.

"The grass is eaten down pretty good on that hillside over there." Marvin acknowledged with a pointed finger.

Adam peered at a distant hillside with anger burning in his eyes. "Let's go."

Forty-five minutes later, they found a large flock of sheep, perhaps a thousand to fifteen-hundred strong, gently grazing on a flat piece of ground that bordered the Lower Flint River. The white wool of so many sheep was an odd sight to see in cattle country. It was not a welcomed sight to any of the three men on horseback.

"I say we shoot every darn one of them," Marvin said, pulling his rifle out of the scabbard.

Charlie held out his hand to stop Marvin from shooting any sheep. "Hold on. Let's talk to the shepherd before we do anything."

The shepherd's covered wagon with a stove pipe coming out of the canvas top was camped on the other side of the flock. The shepherd's two dogs barked, warning the shepherd of the three strangers as they rode slowly through the flock of bleating sheep. The shepherd sat on a foldable canvas stool near a burned-out fire pit, nervously watching the men with his rifle leaning against the wagon. The man stood and spoke to his two dogs in a foreign language, and immediately, the barking ceased, and the two dogs returned to his sides.

"Hello," the shepherd called out with a heavily accented voice. He was brown-skinned with black hair that covered his ears. He was middle-aged and wore a wide-brimmed weathered hat that covered his head, loose-fitting cotton pants, and a cotton button-up shirt. He was barefoot while his boots were set next to his chair. A stringy mustache and beard covered his face. "Welcome, me friends."

Marvin Aggler answered roughly, "I don't know about that. You butchered our bull over there."

The man nodded shamefully. "Si, it was me. Yes."

Charlie had more significant concerns. "Who do these sheep belong to?"

"I work for Mister Fairchild. My name is Sixtos Pizarro. Please, come join me." His accent was heavy but perfectly understandable. His friendly countenance made him a likable man almost instantly.

"Mister Fairchild?" Charlie asked, "Does he have a first name, and where can we find him?" He wasn't being unfriendly, but his natural sternness was made clear.

"His name is Robert. Do you want to sit?" Sixtos waved toward the ground beside his fire from the night before. "I can make some coffee. It will only take a few minutes."

Charlie shook his head. "No. I want to know where I can find Mister Fairchild."

"He lives in Hollister."

Adam pointed at a cleaned and washed longhorn skull with wide horns hanging from four wires on the wagon's side. "That's my bull! Why did you kill my bull?"

"My apologies. The bull attacked my flock twice and spread them in every way. I found most of them. I did not want to kill your bull because he was quite beautiful, but I had no choice. I was hunting for a rabbit or a deer to eat, for all I have is oats and mush. I saw no deer, but your bull charged and left me no choice. I apologize for shooting your property. But I could not risk it injuring my horse."

"Apologizing isn't going to pay for it. Mind if I take my skull?" Adam asked, stepping out of the saddle.

"No. Please. I am sorry for shooting your property, but I had no choice," he repeated uneasily.

"I have a hard time believing that..." Adam said as he unwired the skull from the wagon. The bullet hole was square in the center of the head. "You said it was charging you?"

"Yes. I would not want to kill so large an animal for a day's meal. It was only done to protect myself. My apologies."

Adam moved the coyote skin to the front saddle strings and tied the wide horns behind the cantle.

Marvin watched Adam and suggested, "You should kill a sheep and take a sheep's head home too. That way, your kiddo can play along with nature's way of the coyote killing a lamb."

"Please, don't," Sixtos said quickly. "We moved this way to keep these sheep alive. The ranchers there do not like us and have killed many sheep. It's my job and responsibility to keep them safe."

Charlie answered with a heavy sigh, "We won't kill your sheep, but this our land, and we graze cattle here starting next month. So, do yourself a favor, keep these animals moving east, and don't come back here." He spoke to Adam, "We need to go to Hollister and talk to Mister Fairchild about where to graze his sheep. I say we go home, get some supplies and leave for Hollister in the morning. We can cut across the valley and camp out until we reach Cold Water and take the road from there."

Sixtos pointed east. "My friend Manuel Ayala has a flock of the same size that way, and north you will find the brothers Jorge and Mateo Menza with a much larger flock. Let them know you come in peace if you come across either of those flocks. There has been much trouble, and the brothers have been beaten and are afraid of cowboys. Mister

Fairchild protects his home and family, but we have been chased far from any towns."

Charlie answered, "I don't have a fight with you, but I might if you don't keep this flock moving off my cattle's feeding grounds. Go seven miles that way and keep going. Good day, sir."

"May I ask your names?" Sixtos asked.

"I'm Charlie Ziegler. That's my nephew, Adam Bannister. We own the Big Z Ranch a few miles that way, and this is our foreman, Marvin Aggler. I don't want to sound unneighborly, but those animals will ruin this land."

"I will move them further along to save any trouble."

"I appreciate it. Seven miles at least."

Adam said, "We got dead sheep in our fence. Are you missing some?"

Sixtos nodded. "Your bull attacked the sheep twice, charging through the flock and scattering them. Coyotes are always waiting to grab a lamb, but three wolves have attacked the flock and scattered them a few times. My dogs help, but they are still young and learning. I am the only shepherd and rounded up what I can find."

Marvin couldn't care less. "As far as I'm concerned, the wolves can have them."

Chapter 3

Tad Sperry was angry. His home, his life, had been changed overnight by the appearance of a woman that tore his family apart. Audrey Butler had agreed to marry his uncle Alan but betrayed him for his uncle Morton. The rip down the Sperry home led to the violent deaths of his beloved Aunt Daisy, whom he had grown up with as she was only seven years older than him. And the cold-blooded murder of his favorite uncle, Alan. His uncle Morton moved out of the family home to be with Audrey in Branson, leaving them all behind to carry the burden of the losses.

To make matters just a bit worse, his uncle Henry and aunt Bernice were looking for somewhere else to live and saving their money, which left very little for anyone else. Tad's mother, Jannie, had not quit drinking since the death of Daisy, and his grandmother had aged another ten years and spoke very little in her depths of sorrow. His uncle Vince had become responsible for providing for the family and worked at their uncle Gerry's dairy, cleaning stalls and milking cows. Tad could no longer spend his days frolicking in town with his pals or hoping to get a good word in with any town girls. He was now working with his uncle Vince and the other members of the Sperry-Helms Gang at the dairy. His younger brother Travis had taken Morton's position working with Henry at the tannery. Henry and Bernice had taken custody of Daisy's three children, putting more pressure on Henry to provide for his expanding family. It wasn't the home Tad once knew, and he despised the woman responsible for it and his uncle Morton for betraying the family for a woman.

Gerry Helms was not easy to please nor an easy man to deal with, but he did peer at the bulls delivered from the Big Z Ranch with satisfaction. He had a mix of breeds on his dairy, and the two stout bulls were of good quality for his combination of heifers. He had agreed to the siring fee along with giving any bull calves born to Adam which would become steers. In Gerry's experience, heifers were much more common than bulls during calving season, but if by chance there were more bulls born, it wouldn't hurt Adam Bannister any not to know about one or two that stayed on the dairy to sell or to breed future stock.

"Tad," Gerry said, "I'm not paying you to stand here and gawk. The pig pens need to be cleaned, then feed and water them beasts. After that, you can go home."

"I'll do that. How many cows do you think Mister Ziegler has, Uncle Gerry?"

"I don't know, a couple thousand maybe. They've gotten bigger since Adam partnered with them. You better get a move on; the day's getting late."

Tad walked to the pig barn, a medium-sized single-level building with eight pig pens with a few hogs per pen, except for the large boar at the end. He used a square-tipped shovel to scoop out the manure and toss it in a wheelbarrow to haul outside to the manure pile, which they would spread over the fields and garden in the late fall. When the day's work was done, he found his uncle Vince speaking with their cousin Jesse Helms and gang member Cass Travers.

Cass was speaking, "I believe I'm moving on at the end of this week, fellas. I don't know what I'm going to do, but since Morton's left the gang and Alan's gone, this deal is done. I'll collect my pay from your pa on Friday and leave. You should ride with me, Jesse. This dairy isn't for you, either. I know that much."

Jesse Helms leaned against the dairy barn and shook his head slowly. He was average height and stocky with a powerful frame. He had brown hair that was kept cut close to his head and a goatee that he let grow four inches long. Jesse had a square-shaped face with blue eyes that were gentle with family and friends, but could turn cold as steel in a freezing rain storm at a moments notice with his quick temper. "I don't know if I can. My folks are getting older, and there's always work to do."

Cass scoffed with disgust. "Bull! Your pa has plenty of help. Jesse, this place will kill your spirit if you don't leave here and find another gang to team up with. You and I can rob the Loveland bank together and ride into Idaho until we find a few fellas to join us and start the Travers-Helms Gang or something because you know the Sperry-Helms Gang is history."

"That ain't true," Tad argued. "I've been thinking about it since they brought the bulls over. We could steal some cattle from the Big Z Ranch and they'd never know. We could sell them or butcher them for meat and sell the hides."

Jesse ignored him.

Cass narrowed his eyes irritably. "Why don't you go start your own little gang and do just that? It sounds great. Be sure to cut the brand off the hide before you try to sell it. In the meantime, why don't you go play with the other kids and get away from me."

"I'm no kid," Tad said harshly. "I'll join up with you when you leave. It's better than shoveling manure."

Cass had no interest. "I said go away from me."

Jesse answered Cass. "Let me think about it. My mother is not so well, and I'd hate to be gone if she gets worse. But you're right; I do miss the excitement."

Vince Sperry said, "I can't join you. My family doesn't have anyone if it isn't me."

Cass scowled. "Vince, I didn't ask you to join me. I wouldn't ride with you or your idiot nephew again for any price."

"I'm no idiot!" Tad exclaimed, offended. "I can prove myself on any day against you or anyone."

Cass grinned, slightly amused. "Well, you do that. Go start yourself a gang and prove to me that you're something more than a whining kid. You and Vince are both idiots, and I don't know why you're standing here. I have no interest in talking to either one of you."

Vince expected Jesse to speak up for him, but Jesse immediately looked away. Taking the hint for what it was, Vince said to Tad, "Let's go home."

Vince was deep in thought as he and Tad walked home slowly. He had lost four siblings in the past week, and his heart hurt more than it had ever ached before. He doubted he would ever get over the loss of his younger sister, Daisy, as that was the most painful. Alan was a terrible loss, as they had made plans together, but those plans were now in Vince's mind to bring to completion. While Daisy and Alan lay in the freshly dug graves of the cemetery, Morton was in Branson, starting a new life, as was the youngest Sperry brother, Jack. Without his siblings, Vince felt alone. Vince and Henry didn't have much of a relationship ever since Henry married his red-headed viper of a wife, Bernice.

Vince tapped Tad's arm and waved towards the two bulls in a pen. "Tomorrow, we'll catch one of those bulls and measure the brand. I'm pretty sure I can design a branding iron to change it. I don't think they'd catch us if we took a few beeves, changed the brand, and sold them at the market.

We would just have to make sure it covers the Big Z brand. I'll design something tonight, get the measurements tomorrow and see if Steven Bannister can make us a branding iron."

Tad scowled. "He'll know what it's for. You can't use him."

"No. He won't know. It will be our brand with a big Z contained in it, but it won't be recognizable. You'll see. We could do it and get away with it."

"Then I say we do it and make some money," Tad offered.

***

"Grandma, we're home," Tad shouted as he and Vince entered through the door. "Where is Grandma?" he asked Bernice as she made dinner.

"Where she has been all day, lying-in bed, crying."

"Hmm," Tad said sadly. He walked down the hall and knocked on her bedroom door. He opened it and stepped inside. The window was open, but the curtain was closed, leaving the room dark, stuffy, and smelling of stale feet and body odor. "Grandma, you have to open the curtain and let some sunshine in. It will make you feel better."

"Go away," Mattie Sperry said with a sniffle. Her heart was broken far beyond the ability of the sunshine to repair.

"I got some good news. Uncle Vince and I are going to start our own gang. The Sperry Gang, and we're going to be even better than what the Sperry-Helms Gang was. Smarter too." He sat on the edge of her bed.

Mattie Helms lay on her side facing away from him while another tear fell to the pillow below her head. She did not bother to look at her grandson. Mattie had not eaten with her family or left her room except to empty her chamber pot once a day. She wanted to be alone to mourn the overwhelming losses of her two children. "I told you to go away."

"Grandma, you can't stay in here forever. I'm sad too, but they're gone, and we have to move on. Uncle Alan wouldn't want you to lay in here like this. He'd say Ma, get your butt out of bed and make some food because Bernice is too heavy on the vegetables and not enough meat."

She exhaled emotionally and sniffled. "No," she said softly. "Alan would say go kill that woman that betrayed him and his former brother." Her voice quivered, "And I would."

"Vince and I will do that, Grandma. Uncle Morton's a lawman now. That makes him an enemy."

She turned her head to look at her grandson with penetrating eyes. "Then do it!" she snarled.

Tad slowly smiled. Her tone was strong and defiant like it used to be, and the anger in her eyes burned with venom. "I will, Grandma. I promise you; I will bring justice for Daisy and Uncle Alan. Let me round up a gang, and we'll do just that. In the meantime, open your curtains at least."

Mattie placed a hand on his affectionately. "You're a good boy, Tad. But you're becoming a man now. I want you to kill that woman, but I want you to make her suffer before you do. If you do that for me, I'll give you this property in my will. I want her to suffer, Tad. And Morton too."

"I'll take care of it. It might take some time, but I'll take care of it." He stood and slid her curtains open to allow the bright sunlight inside the dark room. "You still have family left, Grandma. Get up and enjoy them."

***

Elliot Zook had taken a wagon load of cheese and butter into Branson for the stores to sell the day before and returned to Natoma with a load of grain bags for the dairy. Milk, by nature, soured too fast to deliver over long distances in the summer sun. To preserve the milk, they needed to make products that last to earn a living. The Helms Dairy delivered fresh milk to homes and the store in Natoma every day, but they also had a cream and butter room where butter was made and a cheese room on the other side of the wall where they made cheese.

Elliot wasn't surprised to hear Cass say he wanted-ed to leave Natoma, as he'd been talking about it for a while. Elliot was sitting in Avery's Saloon with Cass and Jesse having a drink. He knocked on the table to get their attention, "I went to the Green Toad Saloon last night while I was in Branson and ran across your cousin Jack Sperry and his friends. His pal Bruce Ellison was there with his uncle Wes

Wasson. You remember the man who killed the Indian a while back?"

Jesse corrected him. "I don't know him, but Bruce's father killed Chusi from what I heard. Wes was lucky to be alive by the time Chusi got done with him."

"Doesn't matter," Elliot said. "The point is Wes is now a Blackburn Marshal working up in Hollister for some rich man. He said it was the easiest work he's ever done and making more money than he ever has for less work."

"What's he doing?"

"Protecting the rich man and his property. That's all I know."

Jesse narrowed his eyes. "It was the Blackburn Marshals that shot some of the miners during the mine strike. They shot at my cousin Mark. Mark shot their leader, Blackburn, and he died later. I don't know that I'd want to work for such men after they warred with my cousin."

Cass Travers was of average height and build. He had shoulder-length straight brown hair and long sideburns that reached his lower jaw to cover a large mole on the side of his right cheek. He had a triangular face with three light scars that looked like claw marks coming down his left cheek. He was a rough man, and the years of rough living showed in his cold brown eyes.

Cass wrinkled his nose. "Jesse, your cousin killed his brother. Actually, two of your cousins killed their brother. Alan would have died from an infection from the pitchfork Henry drove through him. You can't take pig and cow manure, run it through a man's guts, and expect him to live. You can blame Morton if you want, but the way I see it, he was doing Alan a favor."

Elliot responded, "Whether that was his intention or not, Morton's now a deputy U.S. marshal and riding with Matt Bannister. I wouldn't welcome him back into your life anytime soon."

"Morton's my cousin nonetheless." Jesse took a drink and rapped his finger on the table. "Nothing is the same anymore. Even my family is changing. My mother is sickly, and Pa's getting weaker, but he won't say so."

Elliot spoke pointedly to Cass, "You and I should ride over to Hollister and see if we can get a job with the Blackburn Marshals. There is nothing here to keep us anymore unless you want Vince to lead the gang." He laughed.

"What do they do? Just stand around and protect a rich man?" Cass asked.

Elliot shrugged. "I guess they do whatever they are hired to do. Here's the way I see it. If we could work for them for a few months, learn the ropes, and start our own gang of marshals or whatever we called ourselves. We could protect rich people and make a good living doing that instead of robbing people and running for our lives."

Jesse's attention went to Elliot as he nodded in agreement. "That is a good idea. I'd be up for that."

"Would you?" Cass asked his friend.

"If we could start a legitimate business like that, yeah."

Cass finished his drink. "I say we cut our ties here, ride to Hollister, and meet up with Wes Wasson. I met him once or twice while at the Green Toad Saloon. He's not a bad man."

Chapter 4

Jorge Menza enjoyed sitting beside the small fire outside the sheep wagon under a clear sky filled with stars. Unfortunately, the wind changed, and the eastern breeze brought a hazy smoke from a distant forest fire that filled the sky with a brownish-yellow color, and the smell of woodsmoke filled the valley. The smoke was high in the atmosphere indicating to Jorge that he did not need to be concerned about moving the sheep as the fire appeared to be far to the east. The smoke created a magnificent red sunset that he and his younger brother Mateo found beautiful. However, as darkness fell, the moon not only seemed more prominent than usual, but it was also blood red and gave a red tint to the darkness of the night. The explanation for the red moon was simple enough, the moonlight was cutting through an atmosphere filled with heavy smoke, but it still sent an eerie chill down Jorge's spine. It was too quiet. The usual singing of the millions of crickets in the prairie grass seemed to have taken the night off. His throat itched and was sore from breathing the smoke, and his brother's throat felt the same as well. Their eyes burned, and they repeatedly blinked to add moisture to their eyes. If the smoke bothered them as much as it did, then it was reasonable to think the heavy scent of smoke had something to do with the crickets remaining silent as well. They would have taken what little shelter the covered wagon may have offered from the smoke, but the two thousand sheep they watched over were restless too. It was an odd night that just didn't feel right.

His younger brother Mateo had been riding his horse around the flock with his sheepdog to protect the lambs born weeks before from the ravenous coyotes and wolves that were always looking for easy prey. A young mountain lion had been spotted roaming nearby the night before and was chased away by the three sheepdogs. For a predator, there wasn't a more leisurely meal than a young lamb, but that is why Jorge and Mateo were there.

From the beginning of creation, sheep had a shepherd to watch over them. The first shepherd was Abel, the son of Adam and Eve. Shepherding is the oldest profession known in the world and one that is still needed across the globe. Abel, Abraham, Jacob, Joseph and his brothers, Moses and even King David, were shepherds over a flock of sheep. It was an admirable profession shared by some of the Bible's most important characters, and even Jesus, the Lord of all, called himself the

Good Shepherd. All were dedicated to caring for the sheep and keeping them safe because sheep are the only animal God created that would not exist without man's protection and care. Sheep have no natural defenses except to run blindly and will run off a cliff to their death in their panic. Unlike other herd animals that stay together, sheep scatter and isolate themselves to become easy prey. Easily startled, nervous, and not commonly known as intelligent creatures, they can be a handful to care for. It makes sense why Jesus called himself the Good Shepherd and used the profession as a loving analogy for his relationship with his followers. The sheep follow the shepherd because they trust him. And a good shepherd knows his flock and watches over them while he cares for their needs. Jesus does the same thing.

Mateo rode his horse into camp and looked at his brother in the fire's light. He pointed at the red, nearly full moon. His unease was clear to see. "I don't like it. It's too quiet, and not even a coyote can be heard. I think it is a bad omen," he said in his native tongue. He looked across the wide-open range of grass and rolling hills, lit with a slight reddish tint of moonlight. "I can't see any flames in the distance, but something isn't right. Not even the crickets are singing, and I haven't been pestered by a mosquito either. The water hole should be full of them."

"It's the smoke," Jorge replied. "Maybe the red moon and smoke bother the insects too. I don't know, but it's fine. I'm going to sleep soon, so if you have any trouble, let me know."

"I miss home. I miss Maria." Mateo was eighteen years old and homesick for their parents and siblings. Their father owned a large sheep farm where the two boys learned their trade. Jorge was a single, twenty-five-year-old young man who was perfectly content in America, but Mateo had a love interest back in Peru who had promised to wait for his return. He promised to return after one year and marry the young lady, but the more he missed her, the more he wanted to go home.

"Think of the money instead of Maria. There are a thousand other Marias in the world. You don't have to marry the first one that you meet."

The sheep were bedded for the night in a wide, relatively flat area not far from a stream that supplied a shallow pond before continuing across the fertile ground. Two of their well-trained and alert dogs wandered along with Mateo and the sheep, while the third, Jorge's black and white-faced shepherd named Keelo, rested beside him by the fire.

Mateo ignored his brother's comment about Maria. "I wonder where the fire is?"

Jorge shrugged. "I think way off. But keep your eye out for any flames in the distance. I'll see you in the morning." Jorge entered the covered wagon and lay on his bed. The wagon was no different than any other prairie schooner, except it had a thin mattress on the floor and a bench seat on each side, with a small cookstove bolted to the floor with the stove pipe exiting out the side of the canvas top. It wasn't too comfortable and was crowded, but it served its purpose better than sleeping in a tent and trying to make a fire to cook in stormy weather. Robert Fairchild had bought the wagons and had them customized to meet the shepherd's needs as they would be out in the wild for months. Once a month, supplies were brought to them from other employees of Mister Fairchild to restock their food and other supplies. It would be hard for the supply wagon to locate the different flocks, but he carried a map with a general area where he should find the three flocks. It was a lonely life; for the Menza brothers, it would have been much lonelier without the other. Jorge settled in to sleep and would wake before sunrise to relieve Mateo of his duties and allow Mateo to get some sleep. They had already decided that in the morning, they would move the sheep a mile south along the creek for new ground before Mateo went to bed.

An hour later, Jorge sat up abruptly at the sound of his dog barking and the unmistakable sound of guns firing repeatedly. It wasn't Mateo shooting at a coyote with a shot or two, but a dozen or more guns blazing away consistently like two enemies at battle in the middle of two-thousand panic-stricken sheep bleating in terror and blindly scattering in every direction. Shouts of American voices, thundering hooves of many horses, guns blazing, dogs yipping, and then Mateo's screaming added to the chaos erupting around the wagon. Frightened, Jorge grabbed his rifle and ran out of the wagon barefoot. He froze when he saw three men pull their horses to a sudden stop and point their weapons at him. The men wore long black dusters and burlap bags over their heads to hide their faces. He couldn't understand their language, but the harshness of their tone was understood. Jorge dropped his rifle and raised his hands.

His heartbeat pounded in his chest hard enough that the drumming of his heart became louder than the gunshots that massacred the sheep. His dog barked fearlessly at the strangers. "Keelo, no! Quiet! Sit!" he ordered his dog urgently.

One of the men on horseback aimed his revolver and shot Keelo in the head, killing Jorge's prized sheepdog that he had trained since it was a pup back in Peru.

Jorge gasped and nearly fell to his knees with the loss of his beloved dog. Yet, Keelo was more than a dog; she was his best friend.

Another rider on horseback dragged Mateo, lassoed by the feet, across the ground to the wagon. Mateo was skinned up from the ground but not seriously harmed. He was freed from the rope, yanked to his feet, and pushed over beside his brother.

The shooting continued as thirty-some men rode and executed every sheep they could find. Some fired guns, and others rode the sheep down, bashing their heads with wooden clubs. The sheep had scattered, and the prairie grass was filled with dead sheep and men chasing the terrified creatures until they were dead. The sound of excited yells of sheer exhilaration and laughter filled the prairie in all directions.

"Do you boys speak English?" a man asked

harshly as he dismounted his horse. Their faces were covered with burlap bags with eye holes cut into them, but their voices revealed no remorse or compassion for the sheepherders. "Huh?" he shouted as he shoved Jorge.

Jorge's eyes watered as he watched the sheep running for their lives. Even the newborn lambs were executed. He watched a man swing a wooden club and break a bleating lamb's head open with a single crack of the club. The man beat the lamb repeatedly until the club was covered with blood. Laughing, the man joined the others at the campfire.

Jorge shook his head with a combination of terror and horror at what he was witnessing. Jorge and Mateo had been attacked and beaten once before by the same men, but they never expected the men to bother them again now that they were a long way from Hollister. He knew they were going to be beaten again. His voice cracked emotionally, "No hablo ingles."

"I thought not," the man who shot Keelo said. "These Mexicans don't speak English, just like the last one. We can't talk to them, so beat the hell out of them. Don't kill them like you did the last shepherd. Just make him hurt and burn that wagon. I'm going to kill some woolies." He rode off towards the continuous shooting, which had spread out in all directions.

The man who clubbed the lamb carried the bloody wooden club forward and cracked the side of Jorge's head with a powerful blow. Jorge fell to the ground unconscious. Not finished, the man swung the club across Jorge's kneecap with a powerful impact.

Mateo watched his brother fall and began to hyperventilate in the bad air with the terror of fearing his brother was dead. "Jorge! Leave my brother alone!" he screamed in his native tongue to stop the man from hurting his brother. Mateo was quickly grabbed by two other men and slammed against the wagon wheel. The men weaved his arms forcefully over the steel rim and yanked his elbows up between the spokes to hold him there while another cowboy with his face covered by burlap and wearing leather gloves hit Mateo's jaw with a hard jarring right fist. A large man dressed exactly the same as the others stepped in front of him and hit Mateo three more times before tearing the front of Mateo's shirt open. He turned to another man with a branding iron heating in the campfire's red coals. "He's ready when you are."

Mateo shook his head to regain his senses. He could taste blood in his mouth and knew his nose was bleeding too, but he felt no pain as his adrenaline was high. He stared at Jorge and called out with a growing terror that his brother was dead. Everywhere he looked, there was chaos between the sheep, the strangers that looked like ghosts in the red moonlight, and his brother Jorge lying unconscious and unmoving while bleeding severely from a head wound on the ground. It was a nightmare that seemed too unreal to really be happening to him and Jorge. Mateo's nightmare increased significantly, and his eyes widened in horror unlike any he'd ever known when he saw a man carrying a red-hot branding iron toward him. With Mateo's arms locked around the wagon wheel, he could do little but kick and struggle to break free, but it did little good.

Mateo screamed in agony before the red-hot branding iron touched his soft skin, but the tone of his screams changed into a high-pitched cry as the branding iron was pressed into his flesh and held there to burn deeper. The sizzling sound, scent, and excruciating pain were more than he could endure, and he fainted. The men let him drop to the ground.

"Stand the other one up and let's brand him too," the one holding the branding iron said as he put the brand back into the fire's coals.

The man holding a bloody club chuckled. "He can't stand; I think I broke his knee pretty good. I was told not to kill him but to hurt him. I'm just following orders." He kicked the unconscious Jorge onto his back and ripped his shirt off. "You can brand him on the ground just like a heifer."

Mateo's eyes opened, and he realized he was lying face down on the grass. All he could do was watch the men lower the branding iron to Jorge's chest and weep helplessly.

"If we can't kill them, let's at least make it so they can't walk out of here. We'll let the wolves and heat kill them. You broke that one's knee; let's burn this one's feet. Yank those boots off that Mexican and let's stand him in the fire. Get those coals exposed.

Let's fry some feet."

An hour later, Jorge opened his eyes, saw the flickering of firelight, and heard the sound of wood burning. The wagon had been pulled into the pond and set on fire where the flames wouldn't catch the grass on fire. Jorge realized his head was resting on a saddle blanket. His brother Mateo was beside him weeping.

"Mateo, are you hurt?" Jorge's head ached severely. He was dizzy and found it hard to move his head.

Mateo's voice quivered painfully. "They branded my chest and burned my feet. I can't walk. My feet are blisters." He began to sob from the pain.

Jorge tried to lift himself, but it was no good. He collapsed back down. "My head hurts. My chest burns." He again passed out.

"Jorge? Jorge?" Mateo looked upwards at the reddened sky full of smoke. "Lord, keep my brother safe. I will crawl if I must, but please, keep him alive and safe. Help us, Lord. I've never hurt so much. Help me, Jesus."

***

Two days later, Charlie Ziegler, Adam Bannister, Marvin Aggler, and Nathan Pierce rode over a knoll and stopped as the sight before them was as gruesome as any they had seen in a long time. A wide swath of grass was covered with the white and red stained wool lumps of hundreds of dead sheep. Some were half-eaten by vultures by the dozens, as well as coyotes and other scavengers making an easy meal of the slaughter. They rode through the sheep, covering their noses as the scent of decaying flesh was strong in the hot sun. Across a wide flat area of grass littered with dead sheep was the frame of a burned wagon in the middle of a pond. The woodstove remained on a single beam between the axel. Sitting forty yards uphill was a man with his head wrapped in a blue shirt. He was propped against a dead horse twenty yards from where a campfire once was. The man's head hung down as he had no protection from the sun except a torn, bloody shirt draped over his shoulders. He appeared lifeless.

They kicked their horses to a gallop and Nathan hopped out of the saddle to approach the man. He knelt and felt the man's neck for a pulse. "He's alive!"

Jorge lifted his throbbing head slightly. His face was covered with dried blood. He whispered through his dry mouth, "Agua..." He tried to lift his empty canteen but was too weak to do so.

Adam knelt on the other side of him with his canteen and put it to Jorge's chapped and dry lips. Jorge had not had more than a few drinks in two hot days and nights sitting there. Mateo had gone for help, but he crawled as the men had taken their boots and socks and thrown them in the fire after burning Mateo's feet. Jorge drank slowly as the water eased his parched mouth and throat. He drank more and could feel his strength growing slowly with each swallow of the lifesaving water.

Charlie looked around and said, "This must be

the other sheepherder Sixtos was telling us about. We need to get him to town. Do you think he has the strength to ride?"

"Not upright," Adam stated. He had removed the shirt wrapped around Jorge's head and looked at the wound. His face was covered with dry blood, and his right knee was swollen so much it was tight against his pants. "He can't walk, and he can't ride like this. If we can find a couple of poles, we can make him a travois and haul him to town. His boss will want to know what happened out here."

"Whoever did this killed his dogs and horses. Marvin, let's see if we can't find a tree or something to make poles with," Charlie stated.

Marvin had been watching the ground for tracks and trying to estimate how many dead sheep there were. "I'd say there's over seven hundred dead sheep."

"Charlie! You better come look at this." Nathan shouted, pulling the shirt back, exposing a fresh brand of burnt flesh in the center of the man's chest. It was a sheep-shaped brand of about four square inches filled with multiple coils to indicate wool.

Charlie narrowed his eyes, repulsed. "Good lord."

Adam gasped at the horror of it. "It must be meant to mark the shepherds as woolies."

Marvin nodded towards the pond. "Sheep smell up the water and cattle won't drink it. My guess is some cowboys saw them here, rounded up their pals, and took care of the problem."

Charlie rubbed his face irritably. "That's not

how we take care of problems. Let's find a tree and see if we can't break some branches for a travois and get this man some help."

Jorge tried to speak to the men, but they did not understand Spanish and were about as lost for communicating with him as he was with them. The best Jorge could do was point north and indicate *that way*.

An hour later, they had Jorge lying on a travois, pulling him northeast. He didn't feel like talking and couldn't get them to understand that his brother Mateo had crawled away for help the morning after they were attacked. Mateo was in bad shape too, but he could crawl. Jorge couldn't even do that. His head ached, and he got too dizzy and vomited if he tried to stand.

They had traveled a rough ten miles when they spotted the first sign of human life. To the west was a covered wagon with a few riders on horseback who had taken notice of them and approached.

"Howdy-do?" the man called as he got closer. "It looks like you have an injured man. It might be the man we're looking for. Sheepherder?"

"That he is," Charlie hollered as the man rode over.

"Charlie, is that you?"

"It is. Martin, it's been a long time. How are you?" he asked, riding forward to meet his old pal. They shook hands with a friendly greeting.

"I'm still kicking. How's that beautiful lady of yours?"

"She's well. Yours?"

"Still feisty," Martin said. "We had a Mexican crawl onto our property this morning, and when he woke up, he kept saying, *Mi Hermano*, which apparently means my brother, according to one of our cowboys from Texas who knows that language. Me and the boys decided we better come looking for another man. Our Mexican has been branded. Yours?"

Charlie nodded. "A sheep brand in the center of his chest. His head has been hit pretty hard, and his knee is swollen twice the size of the other. Whoever did it killed maybe seven hundred sheep from what we had seen and their horses and dogs before burning their wagon."

Martin Pollard owned the Pollard-Lee Ranch on the southeast side of Cold Water. "Let me call my boys over, and we'll put him in the wagon and get him out of the sun. I figure they work for Fairchild. He wants to make this sheep country, and it isn't going well. Let me call the boys." He pulled his revolver and fired into the ground.

"I suppose you and the others have tried talking to Fairchild?" Charlie asked.

Martin nodded. "He hired a bunch of gunmen to protect himself but doesn't offer that protection to his Mexicans watching the sheep. These boys are lucky to be alive. I heard the sheep shooters killed one of Fairchild's Mexicans recently. He moved his sheep further south, but it's still free-range country with good grass and water."

"They were camped at a waterhole about ten miles back."

Martin exhaled with a sense of wonder. "That's a long way for a man to crawl. The kid we found had the bottoms of his feet burned. He can't walk."

Charlie was disturbed. "Who did it? Any idea?"

Martin nodded. "Yeah. A collection of cowboys from various ranches that call themselves the Hollister Sheep Shooters. No one knows who they are because they ride at night and wear black dusters and hoods. I have not heard one word about them or who they may be, but I have a good idea of a few men who probably are involved. Either way, Sheriff Emerson doesn't seem too interested, and now the U.S. Marshal is investigating it. He won't find much because no one is talking. Not even to me, and I live here."

"You're not involved, are you?" Charlie asked.

"You know better than that. None of my sons or employees better be involved in something like that. If you came to the Hollister Cattlemen's Association meetings like you're supposed to, you'd be in the know about all this stuff."

"When they change the name to the Jessup County Cattle Association, I will. We all don't live in Hollister. Does the cattle association support this kind of crap?"

Martin shook his head. "Not officially. But you know how Gunther and the others are. You can bet they support it if not involved in it. Come to a meeting sometime."

"I go to the yearly meeting, but I don't need to attend every monthly or bi-weekly meeting you all decide to have. It's a half-hour of business and six hours of socializing and drinking. I don't have time for that."

"I know. But recently, it's been pretty important. We'll all suffer the consequences if the sheep kill the grass out here. And you know sheep will. I don't believe in violence or ruining another man's livelihood, but it's getting to the point that Fairchild doesn't care about ours. He's a rich man, Charlie. He bought the land around Gibbons Lake and built a large homestead there. That used to be public land where we'd graze and water freely, but now it's all private property. He wants to build a woolen mill in Hollister and change this from cattle country to sheep country. He has already bought out Smith's ninety-acre farm. Now he's pressing others to sell to him."

"Sounds like a fight brewing, but he's a long way from Willow Falls."

Adam spoke, "His sheep were caught in our fence. And that sheepman was on our grazing land. I guess they're not too far from Willow Falls."

"Adam, how are you?" Martin asked with a shake of his hand.

"I'm well, sir."

"You should be coming to those meetings too."

"I might start, depending on what happens on this trip. We're going to talk to Fairchild and get some of this cleared up."

Martin grinned. "I wish you luck. As I said, he surrounded himself with hired guns, and they aren't afraid of trouble. Now those old cowboys over in Hollister ain't afraid of much either, so if they pick a fight with Fairchild's men, it will turn into a bloody feud, and no one wants that. We all have family working for us, and Fairchild doesn't have family, just hired men."

"You said Matt was investigating a shepherd's death?" Charlie asked.

"Not Matt. One of his deputies, Truet. He's been around here several times but never seems to settle anything. Personally, I want to graze my beeves on good grass and clean water and be left alone. I don't want no part of a war or my sons involved in it."

Chapter 5

Matt Bannister sat in a comfortable armchair holding a saucer and matching cup as he sipped the coffee. It was a foreign brand from Peru that tasted much better than the basic Arbuckle's coffee that was commonly brewed. He was in Robert Fairchild's large Victorian home on Gibbon's Lake just outside of Hollister. The stone and wrought iron head gate at the front of the driveway to the house proclaimed it was the Fairchild Estate.

Matt had sent Truet Davis to Hollister three times over the past two months to settle disputes between the ranchers and Robert Fairchild. The conflicts took a deadly turn recently with the massacre of hundreds of sheep and the death of the shepherd that watched over them. Matt came with Truet to investigate the death and find the men responsible. Truet sat beside Matt as they talked with Robert Fairchild in his private office, which was filled with artifacts collected from his travels, such as small sculptures, wood carvings, and colorful pots from South America and elsewhere.

Robert Fairchild was an older man in his late fifties or early sixties with short gray hair and a groomed goatee. He wore silver-rimmed glasses and spoke and acted with the distinguishing character of a man who had been everywhere, done everything there was to do, and did not doubt his abilities. He was dressed in white suit pants and wore a light blue shirt with a white bowtie while leaning against the front of his desk with his palms on the edge of the desk.

Robert looked at Matt admiringly. He was quite familiar with Matt's name and reputation, but he had never had the pleasure of meeting the man. Matt was a much younger man than his colorful reputation had led Robert to believe the lawman was. Matt Bannister was in his mid-thirties, tall with broad shoulders, and appeared to be quite muscular under his tan button-up shirt with the sleeves rolled up above his wrists. He was a handsome man with a neatly trimmed dark beard and mustache that covered the lower half of his strong square-shaped face. His long dark hair was pulled into a tight ponytail that fell below his shoulders.

Robert spoke, "I thank you for informing me of Avery Gaines' unfortunate passing. He was a splendid reporter, unlike any other I have. He was the most daring man I've ever known, except for maybe you. I will miss him." He pointed a finger at Matt. "Tell me, is the scar on your cheek from Frank Walchester's gun when you killed Clay Dobson and the boys?"

Matt narrowed his eyes, curious how Robert would know such a detail. "It is."

"I read about that." He grinned. "You didn't think Avery Gaines went to Willow Falls for fun, did you? It seems some of the townspeople are very forthcoming when a man travels across the country to talk to them. The leather man suit was for surveillance to see who was friendly and who wasn't. Avery went back without his suit and collected enough information for a story. That story was published in all three of my newspapers back east."

A twinge of indignation registered in Matt's eyes. "The article didn't mention Elizabeth's name, did it?"

Robert's brow furrowed curiously. "No. Who's Elizabeth?"

Matt's lips curled upwards, slightly humored. "Then, sir, the town folks in Willow Falls didn't tell him a thing that isn't already known. I'm not here to talk about that anyway."

"True. That is not why you are here. Okay, I lost a good man in my employment, and I want some justice for his family back in Peru. Juan Garza did not speak English, but you would not find a kinder and more authentic man than Juan. He came here to do a job that I hired him to do. Now he is dead, along with over five hundred of my sheep.

"I've spoken to your Deputy Davis many times, and it only worsens. I tried to work with the ranchers by moving my flocks south because my sheep were being cut down hundreds at a time. There are threats to my life and my wife's, so my hired men stay here to protect us from the violence that is threatened. I moved my sheep away from here as a compromise with the ranchers, but no matter how far away my shepherds take the sheep, the sheep shooters track them down. There were no cattle where Juan was found. Conveniently enough, a cowboy found Juan's body the day after the sheep were massacred. My guess is that unnamed cowboy was one of the Hollister Sheep Shooters that did it."

Truet spoke, "The disputes between you and the ranchers that I was summoned to settle really can't be settled without a lawsuit and a judge in the court of law. I told you that then."

Robert looked at Truet evenly. "What about now? I have a dead friend and need to explain this to his family. I want to say his murder is solved."

Matt said, "The chances are we won't find the man that killed him. If they are working as a group of unknown vigilantes, they won't turn on each other. It's hard to convict a man when you can't identify who was there or who pulled the trigger."

"So, you're wasting our time being here?" Robert asked sharply.

Matt answered honestly, "No. I want to find the men who did it. But you'll understand that you're hated in this town. Quite simply, no one likes you or wants you here. If you had a sheep or two, nobody would care, and you'd be a welcomed neighbor. But you brought ten thousand sheep into cattle country, bought up all the land around their lake, and want to build a woolen mill in the capital of cattle country. I don't know what you expected to happen. I really don't."

Robert lifted a finger thoughtfully. "Where in the American Constitution, Bill of Rights, or any other state or federal amendments does it say I can't live where I choose to live or seek a business of my choosing as long as it is law-abiding? Do I not have the right to live here?"

"That's not in question. The question becomes; is it smart to want a wool industry in the center of cattle country? I'm guessing not," Matt said.

"This is my home, and I'm not moving. There will be a woolen mill on the river, built on my property, and the cattle association will have to get used to it. I'm trying to work with them, but they are not working with me. There is a hundred square miles of ground out there and plenty of grass for all of us. I don't harm their cows, but I will if they keep killing my sheep. As you pointed out when you arrived, yes, I did hire the Blackburn Marshals, and if need be, I'll hire more. I'm an easy-going man, Marshal Bannister, but I'm no fool. I know exactly what I am doing here, and this is the greatest environment for sheep. I would appreciate it if you would set up a meeting with the cattlemen's association for me. I have a proposal to make to the cattlemen. I believe our corporate entities never need to cross paths. I have taken the liberty of having a map drawn up of Jessup and Waller Counties, where I hope we can come to a compromise. I am willing to create a border that I think is more than reasonable and will be satisfactory with the ranchers."

"I can set up a meeting with the cattlemen's association tonight to try to reach a reasonable agreement."

"Perfect. I would like that."

There was a knock on Robert's office door, and it opened slowly. An attractive blonde-haired lady wearing a flower-patterned dress spoke softly, "I'm sorry to interrupt. Robert, Ed came to the house to say that the marshal's uncle, Charlie, and brother, Adam, are here and wanted to see you. Apparently, they found more dead sheep and hurt men."

Robert looked at Matt curiously. "Are they with you?"

Matt was surprised. "No. My brother and Uncle Charlie?" he asked the lady.

She smiled kindly. "Yes. Shall I have Ed bring them in?"

"Yes," Robert said. "Do you know what this is about, Marshal?"

"No. I'm curious myself. I don't know what they're doing here."

***

Matt was surprised to see Charlie, Adam, Marvin, and Nathan step into Robert Fairchild's office. He and Truet stood to let Charlie and Marvin have the two seats facing the desk and made the introductions. Curious as to why they had come to Hollister to see Robert, Matt stood back with Truet, Adam, and Nathan to let Charlie explain. The news of the slaughtered sheep and injured and branded shepherds was shocking. Charlie continued to explain the help they offered along with Martin Pollard's kindness. He added, "I don't know how you expect to have a successful business around here with all your sheep being killed and your employees being nearly killed. This is cattle country Mister Fairchild, and sheep aren't welcome."

Robert Fairchild rubbed his temples irritably. "Thank you for helping my shepherds. I appreciate that very much. I get letters from a group calling themselves the Hollister Sheep Shooters, and that's what they say too." He looked at Charlie. "Your nephew supposedly is here to investigate these crimes, and I hope he can identify the men responsible." He looked at Matt sharply. "I have a legal right to buy land. I have a legal right to own sheep and to graze them on public land, just as much as the cattlemen do. I have the right to build a woolen mill on my property and create a business without being harassed, and I intend to do just that. I didn't want bloodshed, but if it must happen, I have the men that can do it! I never wanted trouble, and I have tried to do everything I could to avoid it. But when my employees that I brought from Peru are killed and branded like cattle, I get damn angry!" He took a deep breath and put his focus back on Charlie and Marvin. "I appreciate you and Mister Pollard for helping them. The other ranchers around here would have stomped on their throats. Matt will set up a meeting with the cattlemen's association this evening to discuss a reasonable proposition where we can all profit and stay off one another's toes. Please come to that meeting so I can publicly thank you for saving my men. If you all don't mind, I am quite aggravated and need to find my injured Peruvian friends and speak with the doctor. I will see you all this evening."

Adam spoke, "Mister Fairchild, we also have a financial thing to discuss. Your shepherd, Sixtos, shot my prized longhorn bull for dinner."

"Sixtos shot your critter?" Robert asked questionably. The idea of it seemed out of character for the man he knew.

"Yes, sir. Now he says the bull was charging him, and I can't dispute that because it was not a friendly animal, but I spent good money on it, and now it's dead. The way I see it, the beast may have been charging him, and I won't deny a man's right to defend himself against anything, but if he wasn't grazing on our free-range land, my bull wouldn't be dead. Therefore, if you wouldn't mind, could you reimburse my cost of the animal?"

"Your name is Adam, right?"

"Yes, sir."

"Adam, you seem to be an understanding man. Let me answer like this. If free-range land is public land, then it is not your land; therefore, Sixtos had every right to be there, the same as your prized bull. If the animal in question becomes a threat to a man and the man shoots the animal, be it a stockman's prized possession or, say, a cougar, the man's life has greater value—even the life of a Peruvian man. Wouldn't you agree?" he asked, watching Adam closely.

"Of course. I don't blame Sixtos for shooting it. I'm just out of a lot of money."

Robert smiled slightly. "You're an honest man, and I appreciate that. Legally, I don't owe you a thing; I don't believe. But I owe you far more than the cost of a bull for saving the Menza brothers. Name the price you paid, and I'll write you a check right now."

Chapter 6

Hollister, Oregon, was not a large town but was the center hub of the upper Jessup and Waller County's cattle towns. It was where the cowboys came on the weekends to blow off some steam in the saloons, bordellos, and dance hall. It was where families went for a good meal or a day shopping in the larger stores. There were two churches in town, five saloons, two bordellos, and a dance hall, along with billiards and restaurants among general stores. In the center of town, next to the sheriff's office, stood the heartbeat of the community, the Hollister Cattlemen's Association building. It was a large, heavy-timbered two-story building painted dark brown with a large set of bull horns over the door.

The bottom floor was where the official business was discussed in an expansive room with five seats behind a curved conference table where the elected leadership of the organization sat facing seventy-some chairs lined up in an organized fashion. The President of the Hollister Cattlemen's Association was a rough-looking older man named Gunther Thomas. He was in his mid-sixties, a bit heavy in the stomach, but a large man with black hair that refused to gray and small steely brown eyes on his broad face that was kept cleanly shaven. His voice was deep and powerful as he reluctantly introduced Matt to the rest of the board of directors and the membership sitting in the chairs facing him. It was unheard of for a federal marshal to call for an emergency meeting in the Hollister Cattlemen's Association, and it irritated Gunther to be bothered by such nonsense. It was a mere request for a meeting, but the reputation of Matt Bannister's name was well known and added to the curiosity and urgency to be there.

Matt stood next to a large three-foot square official state map that had been enlarged of Jessup and Waller Counties' free-range land with the towns and other landmarks indicated for scale. It was a map that Robert Fairchild had hired a geologist from Portland to make from the most updated and credible county maps.

Robert Fairchild sat in the front row with two of his gunmen, Matt's old friend, former Deputy U.S. Marshal Ed Bostwick, and gunman Ira Kelly. They were both considered the leaders of the Blackburn Marshals now that Jeff Blackburn was dead.

Knowing the crowd would be hostile, Matt took precautions to have all weapons removed at the front door before entering the meeting room. Taking the crowd of cattlemen into consideration, he spoke thoughtfully, "I was raised on the Big Z Ranch, and we all know we cannot have Mister Fairchild's sheep ruining the prime feeding grounds of your stock. But at the same time, we can't have any more sheep killings or sheepherders being murdered or branded. So, let's talk and discuss how we can find a compromise that will keep your grazing land free of sheep and the sheep free of being killed."

Gunther Thomas refused to have the leadership of the Hollister Cattlemen's Association sitting in the membership's seats like common cowhands. The five board members sat in their elected chairs at the curved conference table behind Matt. Gunther spoke loudly from his seat, "Fairchild can move to Branson and run his sheep in your backyard."

"Yeah!" a few men agreed, some more vocal than others.

Matt chuckled. "My backyard wouldn't feed three sheep. Robert Fairchild has the legal right to live here just like you do. We can make this work to everyone's benefit if you and the others will work with me. Where do you graze your herd, Gunther?"

Gunther didn't like the idea of Matt laughing at him. "East of my ranch. There is nowhere for him to graze sheep. And I won't sit back and let some rich eastern city dandy come in here with his fancy house, eastern ideas and ruin our land. This is our town and our land. It's not sheep that supports this town!"

"Amen!" another rancher agreed.

"I second that. Marshal Bannister, we have enough trouble just raising beeves without sharing the land with stinking sheep," a small ranch owner named Cody Bridges volunteered.

"He owns nearly two thousand acres he can roam his sheep on!" Cody's wife, Laura, stood and shouted. "His sheep ruined a good portion of land we graze our herd on. I don't know what we're going to do now!" Her eyes were watering heavily with emotion.

Gunther spoke, "We'll help you, Laura and Cody. It's what we do here. Marshal, that lady and her husband are just starting out and have a decent little herd of top-bred Angus. They put all they had in their beeves, and now the feeding grounds they counted on are ruined. The sheep ate the grass down to nothing!" he spat out with reddened cheeks and fury evident in his eyes.

Robert Fairchild stood unexpectedly. "Folks," he spoke loud enough to be heard. "I feel bad for this young couple and will compensate them for that loss. I will also have some men go through there with grass seed to replant that ground if I must. I will admit, I had lazy and ignorant shepherds at first, and those shepherds that took my sheep into the Bridge's grazing ground were fired."

"You can't replant the prairie!" someone shouted.

Robert held a hand out to calm the speaker. "Sir, I have thousands of sheep, and there is not enough room for them on my land, just like you and your cattle. You own land too. I want to be fair and work with you all. We are neighbors, like it or not. It would be best if we could be reasonable and work together on an agreeable solution. But if any more of my sheep are killed or my shepherds attacked, killed, or branded!" he yelled angrily. "I will no longer sit back and let it happen without paybacks.

I remind you; your cattle are worth much more than my sheep. So, who knows what could happen to your stock if this maltreatment continues?" He gave a questionable shrug while making a sarcastically innocent expression.

It immediately raised an angry ruckus within the membership. Phil Dawson, the Vice President of the Hollister Cattlemen's Association, stood from the curved conference table, pointed a finger at Robert, and shouted angrily, "Don't threaten us! We aren't killing your sheep, but if any of my cows die, I'll be coming for you personally!"

"Amen!"

"Me too!"

"You got that right."

"Hold on!" Matt shouted over the applause that had broken loose in support of Phil. He glared at Robert Fairchild. "That was a stupid thing to say!"

Robert shrugged again while he remained standing. "Perhaps so. But I have invested a vast fortune in sheep and sheepherders, the best in the world. My sheep have been killed since I agreed to the cattlemen association's suggestion of moving my flocks further south, where my flocks are more isolated. I believe it was a setup, but I will not tolerate anymore. If I need to hire more gunmen, I will. But before I do, let's make an arrangement that works for all of us." He turned to Gunther Thomas and the elected board. "I may be an easterner that's moved into your town, but I'm not afraid of a fight, gentlemen. I'll hire a hundred gunmen if I must, and I assure you, I will win. I always do."

Matt shook his head in disbelief. Robert Fairchild was as calm and softspoken as any gentleman he had ever known, but his words were as cold and calculated as the most confidant gunman he'd ever run across. There was no fear in Robert Fairchild, just plain confidence and surety of his words.

Gunther answered bitterly, "Get your hundred men. If you want a war, you'll have one. By George, you'll be carried out of town in a pine box!"

Matt rubbed a thin layer of perspiration from his forehead. It was a warm night, and with all the men crowded into the room, it was warmer than the dance hall on a Friday night. Matt shouted loudly to end the elevated arguing and bickering among the cattlemen, "Where can he run his sheep?"

"Willow Falls," one of the ranchers volunteered, knowing that's where Charlie's ranch was.

Matt was quickly angered. "Do you gentlemen want a war? Do you really? These men right here, Ed Bostwick and Ira Kelly, are Blackburn Marshals, professional killers. And there are more of them just waiting to ambush someone. Are you ready to lose your sons, Gunther? How about your husband?" he turned to ask Laura Bridges. "You all might kill a good number of Blackburn Marshals, but it will cost you more lives than you may want to lose. I'm warning you now. It doesn't stop with just your cowboys; these men are the kind of people who will burn your houses down in the middle of the night or ambush your wife in the garden. They will do whatever it takes to break you! Life means nothing to them! Now you can avoid that, or you can be prideful and regret it later when you're burying your family members."

"Whose side are you on, Marshal?" someone yelled.

"I'm not on a side. I despise the Blackburn Marshals and what they represent, but I know who they are; you don't. I think there is enough land to support all of you and his sheep. Let's consider Mister Fairchild's proposition and agree to borders between the cattle industry that serves you all and a territory where he can graze his sheep peacefully. Robert Fairchild doesn't want a war or a feud, he wants to live peacefully with you all. Will you at least listen to his proposition and consider it? Otherwise, this hostility will grow, and I guarantee your cemetery will double in size. And if you want to know the truth, I've seen enough needless death in my lifetime that I'd rather not see it here."

After a short silence, Phil Dawson reluctantly said, "The least we could do is listen to Mister Fairchild's proposition. Maybe we can live with it."

Robert Fairchild approached the map he had made. "Thank you. I don't want any trouble, folks. I don't want to interfere with your businesses, either. I believe I have a way of working out our differences that may be suitable for you and me. A compromise..."

***

Matt stood on the back deck of Robert Fairchild's home, staring at the blue water of Gibbons Lake, where a number of ducks swam peacefully next to the dock where Robert's rowboat was tied. The back deck and yard were superbly cared for by a gardener while their cook prepared a steak dinner. It was a beautiful location, not far from the mountains that rose in the northern skyline like a rugged sawblade with a few broken teeth like the flat-topped Windsor Ridge. It was a quiet and peaceful place to relax, and Matt understood why Robert decided to build his retirement home there. Matt could not help but wonder if Christine would choose this location for their dream home rather than the top of the hill outside Branson. He knew she'd love the view of the mountains and lake as much as he did.

"Matt, again, thank you for that passionate speech you gave. I don't believe those uncultured cowboys would have listened to me if it wasn't for you." Robert said happily as he came out of his house holding the hand of the much younger and attractive blonde-haired lady that interrupted their meeting earlier.

"I'm glad a compromise was agreed upon." The cattlemen agreed to let Robert's shepherds graze the sheep on the eastern rim of Donovan's Canyon from Riley Gulch down to Vardis Creek, some thirty miles to the south. It had plenty of land for the sheep to graze and were areas most cattlemen preferred not to graze. When the area was mapped out by Robert, there were few complaints, except for an acceptable path to bring the sheep back to the Fairchild's property, but easements were agreed upon with a financial fee, and Robert could not be happier.

"This is my beautiful wife, Holly. She is my pride and joy," Robert said with a proud smile.

Matt shook her hand gently. "My pleasure." He was surprised to learn that the young lady was Robert's wife and not his daughter.

Her pleasant smile was genuine. "Thank you for your help. It's been frightening with all the hostility towards us. Maybe now, people in town will be a bit more friendly." She was in her mid to late twenties, tall and shapely, with a darker shade of curly long blonde hair that fell over her shoulders. She had an oval-shaped face with large round blue eyes that appeared to bulge just enough to add to her beauty.

"I hope so. I'd like nothing more than to not hear of any more trouble up this way."

Her brow lowered just a touch. "I was wondering if you were ever coming here yourself instead of sending your deputies."

"I assure you I was needed elsewhere. Truet is quite capable of handling most complaints without me being there. Unfortunately, as he stated, the complaints here were more legal disputes than criminal," Matt explained.

Holly's attention went elsewhere. "It was nice to meet you, but if you'll excuse me," she said and walked swiftly away to speak to one of the servant girls.

Robert asked, "Are you still going to investigate who killed Juan and branded my men?"

Matt nodded. "I am. But I have a feeling, from what I gathered in town, that we'll never know.

People in groups like the sheep shooters usually won't admit to being part of the group and took an oath to never say a word about it. Coincidently, no one I talked to knows a thing."

"Of course not," Robert said, discouraged. "You said you despised the Blackburn Marshals, but I saw you and Ed talking earlier and understand you two are friends?"

"I knew Ed Bostwick when he was U.S. Deputy Marshal with me in Cheyenne. We go back a long ways."

"And the others?" Robert inquired.

Matt chuckled. "Well, I beat the crap out of Wes, Henry and Jimmy on a Branson street at the same time, if that tells you anything. I'll let them tell you why, but I wouldn't trust them around your wife." Matt nodded towards Holly, who was talking to one of the servant girls twenty-five feet away.

"Oh. I will ask them," Robert said with a furrowed brow.

"I thank you for a fine dinner, but I must get back to Branson in the morning. When you talk to your shepherds, write everything down and send it to me. That way, I'll know what to look for when I come back. I want to wait a few days to let everyone calm down and get back to normal before I start making people nervous."

Chapter 7

Originally, Ira Kelly was the second in command under the Blackburn Marshals behind the founder, Jeff Blackburn. While hired by William Slater to guard a transport of gold to San Francisco, William decided to cause a strike at his silver mine as a subterfuge for double-crossing another mine owner that rightfully owned the gold. Jeff Blackburn stayed in Branson with Ed Bostwick while Ira and a few others guarded the transport of gold to San Francisco.

When they returned to Branson, Ira discovered the strike had turned violent, and Jeff Blackburn lay dead in the funeral parlor. It came as news that Ed had taken charge of the Blackburn Marshals and signed a contract with Robert Fairchild. Ira was the rightful leader of the Blackburn Marshals since Jeff Blackburn's untimely death and refused to relinquish that title. Outraged that Ed assumed he could take the Blackburn Marshal's future into his hands, Ira and the men with him, Kent Kruse and Ellis McKenna, came to Hollister to confront Ed Bostwick.

Robert Fairchild, being a fair man, hired Ira and the others. Robert explained that he wanted Ed Bostwick and Ira to share the responsibilities as co-leaders because he wanted to grow the Blackburn Marshals into a much larger entity. Robert envisioned a nationwide police/detective agency for hire that would rival the Pinkerton Detectives. With Robert's political contacts, funding, and knowledge, he had no doubt that his vision for the Blackburn Marshals would be a significant success and make both Ed and Ira, as equal co-owners, wealthy men.

Ed Bostwick was forty years old, almost six-feet-tall, lean, muscular, and as tough as a man can be. His straight light-brown hair fell to the top of his shoulders, and he wore a well-groomed goatee that had traces of gray on his oblong face. His brown eyes revealed his hesitancy as he scratched inside his ear while clenching a hesitant grin. "I think we screwed up, Mister Fairchild. The cyanide we threw in Thomas's waterhole will be discovered if it hasn't been already." Robert Fairchild had instructed them to take two bottles of soluble cyanide powder six miles out of town in the middle of the night to throw into a pond on the Long T Ranch, which belonged to Gunther Thomas.

It was a bold move that guaranteed trouble, but it was payback for the dead sheep and the death of Juan Garza. There was no doubt in Robert's mind that Gunther Thomas was involved, if not the leader of the Hollister Sheep Shooters. The cyanide bottles were opened and thrown into the pond, where the powder would slowly dissolve and poison the water. The bottles were thrown in last night, and it was too late to turn back now. If he had waited just one more day, it would have avoided the trouble that would surely come. He was not expecting the arrival of Matt Bannister or his ability to keep the peace while Robert made his grazing proposition to the cattlemen, which the ranchers agreed to. But it was too late now; the Long T Ranch's spring calves and nursing cows would die before long, if not already.

Little did Robert know about the Mendez brothers being branded and injured severely or hundreds of his sheep being slaughtered at the time when he made that decision. On the one hand, he regretted poisoning the water hole because it voided any peace that tonight's meeting had promised. Still, on the other hand, after visiting with Jorge and Mateo Mendez in Cold Water, Robert wanted to poison other water holes and get some revenge for the two young brothers. In the barn, hidden behind grain bags, was a wooden box with ten other bottles of powdered cyanide. It was meant for other ranchers if the sheep continued to be killed. Robert figured he could afford to replace his sheep at a greater pace than the cattlemen could replace their herds of cattle. And he could kill cattle faster with poison at more significant numbers without putting his men at risk.

Robert sat behind his desk, facing Ed and Ira Kelly. The two men wanted to talk to him earlier, but Robert was hosting Matt and his family. When his guests had left, he called the two men into the house.

Robert rubbed his goatee thoughtfully. "Yes, I know, Ed. We acted just a little too soon. I wasn't expecting Matt Bannister to give such a moving speech about you and your cohorts. You two must have earned his respect at some point. Well, if there is anything I have learned from my thirty-plus years in the newspaper business, it is people will do about anything to get rid of a person they hate, despise, or sometimes love if money or a more passionate love is the motive. It goes back centuries. In the sixteenth century in Europe, a person could simply accuse another of witchcraft, which was a certain death sentence. Feuds were indeed settled that way, and coveting a man's wife, husband, or property were all gained by such means. So..." He tapped his desktop with his fingertip. "When we are accused of poisoning good ole' Gunther's stock, we will turn it around and ask why we would do that. We got all we could ask for last night and have no reasonable motive to do so. But who would gain from poisoning the man's stock?"

Ira Kelly was a medium-height man with medium-length light-brown hair and a well-groomed mustache on his oval-shaped face. He wasn't a broad man but a muscular, blue-eyed fellow. He was in his early forties and was normally the more vocal of the two men, but he slowly shrugged in answer.

"Any idea, Ed?" Robert pressed. He liked Ed Bostwick from the start and intended to take the former lawman under his wing and teach him to be a businessman. He could not say the same for the reckless and contentious Ira Kelly.

"Someone who doesn't like him?" Ed questioned.

"Yes, but also the Hollister Sheep Shooters. Or at least that's who we'll accuse. Our reasoning is they did it to create an uprising against us and start a fight. They hate sheep, and they hate me. They've made that known. Instead of making a false accusation that I'm a witch, they poison a cattleman's stock and point the finger at me to arouse everyone else's anger and wipe us out completely. It's a different time in history, but the same treacherous technique. They would gain my land along the lake, my house, and no longer be troubled by sheep."

Ira was skeptical. "The people in that group will know they didn't do it."

"Yes, but then we might know who they are and let Matt know. The good Marshal will be on our side because, again, we never wanted any trouble and have everything we wanted." He laughed lightly. "What would I gain by poisoning the president of the Hollister Cattlemen's Association's cattle after I made a peace offering? *That,* gentleman, is our defense. The depth of the sheep shooter's hatred for us is their motive to set us up to take the blame and continue their acts of terror. If my plan goes well, it will cause a wedge between the ranchers who are part of the sheep shooters and those who are not. Subterfuge, gentlemen; it will come in handy in

your future as co-owners of the Blackburn Marshals. In the meantime, prepare your men to do
their jobs as a new and unknown disease is right
now affecting Gunther's cattle."

Chapter 8

The 1878 Saloon was so named because it was opened in 1878. The simplicity within the town of Hollister was plain to see, from the Hollister Hotel to a pink two-story house with a sign proclaiming, The Pink House. Matt learned it was a bordello and initially went by another name, but the cowboys kept referring to it as the pink house, so the madame changed the name. They had a good dinner at Robert Fairchild's home, but there was a restaurant in town simply named Mel's Good Food. The businesses didn't try to impress the potential customers with unique or catchy names; they just stated their business as plain as day.

Nathan, Adam, Matt, and Truet sat at a table in the 1878 Saloon, having a drink or two to break the monotony of staying at the Hollister Hotel, which offered a bed or two per room and not much more. They were parting ways in the morning to go back home, but the four of them could relax and visit over drinks for a few hours.

Nathan Pierce spoke, "Becoming a father is life-changing. You'll find out when you and Christine get married and have a baby. The first time you hold your baby in your hands, it's an amazing feeling. I looked into little Cal's eyes, and he just stared into mine. I now understand what love is in its truest definition. And, of course, Sarah's old maid, Miss Jane, is there to help because I don't know what to do when Little Cal wakes up screaming. Miss Jane is a blessing and always reminds me that the love I have for my son is a fraction of how much God loves us. She believes God gives us children so we can understand the depth of God's love for us. And you know, it makes sense. I rode out alone one day to watch the sunset and thank the Lord for his blessings in my life. I mean, look at me, I'm sitting here with friends that have become my family, Sarah and I have a home, a job I love, and now a son, a maid I don't pay for, and my wife's parents aren't trying to kill me anymore," he grinned. "The Lord's given me everything I always wanted, and I'm so thankful."

Adam asked Matt, "Are you and Christine anxious to have a baby?"

Matt shook his head slowly as he replied, "Doctor Ryland doesn't think Christine can have any children. So no, we're not expecting to have any." He could see the questionable expression on Nathan's face. He explained, "When Martin Ballenger shot her, it damaged her ovaries. One was taken out, and the other was damaged. Her chances of getting pregnant aren't too good; if she did, it would probably end in a miscarriage. She's more optimistic than I am, though."

"Sarah and I will be praying about that. Well," Nathan said, raising his glass, "here's to trying anyway."

Adam set his drink down and peered at Truet. "And what about you? Are you going to marry my sister or not?"

Truet grinned as his face reddened a touch. "There's nothing quite like putting me on the spot, huh, Adam? I intend to, but I didn't want to bring it up until after Matt's wedding. This is his time, and I don't want to take away from that."

Adam raised his eyebrows while taking a deep breath. "I don't want to be the bell tower of gossip, but there may be another wedding on the ranch soon enough. Nathan's maid, Miss Jane, has sparked the attention of Darius. That old man has been reenergized since she's shown up. There might be a bit of a romance blooming there. Isn't that right, Nathan?"

"Yeah, there's a spark, alright. The best way to explain it is when I asked Aunt Mary what she thought about how giddy those two were, she said their age is irrelevant because falling in love is always timeless."

Matt smiled slowly. "I can believe that." His eyes went the bat doors as Wes Wasson entered the saloon with two Blackburn Marshal friends, Jimmy Abbot and Henry Dodds.

Wes nodded his head at Matt before approaching. The other two went to the bar. "Matt, I heard you were in town. I just got back myself from Branson. Rumor has it you made Morton Sperry a deputy marshal. I heard there is a lot of bad blood between Morton's family and him now, and you for hiring him."

"I don't know about that, but I did hire him."

"Is Morton here?"

"No. He's in Branson with Nate and Phillip."

Wes offered a smug hint of a grin. "That's too bad. The boys over there and I owe him one for jumping us after our fight with you on Rose Street that night. I hate to admit it, but you beat us pretty well that night in our drunken state. I don't think you could do it when I'm sober. But Morton's the vulture that jumped us at our weakest. I want to face him when I'm at my best."

Matt had discovered that Wes and his friends pretended to be Matt and his deputies while raping a former prostitute in the Monarch Hotel. The beating Matt gave Wes and his friends in the middle of Rose Street was what Wes was referring to. Morton Sperry and his friends took over, beating the three Blackburn Marshals after learning what they had done.

Matt answered, "Maybe someday you'll get the chance to prove yourself. In the meantime, let me ask you, what do you know about the sheep shooters? Do you have any names that you know are involved?"

Wes Wasson was five feet and ten inches tall, with a stout body build and broad shoulders. He had short straight brown hair with an ugly scar along the hairline and a square face with broad cheekbones. His eyes were small and far apart, with lines at the corners from his laughter over the years. He had a concave nose with a scar on both sides from his upper lip to the bridge of his nose. Wes wore a goatee, but his face was covered with a week's worth of whiskers. He snorted as he looked around the saloon. "Probably every cowboy you see in here and around town."

"I notice there haven't been any dead cowboys from you, Blackburn Marshals, yet."

Wes chuckled softly. "We are under strict orders from Mister Fairchild to not cause any trouble and walk away from any when we can. We can lose our job if we start a fight or don't make a strong effort to walk away. That's coming straight from Ed and Ira. We'll be fired from being a Blackburn Marshal. Mister Fairchild is all about getting along with his neighbors, and we are a reflection of him. So, we sort of coexist in a world of growing hostility on both sides, if you can understand that."

"Maybe now that the grazing boundaries have been agreed upon, that hostility will decrease, and you won't be needed anymore, so you all can move on," Matt said.

Wes nodded in agreement. "Maybe so. You have a good night."

"Friend of yours?" Nathan asked Matt.

"No. That's Wes Wasson. He's the one that courted Billy Jo and bragged about massacring Chusi's tribe on Bear River. He started harassing Chusi and got him killed. It's his fault Chusi is dead."

Adam turned his head to watch Wes at the bar with his two friends. "Huh."

A group of cowboys entered the saloon with a laugh over something and approached the bar to order some drinks. They stayed a reasonable distance away from Wes and his pals. One of them looked at Matt and shouted, "Marshal Bannister! It's been a long time." He approached the table to shake Matt's hand. "How are you?" He noticed Truet, and his grin faded. "Truet?" he paused to question Truet's reaction to seeing him.

Matt stood. "Barry McCracken. I heard you went to Wyoming after leaving Sweethome?"

"I started that way and wound up working on the Dawson Lakes Ranch. I'm a..." His eyes shot nervously at Truet. Truet stared coldly at him. "I'm a... just working." He sighed and turned his full attention to Truet. "Truet, I told you at the time I am so sorry about Jenny Mae. I had nothing to do with what happened to her. I didn't know what AJ and the boys had planned, or I would have tried to stop it. That's the honest truth. Jenny Mae was such a beautiful and sweet lady. I never would have let anything happen to her."

Truet's jaw clenched tightly. It was a year before, within days of Jenny Mae's death at the hands of AJ Thacker and his cowboy pals. Barry McCracken was their good friend and fellow cowboy on the Thacker Ranch. Seeing Barry again brought the reflection of AJ's face to mind and the others that Truet had killed. A fury from deep within began to rise within Truet. He forced it down as he knew Barry had never harmed Jenny Mae and came to a hotel to warn Matt and him of a pending ambush. Barry wanted nothing to do with it, quit the Thacker Ranch, and left town that night. Truet did not stand or reach out a hand to shake. His eyes turned fierce as he said, "I know that, or you'd be as dead as AJ."

Barry nodded uncomfortably, understanding that Truet did not want to speak to him. He turned back to Matt. "Well, you two take care."

Truet stood. "I'm calling it a night." He didn't want to hear Barry's voice or see him because the memories would take him back to his life in Sweethome with Jenny Mae.

"I suppose we better too. We have a long ride home tomorrow," Adam said to Nathan.

***

Wes Wasson watched Matt and his pals leave the saloon to go to the hotel for the night. What he had told Matt was the truth for the most part, but he neglected to tell the whole truth. He did know three people who were sheep shooters, but any vengeance would come from the Blackburn Marshals and not the law. There was the lawful way to take care of things, and then there was the Blackburn way, which was quieter and swifter than a trial. There were several cowboys from various ranches that belonged to the sheep shooters. Still, there were a few cowboys that had gotten on Wes's bad side over the weeks, and none was more at odds with him than the son of the president of the Hollister Cattle Association, Bode Thomas, who had just come into the saloon with some of his friends, including Barry McCracken. There was tension between the local cowboys and the Blackburn Marshals, but so far, there had been limited fist fights and threats, no guns had been drawn by either side. The hired gunmen were ordered to stand down and weren't there to cause any trouble with the cattlemen. They were just hired to protect Mister and Missus Fairchild.

"McCracken," Wes called, "how do you know Matt and Truet?"

"None of your business," Barry said with as much interest in talking to Wes as Truet had in talking with him.

Wes continued, "They don't like me much either. I know that look on Truet's face. He despises you."

"He probably has reason to," Barry said with a sense of guilt. He could not help but feel guilty for what happened to Jenny Mae Davis. She was a special lady, and the tragedy and hideous crime done to her had always haunted him. His friends had hurt her, and he took part in the cover-up that followed, and that alone made him feel guilty.

Wes continued, "It must be personal. I courted Matt's cousin, Billie Jo. She told me a bit about Truet. He's courting Matt's sister now, but I heard Truet's wife died. Do you know about that?" He had overheard Barry's conversation with Truet.

Barry narrowed his eyes with hostility but ignored Wes. He said to his four pals, "Let's get a table and play some cards, fellas."

Wes chuckled. "I hit the nail on the head, huh?"

Twenty minutes later, Adam Bannister walked back into the saloon with his bushy dark hair under his worn hat and thick beard. He spoke to Bode Thomas and the other cowboys for a moment before introducing them to his friend, Nathan Pierce. Nathan's long shoulder-length brown hair and thick beard made him look more like a miner or a trapper than a ranch hand. After a short conversation with Bode, Adam moved to the bar to an empty space beside Wes. He ordered a drink for Nathan and himself and then tapped Wes on the shoulder. "Matt mentioned you were part of the Bear River Massacre. I was in the Battle of Coffee Creek, if you've heard of that. I took an arrow in my leg and chest, another in my back."

Wes was immediately interested. "Yeah, I've heard of it. That was quite a fight, I understand. You should be dead if you took that many arrows."

"Probably, but the danger wasn't just arrows; it was being overrun. We were heavily outnumbered, resulting in a lot of hand-fighting. So, you were really at Bear River?"

"I was. We rode in and shot them scavengers like pigs in a pen. Men, women and children. You look like Matt. I take it you're brothers?"

"Adam Bannister." He put up a hand to shake. "Nice to meet you."

Wes was slightly taken aback. "Wes Wasson. You're part Indian, too, right?"

Adam nodded. "Yeah, but the ones I killed at Coffee Creek and elsewhere during the Snake War didn't care about that."

"Your brother seems to have a soft spot for Indians," Wes said slowly. He was trying to size Adam up.

Adam snorted. "My little brother was never in the cavalry or warred against them. I did, and I have the wounds to prove it. He even made friends with that drunk one in Branson, Chusi. I heard what happened between you two. Trust me. You didn't do anything I wouldn't have done if my brother wasn't the marshal." He turned to Nathan. "Isn't that, right? This is my good friend Nathan. He works for me. Nathan was in the cavalry in California too, but I don't think he ever got the opportunity to kill an Indian. I personally believe every one of us that did should get a medal. Let me buy you a drink."

"I won't deny a drink from a like-minded man. Thank you," Wes said.

Adam motioned to the only empty table in the saloon. "Wes, I ran into a bit of money today, so I'll buy the drinks if you want to join me and Nathan and swap war stories. I miss the good ole days in the cavalry. Do you know what I mean? The camaraderie of the men, the friendships becoming a brotherhood. I think that's why Nathan and I get along so well; we're both cavalrymen. It's my experience that we cavalrymen are a unique breed of men, Wes, and that's probably why we have so much in common." He smiled and pointed a finger at Wes,

"Do you know what I miss? The jokes we'd play on each other when our buddy drank too much," he said with a friendly grin.

Wes laughed loudly and slapped the bar with excitement. "I know exactly what you're talking about! It wasn't long ago my pals here and I got a bum drunk and crucified him naked across the front door of his father's church," he laughed.

"That's funny." Adam laughed. He put a large hand on Wes's shoulder. "On a serious note, I want to thank you for trying to get my cousin Billie Jo away from that piece of crap, Joe Thorn. I think she would do a whole lot better with you. Matt may not like you, but I think you're alright."

Wes's laughter faded as he said, "I think Billie Jo made a bad choice too. But I'm not done yet trying for her hand. She's an exceptional lady."

Adam glanced at his old friend Bode Thomas. "Why don't you and Nathan grab us that table, and I'll be right back." He spoke into Wes's ear, "Let's see if we can't get him to pass out, huh? I'll be right back; I need to use the privy."

Adam walked out the bat doors of the saloon into the warm night and then peeked back inside to get Bode Thomas's attention. He motioned for him to step outside.

"Adam," Bode asked curiously, "what are you doing?"

"Bode, I need a little help. I need about twelve feet of strong twine if you have it, and a straight razor. And if you can come up with something to put a man to sleep for a while, I'd appreciate it. Can you help me?"

Bode chuckled. "I know you well enough to know you're up to no good. What do you have planned?"

Adam shook his head with a scrunched-up grin. "Just having a little fun."

"With that Blackburn Marshal?"

"Yeah. He seems like the type of fellow that can take a joke," Adam said hesitantly.

Bode chuckled. "I can't stand that man. Yeah, I think we can gather most of that between my friends and me. Tim's brother is the town doctor, so he might be able to come up with something to make a man sleep. What do you want me to do?"

Chapter 9

The chill of the morning and an ache in his arched back were bothersome, but it was the abrupt kick in the ass that jarred Wes Wasson from his uncomfortable slumber. It took a moment for him to figure out that he was staring at the hardened ground of the street when his eyes adjusted. A pile of half-digested food was next to the bottom of a post that he was hunched over. His hands were tied with hemp twine to the post of a hitching rail outside the 1878 Saloon in the center of town. He couldn't move his hands or slide the braided twine up the post to an upright position as the knot also bound his feet to the post in such a way that he was helplessly tied bent over the hitching rail. To make matters just a bit worse, his pants had been pulled down, exposing his dirty drawers to the town street. Whoever had tied him was good enough to leave his drawers around his waist, but the backside of his drawers was cut wide open in a square to expose his buttocks to the world. His Blackburn Marshal badge had been removed from his shirt and pinned to the back of his drawers to add to his humiliation. Wes had no idea how he got there or who tied him, but at the moment, he cared more about being cut free. He could hear a few fellas laughing behind him, one of whom had kicked his rear.

"Hey!" Wes yelled at the men that he couldn't turn around to see. "Cut me loose. This is not funny! Cut me loose."

"That was a good kick, but watch this," one of the men said and then delivered a painful blow that drove the tip of his boot between the space between Wes's legs. The impact lunged Wes's body upwards as far as the tight binds allowed.

Wes cursed loudly and spouted out inappropriate words, even for a rough cattle town. "Cut me loose and face me like a man, you bloody cowards! Cut me free, and we'll see how tough you are. Kicking a bound man is what a woman would do, not a man. Free me and show your faces, you cowards!" The sun was rising, and people were waking up to start their day. Wes feared becoming the morning's entertainment for the town folks, and being seen in such a compromising position by the ladies of the town was a horrifying thought. He tried to jerk the twine to snap it and free himself, but the braided hemp refused to break. "Cut me loose!" he demanded.

One of the gentlemen behind him grabbed a part of his drawers that was left and yanked them up with enough force to lift Wes's bound feet off the ground as far they could go. The man laughed hysterically as the cotton drawers, even with a square cut out, took the shape of his buttocks. "Didn't your mama ever teach you to cover your butt?" the man teased while laughing with his buddies.

Wes growled as he desperately tried to jerk his hands free. "I'm going to kill you when I get free!" he hissed in a rage.

"We better leave you here then," one of the men said with a chuckle.

A middle-aged lady carrying a bag of flour towards Mel's Good Food on the wood slab boardwalk glanced nervously at Wes with a troubled expression.

"Dora," Wes called to her, "get a knife and cut me free."

She shook her head nervously with a glance at the men behind Wes and kept walking.

"Dora!" Wes shouted angrily. In a storefront glass window, he saw his reflection and was horrified. The right side of his head was shaved bald, but the left half still had hair. The left half of his mustache and goatee had been shaved off, but the right side was still there. He stared in disbelief at his reflection, trying to remember who had done such a heinous thing to a man's hair. He couldn't figure out why his two friends had left him alone. It was against the Blackburn rules to leave a fellow marshal alone in town whether he wanted to stay or not. And yet, he was alone. Humiliated and tied in a compromising position where he was helpless. Wes could see the faint reflection of three men standing behind him but could not make out any details in the window's reflection other than himself.

One of the men behind him said to his friend, "He's going to attract attention the more he yells, and people are waking up. Some of his friends might come looking for him, and the real marshal is in town too, don't forget. I think we should leave him here like this."

"I think we should cut his binds and let him go free. Those Blackburn Marshals might want to get even if we don't," Another one of the men suggested. He sounded younger than the other two.

"I suppose you're right," the third man with a deeper voice said. "We better free him while we can. But probably not the way you're thinking."

Wes was desperate to be cut loose so he could confront whoever cut his hair and humiliated him. "You better free me! And you better do it now!" Wes was furious. His mouth was dry, and his head ached. He had vomited at some point, but he didn't remember it. The last he recalled, he was drinking with his new friends Adam and Nathan at a table. He vaguely remembered his friends Jimmy and Henry wanting to take him back to their bunkhouse on the Fairchild Estate, but Wes was having more fun with Adam than his usual companions and accepted the invitation to sleep on the floor of their hotel room when Adam bought another bottle of whiskey. That was all Wes remembered. "Hurry up and cut me loose!" he screamed.

The man with the deeper voice spoke callously, "You Blackburn Marshals have no business being here, and I'm tired of your mouth making threats towards my friends," the man said as he walked around the hitching rail.

A chill ran down Wes's spine when he saw a big man dressed in a long black duster buttoned to the top and a burlap sack over his face. He held a blood-stained oak club about thirty inches long in his hand. The other two men were dressed the same way.

"So," the big man continued, "maybe someone will cut you loose and toss your sorry carcass in a box."

Wes could hardly breathe. There was no saliva to swallow or sound aside from the pounding of his heart flooding his ears at the sight of the three Hollister Sheep Shooters and their killing club stained with sheep's blood. Wes's chest tightened as he struggled to keep from sobbing as he knew he was as helpless as a lamb among wolves. His eyes watered as he choked out meekly, "I'll quit the Blackburn Marshals and leave town right now. I'll leave and never come back. Just please, let me go."

One of the men looked around the town anxiously, "We haven't got much time. You scared him, and he's leaving town. We should just cut him loose and let him go."

The man holding the club spoke, and the voice became recognizable to Wes. "This was a fine oak table leg, thick and sturdy, but I broke the table up and made four of these clubs for knocking the sheep in the head. You'll be interested to know I drilled out the center and melted lead into it. It only takes one solid blow to kill a sheep, but I don't hate sheep as much as I hate you and your friends."

"Listen," Wes couldn't help his emotions as the desperation to live was stronger than his pride or toughness of being a man. "I haven't hurt anyone. I'll leave. Please, give me a chance to run," he begged with an uncontrolled sob. "I'll never come back if you just let me go, please..." he began to weep.

"Look, boys, this tough-talking hired gunman is begging like a woman."

Wes's hands shook rapidly, and his voice was strained as he spoke through uncontrolled heavy breaths, "Wait! I'll pay you... I'll give you..."

The big man swung the club overhand as hard as he could across the back of Wes's head. Wes's body went limp, whether unconscious or dead, it was hard to know. It didn't matter; the big man repeated the vicious blow until the back of Wes's head broke open and became a bloody mess splattering across the ground and staining the club with a fresh coat of red. Wes Wasson was left tied over the rail with his head bashed in, dead.

***

Matt Bannister was angry. He was sitting at a table for breakfast at the hotel with Adam and Nathan when they told him what they had done to Wes the night before. They thought it was funny and laughed as they explained that Bode Thomas's fellow cowboys collected the twine and straight razor while the doctor's younger brother returned with a small bottle of Chloral Hydrate. Adam poured some into Wes's drink to cause him to pass out. The only difficulty they ran into was getting rid of the two other Blackburn Marshals, but it was easy enough to convince Wes to stay and drink with his new friends as it might be the last time they'd be able to. War stories, whether true or not, kept Wes interested in staying later, and he accepted an invitation to sleep on the floor of Adam and Nathan's hotel room. Once Wes passed out, they laid him on the table and shaved half his head and half his goatee and mustache. They tied him over the hitching rail, ripped his pants down, and cut a handy square out of his undergarment to reveal his buttocks.

Sitting at the breakfast table, Adam and Nathan laughed heartedly about it.

"Why would you do that?" Matt asked, not at all humored. "Do you not realize he was a Blackburn Marshal?"

Adam chuckled. "It was just for fun."

"Fun? Wes is a Blackburn Marshal, Adam. You have no idea what kind of danger you just put yourself in." Matt raised his voice as he set his fork down and stood from the table, "What were you thinking?"

Adam chuckled. "Well, actually, I got the idea from reading 2 Samuel Chapter 10 of the Bible. You know, when King David sent his servants to greet King Hanun, but Hanun mistook the servants for spies and humiliated them by shaving off half of their beards and cut off their garments at the waist and sent them out in public butt naked. You know that story, right? Well, Bode and those pals of his didn't know that Bible story. I figured the best way to teach cowboys is hands-on, so we recreated it. On the bright side, I think they're interested in the Bible now."

Nathan spat out a mouthful of milk across the table as he dropped his head into a palm on the table with a roar of laughter.

Matt's harsh eyes moved from Nathan to Adam. "Did you tell them the rest of the story, or did you forget that King David was angered by the treatment of his servants and it ended up in a war David didn't want? You might have just done the same thing here. You don't humiliate a member of a violent group and expect it to end well. Is Wes still there?"

"I don't know. Relax, Matt, he'll understand it was just a joke among old cavalrymen," Adam said as the hotel door opened and Charlie Ziegler and Marvin Aggler stepped inside.

"Matt," Charlie said, "the sheriff asked me to come get you. There's a dead man tied up in front of the hotel."

"What?" Adam gasped. His humored grin turned to concern quicker than a hummingbird's wings.

***

Matt stared silently at the body of Wes Wasson tied over the hitching rail and the blood splatter on the ground under his head. There was a large crowd growing to gawk curiously at the gory sight. The blood was fresh, and the body was still warm.

The Hollister Sheriff, Pat Emerson, stood with his two younger deputies and a growing crowd of curious onlookers. He let Matt get a good look at Wes before he said, "Marshal, there was one witness, Dora Abrams. She's the breakfast cook at Mel's Good Food restaurant. She said the three men that did this were dressed in long dusters and had burlap bags over their heads. They killed Mister Wasson with a club. It had to be three members of the Hollister Sheep Shooters that did it. That being said, it could have been anyone. Dora didn't see which way the individuals went."

Matt cast his eyes to his brother Adam. "I'll talk to her soon. Sheriff, do you folks have a funeral parlor?"

"We have a carpenter in the livery stable who makes coffins and digs graves for a price. He doesn't work for free. I'll have Hank take the body to the livery stable and make a coffin, but I don't know what you want us to do with him from there?"

"I'll arrange for his body to be returned to his family in Branson. Right now, I better go notify Fairchild and tell them what happened. You have no idea who did this?" Matt asked pointedly while peering into the sheriff's eyes.

"No, Marshal, I don't. The only people who know who the members of the sheep shooters are, are the sheep shooters themselves. I'm the sheriff here, and

I don't even know who is in that group or who isn't. All I know is three of them did this."

Matt spoke irritably, "You can spread the word for me and hope it gets to the men responsible that with the borders being established last night, the Blackburn Marshals had no reason to remain here. Now they do." Matt motioned towards Wes's body, "This is…an invitation for a group of men who kill for a living to strike back. You let whoever did this know that. The best way to keep the peace is for them to turn themselves in. I'm going out to Fairchild's to let them know Wes was murdered, and in the meantime, you better be trying to find the men responsible." He turned away and pointed at Adam. "And you are going out there with me! You too, Nathan."

As they walked towards the livery stable, Matt asked Truet quietly, "Did you notice anything out of the ordinary?"

"Besides a man's head being broken open at a hitching post? No."

"The sheriff's boots were clean. Too clean for a dusty town."

Truet offered a troubling hint of a smile. "He washed the blood off his boots?"

"I suspect so."

"What are we getting ourselves into, Matt?"

"We'll find out soon enough. I'm just hoping the Blackburns don't hold Adam responsible for what happened to Wes. Keep your revolver handy today."

Truet exhaled heavily. "Your brother's sense of

humor is finally catching up with us," Truet said, displeased.

"Yeah. But if you marry Annie, he'll be your brother too."

***

Matt, Truet, Adam, Nathan, Charlie, and Marvin rode out to Robert Fairchild's home on Gibbins Lake and waited in the large family room while Robert had Ira Kelly and Ed Bostwick summoned to the house. When they arrived, Matt explained what had happened to Wes Wasson.

Ira Kelly reacted angrily and shouted a few indirect threats toward the sheep shooters that were mainly ignored. Ed Bostwick remained quiet and thoughtful as the news took root.

Robert Fairchild was quiet for a moment, but a troubled expression brought the question, "Why was he tied up anyway?"

Matt looked at his brother. "I already told you it was meant as a practical joke. It was just supposed to be funny." Matt neglected to tell them that half of Wes's hair and goatee had been shaved off or that his buttocks were exposed. The news was bad enough without offering the full details.

Robert furrowed his brow and twisted his lips slowly. "When I was a teenager, my friend stole a bottle of rum from his father, and we drank it beside a creek. His little brother passed out, and we thought it would be funny to put a crawdad in his pants. We laughed hysterically until his father found us and whipped all our hides with a switch. That friend is Louis Sorenson, the owner of the Branson Gazette. My life-long friend." He looked curiously at Adam, "Wes was a Blackburn Marshal. What would convince you that it would be a good idea to leave him tied up in the center of town? Did you not fear him being angry in the morning?"

Adam rubbed the corner of his eye. "In the cavalry, sometimes there wasn't much to do except drink, and humiliating the first person to pass out was our entertainment. Wes, Nathan, and I were sharing stories about doing that to people, and Wes suggested we should tie Nathan to the hitching rail when he passed out. Unfortunately, Wes passed out first. What's good for the goose is good for the gander, right? So we tied him there. Of course, I knew he'd be mad in the morning, but I figured he'd want his chance to get even by topping what I did to him. Competitive humiliation. I never thought anything bad would happen to him. That was the furthest thing from my mind."

Robert replied, "I expect kids to do that kind of stuff, but not forty-some-year-old men."

"Well," Adam replied with a slight smile, "you got to have fun." He was not being completely honest. Adam despised Wes Wasson for what he had done to Chusi Yellowbear. The fact was, he was ashamed of what the cavalry had done in Bear River and other Indian massacres. Fighting man against man in a fair fight, warrior against warrior, was honorable, but to attack men, women, and children unexpectedly and leave no survivors was incognizable.

A man that bragged about doing that, the way Wes did, was a man Adam could never respect, like, or want anything to do with.

Adam's whole purpose of returning to the 1878 Saloon and getting to know Wes Wasson was calculated to do exactly what had been done. Adam knew he could not kill or harm Wes, but he could humiliate him enough that Wes wouldn't want to show his face in town anymore. Adam didn't spend much time thinking about how Wes might react in the morning, he just thought it would be funny. Adam was a beast with hand-to-hand combat and a superb marksman with his rifle, but his weakness was being a sub-par shot with a revolver. He carried one, but he generally missed unless he closed one eye and took careful aim. How Wes would react to being tied up was up to him. If he wanted to fight, Adam was willing to do so, but he doubted Wes would. He felt that Wes could take a joke without demanding blood among friends, which Adam was pretending to be. However, there was a line even among friends, and shaving his head and goatee probably would have crossed it. He reluctantly admitted to himself that he may have gone too far.

Ed Bostwick spoke calmly to Adam, "I suggest you leave town. I understand it's not your fault what happened to him, but if he weren't tied up, he'd be alive right now. It's true; Wes enjoyed doing stupid things like that. He and a few boys stripped the reverend's son naked and tied him to a cross in front of his father's church in Branson after they got him drunk. Wes sure thought that was funny, and so did the other boys out there. But they may not see it being funny this time and blame you. Matt is an old friend of mine, and I'd hate to see any bloodshed come between us. So Adam, please, leave town, and we'll tell the boys the sheep shooters did it all."

"The hell we will!" Ira Kelly shouted. "He's as much to blame as the man that killed Wes. How do we know that he didn't kill Wes?"

Ed answered, "He didn't kill Wes. Everything Adam said makes perfect sense. You didn't like Wes anyway, Ira. Let's tell the boys the sheep shooters tied him up and save any hostility towards Adam, who is innocent enough."

"I didn't like Wes. But that's not the point; the point is those two," he pointed at Adam and Nathan, "disrespected a Blackburn Marshal. They made a mockery of our badge in public, and that puts a bad taste in my mouth. I won't allow it!"

Matt asked, "What do you plan to do about it?" His cold eyes watched Ira warningly.

"I don't have any plans!" Ira snapped. "But we won't be disrespected like that, not by anyone. Maybe we'll tie his feet and drag him through town to show people what happens when you touch one of my marshals."

"No, you won't," Matt said calmly. "I beat the snot out of your deputies on the street, and that's a bit worse than tying one of them up. I knocked out two of Henry Dodds' teeth and left them bleeding on the street. I'm right here if disrespect is your catalyst for violence and retribution."

"Gentlemen," Robert Fairchild spoke to settle

the matter, "there will be no conflict between you two while the Blackburn Marshals are under my employment. What happened to Wes is cold-blooded murder, but no one in this room committed that murder or will be blamed for it. Ira, I believe it is best to listen to Ed and not let the other marshals know Adam is the one that tied Wes up. Without a name to pin on the murderer, it would be easy to condemn Mister Bannister, and I believe his intentions, however juvenile, were meant for good fun without malice. Don't you agree, Ira?"

Ira Kelly took a breath and nodded reluctantly. "I guess."

Robert turned his attention back to Matt. "That is settled. Now, how do we find the man responsible?"

Matt raised his brow thoughtfully. He had reasonable suspicion, but it was best not to vocalize it. "Let me get to work on it. I'll do my best to find out."

Chapter 10

The Hollister Sheriff's Office was surprisingly more prominent than the Branson Sheriff's Office and had a good desk area with three desks and a private office for the sheriff. A heavy door separated the four jail cells from the front of the office. Two prisoners were jailed at the moment.

The sheriff, Pat Emerson, was a cowboy that worked for the cattle trails for a good portion of his life until he came west and was hired on with the largest ranch in the area, the Long T Ranch, owned by Gunther Thomas. Three years before, Pat ran for sheriff and was elected unanimously to put an end to a ring of cattle thieves. Pat and his two deputies, Lenny Clinton and Russ Garvin, along with a volunteer posse, had done just that by arresting and handing out death sentences to the men involved in the crimes. Pat had since gained a strong reputation around the surrounding towns in the county, including Branson, as a tough and capable lawman.

He was the kind of lawman that Matt was glad to have in the county until he noticed Pat's freshly washed black boots that morning.

Matt and Truet now sat across the desk from Sheriff Emerson to talk about the murder of Wes Wasson.

"This is your town, and I'm sure you know just about everyone around here. Certainly, you have suspicions of who may belong to the Hollister Sheep Shooters, right?" Matt asked. "I spoke to your town doctor, and he says those two sheepherders, Jorge and Mateo Menza, will survive, but both men now have a sheep branded on their chest. Juan Garza was murdered, and we're looking at over a thousand sheep killed so far, and this morning, bright and early, Wes Wasson was killed. You can't tell me you're blind about all this. Your reputation as an honorable lawman doesn't line up with a claim of being deaf, blind, and dumb."

Pat Emerson was offended by Matt's words. "Marshal, do you know every criminal in your city? What about the county? I'm sure you don't. The Hollister Sheep Shooters are a mystery. They certainly don't wear their costume as they walk through town or wear sheep shooter badges on their chests. No one has seen them without a hood or a brand on their horses. If those Mexicans could tell me a brand, I could narrow something down, but how do you chase a ghost?"

"Three of those ghosts walked into town and murdered Wes Wasson right under your nose. How did they know Wes was there? This morning my brother told you that he and Nathan, Bode Thomas, and a few other ranch hands were the ones that tied up Wes. Have you made an effort to talk with Bode and his friends? They would seem like prime suspects, wouldn't they?"

"I have not spoken to them yet," Pat answered.

"I'll be talking to him," Matt replied frankly. "I intend to find the men responsible and get some answers about Juan's death and the assault on the shepherds. I understand the Hollister Sheep Shooters wear long black dusters and burlap bags as hoods, right? I find it hard to believe that the group is so secretive that no one around here knows anything about it or thought of questioning the mercantile and other stores to see the purchase orders on who bought dusters. I know you're all friends up here and want to do things your way, but there are still laws. I don't want to step on your toes and get your clean and shiny boots dirty, but I need names. I want the branding iron that scarred those two men and the man that owns it." Matt looked awkwardly at the sheriff. "Seriously, not one person comes to mind?"

Pat answered slowly, "No, Marshal; no one comes to mind. My money says they are cattlemen, though. Good luck trying to tell the difference between the innocent and guilty men."

"Pat!" Gunther Thomas yelled with a deep and demanding voice as he barged into the sheriff's private office, interrupting Pat's conversation with Matt. He shouted, "Somebody poisoned my waterhole and my stock's dying one after the other. I have forty-seven dead cows and calves and fifteen more showing signs as of right now. I know it's the water because Malachi, my dog, ran down there and got a drink, and twenty minutes later, he was doing the same damn thing. My dog is dead! I had the boys run all the stock out to Hanson's Creek. But by George, my water hole is poisoned!" The man shook with anger as his chest rose and fell heavily.

"What? How?" Pat questioned with concern as he stood to address his former employer.

"I don't know! I had my spring calves on the upper T, and they're all dying. They're frothing at the mouth, stiff-legged, falling in convulsions, rapid breathing, and then dying. My pup did the same thing, only quicker. The pond doesn't go bad overnight. Somebody poisoned the water. I'm getting some supplies so I can have a few boys throwing rakes into the pond to see if there is anything in there. I don't want those boys going into the water until I know what's in it." He lifted his hands in disbelief. "I lost thousands of dollars, and my best watering hole may never be useful again. I'm going to kill them. This is the last straw!"

Sheriff Emerson was very aware that Matt and Truet were listening. He motioned with his hands for Gunther to calm down. "We must prove that someone contaminated your watering hole before we can accuse anyone. Calm down, take care of the animals that are okay, and if your hands find something in the water, let me know. Right now, I'm going to send Lenny and Russ around the other ranches to see if they have any strange cattle deaths.

We'll get it figured out, Gunther."

Gunther shot a hostile glance at Matt and then shook his head with disgust. "There is only one person to blame. And Marshal Bannister, you better not be protecting him when we come to collect what he owes."

"Let's prove your water was intentionally poisoned before we point fingers," Matt suggested.

Gunther shouted, "Do you think I don't know what poisoned stock looks like when I see it? We poisoned the wolves around here using strychnine and cyanide on dead carcasses, and I watched wolves and coyotes do the same thing my cattle are doing. There's no doubt about what it is or who did it! I demand you to go out to the sheepman's house and bring back the ones responsible for doing this or get back to your fancy city and let us do the talking. You're not needed here. The way I see it, you're more of a traitor to us than Benedict Arnold. You grew up on a ranch and now stab us all by siding with that sheepman. This whole territory will become a wooly back paradise because of fools like you. They say you found a dead Blackburn Marshal today. I can't say I'm sorry to hear that. None of them are welcome here anyway."

Pat asked Matt, "Have you ever dealt with poisoned stock before, Matt?"

Matt shook his head. "No. I'm sorry to hear about your water, Mister Thomas. If it's proven to be poisoned, I'll do everything I can to find the person responsible."

Gunther glared at Matt and spoke frankly, "The

best thing you can do is go home and let us be. Pat, I'll talk to you later."

"You bet, Gunther." The sheriff looked at Matt. "I think we're done, Marshal. I have a lot of work to do."

Chapter 11

Morton Sperry sat at the desk that once belonged to Deputy Jed Clark. Morton preferred to have his back against the wall, so he turned the desk vertically to the room near the woodstove. His job as the newest deputy marshal had been to assist Nate Robertson with whatever Nate was doing or run errands for Phillip Forrester. Morton had a lot to learn and was anxious to learn more and do what he could.

It had become bigger news than he expected for the people of Branson to learn that he was now U.S. Deputy Marshal Morton Sperry and not the leader of the infamous Sperry-Helms Gang. His change of heart was met with suspicion or awe, depending on who heard it.

For Morton, it was exciting to start a new beginning in life. He had found a small apartment in the Dogwood Shacks to rent that was already furnished. He was meeting new people that encouraged him in his decision to be a deputy, and he found himself smiling more than ever before. A large piece of the puzzle as to why was a lady named Audrey Butler. Although they were not technically engaged, they were courting, and Morton could not be happier than he was when he was with her.

The door of the marshal's office opened, ringing the cowbell mounted above the door. Morton lifted his head from reading a book about the law he was hired to enforce. John Painter entered the office from working at the Fasana Granite Quarry. He was serving a sentence and lived at the jail while allowed to leave to go to work until he paid his debts. He had gone to the Monarch Hotel to bathe after work and now returned to the jail. Slowly, he was earning more privileges and free time as he paid his fees back.

John waved tiredly at Morton as he entered the partition gate and sat down at the lunch table not far from Morton's desk. "How are you doing today, Morton?"

"Not bad. You?"

"Tired. Where are Phillip and Nate?"

"Off doing something, I don't know what. So, I'm here alone."

'Hmm. I was thinking about our conversation from yesterday, and to answer your question, I think of all the amazing things in the Bible that if I could go back and witness in person, it would be when the angels appeared to the shepherds on the hill to announce the birth of a savior. I can't imagine what it would look like or sound like to have so many angels in the sky singing in unison. That would be the most amazing experience I could imagine. Secondly, I would like to see Jesus hanging on the cross. That way, the image of him suffering for my sins would be burned into my memory, and I wouldn't take his sacrifice for granted. You just started reading the Bible recently, but what about you? What would you have liked to have witnessed?"

Morton took a deep breath. "I'm not finished with the book of Genesis or the Gospel of John. To be honest, I haven't read the Bible in a couple days now. I told Audrey I'd start reading the Bible, but I get home and I just haven't," Morton explained.

"Can I tell you a secret? Leave your Bible open beside your chair, and it will remind you to read it. It's the only book in the world that will do that, and that speaks for itself as being God's Word. He wants us to read it and draw closer to him. One day of neglecting to read your Bible easily becomes two, three, and then weeks. You have to read it. So leave it open, and it will invite you to read. Have you read any parts that would have been amazing to witness?"

"The creation of the world, I think. I'm a little confused. Chapter one is the creation, but chapter two is also the creation. You'd think it would explain more about how this huge world was created."

John grinned. "No. Moses wrote the first five books of the Bible, also known as the Pentateuch, the books of the law. Here is the thing: the earth's creation is probably far more complicated than we could understand, but Moses wasn't wandering in the desert for forty years during the exodus, pondering on how the earth was created. He wandered in the desert for forty years to write the Pentateuch and gave us a quick summary of how the earth was created along with Adam and Eve. God didn't have Moses spend a lot of time writing about the world's creation because what happens after chapter two is what we need to know about. Sin entered the world through Adam, and that makes us all sinners. God cares far more about his plan for our salvation than he does about explaining creation. Even if you knew every answer about creation, it would still not compare to the knowledge of salvation through Jesus, which the Bible focuses on from Genesis to Revelation."

"I have a lot to read still," Morton said. "I would have liked to have seen Noah's boat."

John slowly grinned. "The ark, yes..." He looked up as the office door opened, and three rough-looking men wearing gun belts stepped into the office.

Morton stood slowly. "John, go into the jail." He spoke to his cousin, Jesse Helms, "Jesse, Cass, Elliot, what are you all doing here?"

Jesse leaned his hands on the partition and smiled sadly. "We just wanted to come in and say goodbye. We're leaving the area. I can't believe you're a deputy marshal, Morton. I remember when even speaking to a deputy marshal was a danger to us. Now you *are* one."

Morton nodded. "Hard to believe, isn't it? I'll tell you; it feels better to be with the law instead of against it."

Elliot Zook was the tallest of the gang members at an even six feet. He was thin, lanky, and loyal. He had thick black hair that reached the bottom of his ears and a thin mustache on an oblong face that appeared too long and narrow for his wide brown eyes. He said with a sigh, "Well, Morton, I never thought I'd see the day, but if your happy, good for you."

"Thanks, Elliot. So where are you all heading to?"

Jesse laughed. "You're a deputy marshal; we can't tell you that. I love you, Morton, but I don't want to see you on our trail. I just wanted to say goodbye and thank you for being my friend all these years."

Morton peered at Jesse fondly. "Well, you're my cousin; I had to be. You fellas, be careful wherever you go. And I hope you all choose to hang up your weapons and go straight. Life is easier that way."

Cass spoke for the first time, "Now you even sound like a lawman. Take care, Mort."

"Cass, take care of my cousin."

Jesse chuckled sadly. "I don't need him to take care of me." He hesitated. "Your family is a wreck. Your mother hardly gets out of bed, Jannie hasn't stopped drinking herself nearly to death, and your fat brother and idiot nephew are planning on starting their own gang. I imagine it won't be long until you're on their trail."

Morton frowned as a wave of guilt swept through him. "How is Henry?"

"Henry is fine. He's working, and Travis took

your place working with him. If you want to know the truth, he and Bernice took in Daisy's children and Jannie's too. What happened in that barn changed everything."

Morton's lips tightened. "I know. I wish it all ended differently. I don't know if my ma would want to see me?"

Jesse shook his head with a hesitant grimace. "I don't know how to tell you this, Morton, but your mother wants you and that woman both killed. I went by to say farewell, and she had the gall to ask me to do it. I'm sorry to tell you that."

The strength went out of Morton's legs, but he remained standing and straight-faced. His voice masked the turmoil inside him. "I'm sorry to hear that. But thanks for letting me know."

"It's the least I could do. Take care, cousin."

"You, too." He watched the three men walk outside, mount their horses, and leave, pulling a pack horse behind them. Weakened by the news of his mother, Morton sat heavily and buried his face in his hands. He felt like his stomach and intestines were twisting into a braided mess of organs, leaving a vast space for the emptiness to grow and haunt him. He could not get the memory of shooting his brother Alan in the head at point-blank range out of his mind or the sound of his mother's scream that followed. Pulling the trigger wasn't easy, but it wasn't hard; it was necessary. Alan was intent on murdering Morton and had shot at him several times, and there was still a healing new scar from being grazed across his back by one of Alan's bullets. A stray bullet killed their younger sister, Daisy, and Alan showed little remorse. Their brother Henry grabbed a pitchfork used for cleaning the stalls and rammed it through Alan's abdomen, all the way through, until the tines pierced the boards of the barn wall. Alan would not have survived the infection that was sure to follow or the internal injuries the pitchfork caused. Morton wanted to save Henry, who had never killed anyone, the burden of carrying the weight of killing his brother. Morton held Alan's revolver, pointed it at Alan's head, and pulled the trigger.

In hindsight, he wondered if pulling the trigger was done in malice for what happened to Daisy, in self-preservation, to save Henry the burden of killing his brother, or in mercy to save Alan from a slow and painful death. The truth was probably a combination of all four, but there was no joy, victory, or reward. There was only sadness and regret that they couldn't have had a better relationship where the fighting never existed. It had to be done for several reasons, but he was the one paying the price for pulling the trigger. The cost was his guilt and the knowledge that he no longer had a mother who would welcome him home with open arms. She wanted him dead, and sooner or later, she would talk somebody into killing him, perhaps his nephew Tad. The weight of it was a lot to carry.

"I couldn't help but overhear," John Painter said softly while coming out of the jail. "I'm sorry, Morton. I know I brought a lot of shame to my parents, but my parents never gave up on me."

Morton lifted his face from his hands. "I don't come from that kind of family. My mother didn't just give up on me. She wants me dead. There's a little bit of a difference." He smiled sadly. "I suppose I am dead to her now."

John returned to the table near the desk. "I wonder if that's how Jesus felt when God left him on the cross? You'll read about it later in the Book of John. While Jesus hung on the cross, he cried out, *'Father, why have you forsaken me?'.* It wasn't the illegal trial and conviction, nor the hitting, beard being pulled out, or the whipping that tore his flesh up, or even the spikes being driven through his hands and feet, or being hoisted up the cross that he screamed those words. On the contrary, while enduring all that unimaginable pain, he prayed, "*Father, forgive them, for they know not what they do'.*

"Jesus cried out those agonizing words, *'Father, why have you forsaken me?'* when God turned away from his son and left him while the world's sin was placed upon Jesus. That moment of separation from God tore Jesus apart while the weight of the world's sin was poured out upon him. I can't think of a more fitting picture of what that moment must have felt like than when a child learns that their mother or father wants them dead."

Morton looked at John evenly. "You're not helping much. I think I'd like to be alone for a while."

"Morton, Jesus knows what you're feeling because he felt it too, but to a much larger degree. You're not as alone as you might feel."

"Oh yeah?" Morton asked bitterly. He stood and

began pacing the room while speaking heatedly, "Do you think Jesus knows what it's like to shoot my brother in the head? Do you think he knows what it's like to grow up in a family where all you know is violence and how to hurt people? I think my mother had my father killed; that didn't happen to Jesus, did it? There is no one that can know how I feel or what I have stored up inside of here," he beat his chest. "Maybe I'm just fooling myself and don't belong here. I don't know. All I know is that I hear about Jesus from Audrey, Matt, you, and everyone else around me, and it isn't clicking. The Bible doesn't hold my interest, and maybe I'm just wasting my time with Audrey and this place. I'm a criminal! That's what I am and what I was raised to be." Moisture warmed his eyes as he stared out the window towards Main Street.

John spoke softly, "I was raised in the church by a reverend father and went clear to Massachusetts to study the Bible. But I was told I would never be a reverend and left it all behind to drink, gamble, and fornicate. I cheated on my wife, stole money, and lost my family. I became a blemish to the Painter name and came home to be a humiliating son to my parents and the church my father pastored. My father almost lost his job because of me. God forgave me, and he will forgive you too. Jesus can make you a new man, Morton, he did me, and I was a mess."

Morton chuckled bitterly. He turned around to face John with a doubting smirk. "Did you ever kill anyone, John?"

"No."

Morton shook his head emotionally. "I'm a kill-er. I have murdered men for so little that it would make you sick if you knew everything I have done. There are families out there waiting for their hus-bands and sons to come home, and they never will because of me. John, I tried to read the Bible for Au-drey's sake, but despite how much I like her or love her, I know deep down inside that I'm nothing like her. I'm the worst man in the world for her. God wants nothing to do with me, and I already know it. I'm a killer, John. I even killed my own brother, and if my nephew tries..." He sighed, "I'll kill him too. It's what I do and who I am."

John stood and spoke pointedly, "It's your choice to walk away from all of this and keep listening to the lie that you're not good enough for God to love if you want to. But if you accept Jesus as your savior, God will forgive you, and you will no longer be a killer but a child of the living God. The Bible says you will become a new creation in Christ, and your sins will be forgiven and remembered no more. You'll be free and a new man with a clean slate. You could walk away from that identity you have for yourself and discover a new life where the Bible is suddenly alive. You don't read the Bible or serve Jesus for Audrey; you do it for you and your relationship with Jesus. He can be your best friend if you give him a chance. Morton, you carry a lot of burdens; why don't you pray with me right now and give those burdens to the Lord? What have you got to lose?"

Morton was hesitant but thoughtful. "I don't

think now is…"

John interrupted him, "You're at a crossroads. If you keep saying you're not ready, then you may never be ready and keep telling yourself you're not worthy of forgiveness and let every crossroad go by until there are no more. And all along, these people are reaching out to you to offer a new beginning, and you don't see that it is Jesus reaching out to you because he wants you to come to him. He has a plan for your life, and from where I stand, it looks pretty good. But listen to yourself; you're about to throw it all away. Don't! Choose who you will serve today, your old life as a killer, or a new life with freedom that comes with choosing Jesus. You've put it off long enough. I'm just a prisoner here but make up your mind! Either leave that badge on the desk and ride off with your cousin or accept Jesus as your savior and be courageous enough to see what Jesus has in store for you. I'll accept the responsibility if Matt returns and you're gone, but I know he'd be excited if you stayed as a brother in Christ."

Morton stared at John with watering green eyes. "I don't know how to pray."

John smiled slowly. "It's the easiest thing in the world. You only need to be sincere. Let's pray together."

Chapter 12

"Steven, are you busy?" Vince Sperry asked in a husky voice as he stepped through the open double doors of the blacksmith shop. His nephew Tad was with him. Their horses were tethered to a hitching rail out front.

"Not terribly. Do you need your horses shod?" Steven asked. He was leaning against his workbench with his arms crossed.

"No. Could you forge a branding iron? We are getting into the cattle business and want our own brand. I made a sketch with measurements. The measurements need to be precise. Here's the sketch. We named our ranch the Square X."

Steven took the paper and looked at the sketch. It was a large square with an X in the middle of it. "I can do it, but it will take me a day or two."

"No sooner?" Tad asked. "The measurements must be exact. We won't pay if they are not exactly what Uncle Vince wrote down."

Steven nodded in agreement. "What's ordered is what you'll get. I should have it done in a day or two. I have everything I need here."

"How much do you think?" Vince asked.

"Well, as broad as you want it, it's going to take heavier iron, increasing my standard fee for a branding iron. I could go cheaper with a standard three-eighths brander, but if you want a half-inch burn over a six-inch square, that's a big brand. Are you sure you want to burn that much hide?"

"Yep!" Tad said with a sense of undue excitement. "And it must be exact, or we're not paying."

Steven eyed him irritably. "So, you said. Well, it's not going to be cheap."

"How much?" Vince asked. "It's just a branding iron."

"My brother Albert over in Branson makes them cheaper than I do; I'll tell you that upfront. He doesn't have to travel a full day to buy the iron; I do. I charge five dollars for a basic three-eighths inch brander, but with your dimensions, this one takes a heavier gauge iron and time, so we're looking at about eight to nine dollars. We'll call it eight-fifty."

Tad waved his hand around the shop, curious about the forge and black bellow, along with various tools hung on the wall and lying on three different work benches. "Where did you learn how to do all this?"

"My uncle Charlie taught me a lot, and I was an apprentice under Albert for three years while he owned this shop."

Vince said, "I wanted to talk to Charlie about ranching. We're just beginning, and any advice he has might be worth hearing. Do you think it would be okay if we went out there? I always heard people weren't welcome on the Big Z."

Steven yawned. It was one of those days where he had little to do and too much time on his hands. "That's true to a point. But you're not going to get shot for crossing the head gate onto Big Z property if you want to talk to him. If you go out there, you'll find someone that can point you in his direction."

"Do you think he'd be willing to show us around?"

"You'd have to ask him or Adam."

"Hmm," Vince grunted. He and Adam didn't seem to get along. "Well, I'll make you a deal; I'll pay an even ten dollars if you can get that brand done by tomorrow afternoon," Vince offered. "We have a dozen beeves on the property and more coming, so I'd like to get them branded before they're stolen."

Steven gave a half-smile. "Do you have a lot of cattle thieves over there, do you?" He knew there wasn't a widespread cattle rustling problem in their area. He had doubts that the ranch the Sperry family was starting would become much more than big dreams with a small field of old worn-out dairy cows from the Helms dairy.

Vince appeared unamused. "It's just a precaution. Can you get it done by tomorrow?"

Steven nodded, thankful to have the work. "I can. I'll get started on it today."

Vince waved a thumb down the road. "I suppose we'll see what we can learn from your uncle. I'll come back tomorrow afternoon and pick it up."

***

The Big Z Ranch headgate was two miles north of Willow Falls, indicating they were crossing onto Charlie Ziegler's property. Crossing the property line made Vince a little uneasy as he had always been told to stay off the Big Z Ranch. He and Tad rode slowly along the road, not knowing where it was leading or what they would find at its end. They stopped at the top of a hill to gaze at their first view of the Big Z Ranch. A large red barn along the road was the first thing they noticed as a rearing and bucking horse was being broken by a skilled rider in a round corral alongside the barn. Across from the red barn was a much newer gray barn that was shorter but broader, with a maze of holding pens, alleys, gates, and separated fields lined with post and beam fences. Several horses were grazing in each pasture beyond the newer gray barn while others were penned in corrals. A road separated the two barns and led to the two-story yellow house, which Vince guessed was Annie's house, and nearby, the older two-story white house that must have been Charlie and Mary Ziegler's home.

A dog barked continuously as Vince and Tad rode slowly toward the homestead. They pulled the reins to a stop when a young man in his late teens came out of the red barn pushing a wheelbarrow of used straw and manure. The young man stopped, wiped his brow free of sweat, and looked at them with surprise. "Tad, what are you doing here?"

"I didn't know you worked here," Tad stated with a slight smile to see Eli Barso working.

"Gabriel, Evan, and I all work here, but Gabriel took Evan and went to Portland to visit his grandfather for a week or so. Now I'm stuck cleaning stalls in all the barns. It's never-ending." Eli Barso said without much enthusiasm. "I'd rather be going to Portland with them."

"Me too," Tad agreed.

Vince didn't know Eli personally, but he did know Eli's father was the Willow Falls sheriff's deputy, Johnny Barso, and knowing that put a sour taste in his mouth. "We're looking for Charlie," he said, uninterested in talking with Eli.

Eli shook his head. "He's not here. Charlie, Adam, Nathan, and Marvin went to Hollister for a few days. They found some sheep grazing on Big Z land and went to warn the owner to get them out of here, I imagine."

"Who is the boss around here, then?" Vince pressed.

"Right now?" Eli asked with a shrug. "Annie, I suppose. Maybe Paul or Jordie, I don't know. I'm just doing what I was told to do until they get back."

"Where's Annie?"

He pointed across the road to the gray barn. "Over there. I'll get her for you."

A few minutes later, Eli brought Annie out of the new stable for the Big Z Horse Company. Annie wore baggy denim blue jeans held up by a belt and a brown cotton pullover V-neck shirt. Her long hair was in a loose ponytail.

"Vince, Tad, what can I do for you?" she asked curiously. There was none of her usual lightheartedness in her expression. Her attention drifted to the cowboy breaking the mare in the stall across the way. The snorting of the animal and hooves pounding the hardened dirt traveled across the short distance.

Vince spoke, "Annie, we are starting our own ranch and were hoping to get some advice or maybe be shown some ideas of how to keep the cattle from wandering?"

Annie grimaced noticeably. "You mean a fence? How many head do you have?"

"A dozen right now, but more coming."

"It shouldn't be hard to keep that few contained. You don't really have the acreage to run that many more, do you? Isn't your land mostly forested?"

"It is. That's why I need fence ideas. Could you take us around and show us how you all do it?"

She shook her head. "No. We have too much going on. Sturdy posts and barbed wire should do you well. That's my advice."

Vince waved towards a cowboy approaching them curiously from across the way. "How many ranch hands have you got now?"

Annie answered shortly, "Just enough to keep them busy."

"Is everything alright, Annie?" Jordie Pulver asked. He was a thirty-three-year-old buckaroo from Nevada. He was a handsome man with short sandy brown hair and light blue eyes that matched the color of the sky. He kept his square-shaped face clean-shaven and had a stocky and muscular build. He walked a little bull-legged, but there wasn't a better buckaroo on the ranch. He had worked with Marvin Aggler for a short time and had received a letter from Marvin inviting him to come work for Annie.

"Yes," Annie answered. "These gentlemen just wanted to ask a couple of questions, but I think we're good now." She spoke to Vince, "Good luck with your ranch."

Vince scanned the area before answering, "Thank you."

As the two rode away, Jordie watched them carefully with his observant blue eyes. He said, "They look like trouble."

Annie sighed as she licked a fattened upper lip from being accidentally headbutted by a colt. "You're right. The big one is Vince Sperry, and the other is his nephew, Tad. Have you heard of the Sperry-Helms Gang?"

"No."

"Well, they're part of it. It appears they are entering the legitimate ranching business but aren't sure how to build a fence," she stated doubtfully. "I believe we've been scouted."

Jordie grinned as he watched them ride up the hill and turn back to look the ranch over from a higher elevation. "I'll let the boys know."

Chapter 13

Eli Barso walked the two miles toward town after getting off work. He was hot and sweaty and looked forward to jumping into the water of Pearl Creek as he did on most days with Gabriel Smith and Evan Gray after working in the hot sun. Eli wished his friends were with him, but there would be other people from town at the swimming hole to talk to. Eli's family owned one horse, but his father kept it in the stable for when he needed it as the town deputy. One of the benefits of working at the Big Z Ranch was getting to know the owners on a personal level. Annie Lenning had made Eli a deal to buy a mature bay mare for thirty dollars, including the saddle and tack. He had saved up half that amount and expected the long-extended hours of hay season would help double that amount. It was perhaps a bit of charity on Annie's part, as the mare was a fine animal, gentle and healthy. But that was a benefit of working for the family. They treated their employees well.

The road home dipped into a slight gully and crossed a short heavy beam bridge over a dry stream bed, and that's where Eli noticed Tad sitting on a boulder in the shade of an old apple tree twenty feet off the road. Seeing Tad there reminded Eli of a blonde-haired troll waiting for the *Three Billy Goats Gruff* to pass by.

Tad waved with a large grin. "Eli! I have been waiting for you. You tried to shoot Matt Bannister last year at Christmas, didn't you?" He remained seated on the boulder.

Eli left the road to enter the shade. "Christmas before last, yes. But I don't want to hear about it. It was a stupid thing to do, I know." There was nothing except humiliation in his voice. In his desperation to become known for more than being a kid from Willow Falls, he had made the dumb decision to try to ambush Matt Bannister outside of McDermott's Mercantile; it nearly got him killed. Since then, he had been called everything from a simple-minded fool to an idiot by everyone in town. Charlie Ziegler and Annie Lenning had been merciful enough to forget his past stupidity and allow him to work on the ranch with Gabriel and Evan.

Tad shook his head slightly. "No. I think it was brave. It takes courage to do something like that by yourself. Do you like working at that ranch?"

He nodded tiredly. "It's not bad. It's a job."

"How do they treat you? Are you making money?"

"They pay alright. Why, do you want a job or

something?"

"No. We just wanted to see the ranch. We're starting our own ranch and were curious about what we need to make it work. How many fences does the ranch have? Is the whole property fenced?" Tad asked, probing his acquaintance for more information than they had before. The truth was they knew nothing about the Big Z Ranch.

"It's too big to fence all of it. We have plenty of fences, though. We built a fence around Charlie's backyard to keep Annie's goats out of Mary's garden. Her goats wander free and get into everything. It's kind of funny; Marvin keeps threatening to shoot them all. He says goats and sheep aren't good for anything except dog food. But they're Annie's, so no one touches them." He laughed.

Tad offered a polite laugh. "Is there a fence along the property line? How do they keep people from riding in and stealing cattle? Where are the cattle? I didn't see a single cow."

"The cows are way out there somewhere." He waved towards the northwest. "They have a lot of them, but I don't work with the cattle, and we stay closer to the homestead doing work around the houses like gardening, corral building, cleaning stalls, whatever they want."

"So, where are the cows?"

"I'm not sure."

"Can you find out?" Tad asked.

"Why?" Eli asked curiously.

"Because I need to know how things work on a ranch, and Annie wasn't up to sharing anything.

We're competition, and you know how people are. It's not like we can compete with the Big Z, but she was rude."

"That surprises me. She's usually pretty friend-ly."

"She apparently doesn't like us. Do you ever think about trying to kill Matt again?"

"No!" he exclaimed. "I learned my lesson."

"What about joining a gang? I remember when we met, you were interested in joining the Sper-ry-Helms Gang. Are you still?"

Eli wrinkled his nose and shook his head.

"So, you're just going to build fences and shovel crap for meager wages when you could get wealthy and never get caught?"

"You're not wealthy, nor is your family," Eli re-plied.

"No, but we were for a short time. At least rich enough. We have a new plan that we can't go wrong on. Uncle Vince and I are starting a new gang, and I want you to join us."

"Doing what?"

Tad smiled. "Taking a few cows at a time, chang-ing the brand, and selling them. Come back here, take a few cows, change the brand and sell them." He waved towards the Big Z Ranch. "They won't notice four or five cows being gone. We'll take them to the Branson auction, sell them, take a few more and earn some good money. You could keep working here and let us know when and where to grab a few cows to sell. We'd never get caught with you telling us when and where to find the cows."

"Ahh, that's…" Eli hesitated. He couldn't believe what he was hearing, and it left him dumbfounded.

"A good plan," Tad finished for his acquaintance. "You said it yourself, the place is too big, and the cows are out of sight to graze. Eli, it's easy money, and our brand will fully cover the Big Z brand. It's foolproof. We're not taking twenty cows, just a few at a time. Maybe five at most. Look, they're rich people and have more than their share of cows. What do they care if five or ten go missing?"

Eli was nervous, and it was reflected in his stutter, "Y…y…you do know, they'll hang you if you are caught? Charlie, Adam, Marvin, any of them, they won't bother calling for the sheriff or my father."

"That's why I need your help. You don't have to do any stealing; I'll make sure you get your share just for telling us where the cattle are and when to steal them. You'll make good money for hardly anything, and no one will ever know you're our spy. I promise."

"How much?"

"I don't know for sure because I've never done it before, but I'd probably say twenty dollars every time we take the cows to auction or close to that. I'm figuring we could sell them for a good price. I don't know how much cows are worth, but the point is you'd get paid well for working with us. And we'd pay you well to tell us what we need to know and keep quiet. What do you say? It can't go wrong."

"The cattle are all branded. I watched them branding the calves."

"We're having a brand made for us right now that will cover theirs perfectly. They won't be able to prove the cows were theirs. Come on, Eli, it's the perfect plan, and you can be in with us from the start or keep shoveling crap for the rest of your life."

Eli nodded in agreement. "Okay. I'll find out where the cattle are, but how do I let you know?"

"Uncle Vince and I will be right here tomorrow at this time."

Eli shook his head. "No. I don't want to be seen with you. Follow me, and I'll show you where the swimming hole is. I'll meet you there."

Tad reached out a hand to shake. "Deal. You'll see, we'll be rich in no time."

126

Chapter 14

Audrey Butler had worked a long day in the kitchen of the Monarch Restaurant. She was hired to work the morning breakfast to lunch shift but ended up staying to help the dinner staff as the main cook had fallen down his stairs at home and sprained his wrist and ankle. After working thirteen hours in the kitchen making meals, Audrey had no ambition to make dinner for Joel Fasana when she came home. Instead of cooking, she brought dinner home from the restaurant. It wasn't that Joel couldn't make his own, go to one of his children's homes for dinner, or even afford to buy his dinner; he could do any of those. Audrey cooked dinner for Joel because he was kind enough to let her stay in his home for no cost. He didn't ask for anything, but the least she could do was cook and clean for him.

Joel had become a good friend and was a bit like a father in the absence of her own. It came naturally to him as he had had several daughters and offering advice and wisdom to a young lady was what he naturally did. His kind smile and gratitude for bringing a fine dinner home was always a good feeling that helped lift her tired spirits.

Joel sat at the dinner table over a large plate of breaded chicken breast, green beans, a garden salad, and a large baked potato soaked with butter and a touch of grated parsley. Knowing he liked sweets, Audrey brought him a piece of chocolate cake with dark chocolate frosting.

"Well, that looks good," Joel said. "Audrey, I've never eaten better since you came here. Thank you." His grin was broad. "By the way, Morton has come by twice. He seemed anxious to talk to you."

Audrey smiled. "You eat while I go freshen up. I'm sure he'll be coming by again."

A few moments later, a knock on the door brought Joel out of his seat to open it. "Oh, Morton," Joel said, finishing the food in his mouth. He swallowed.

"Is Audrey back yet?"

Joel sighed empathetically. "Morton, you just missed her. I'm afraid she went for a buggy ride with that man…" he paused, "what is his name, Walter? You know, the handsome one that she works with every day. I think it's Walter. Anyway, they left."

"What?" Morton asked as all the wind and life drained out of him like the yolk of a broken egg. He felt like his heart and strength were melting onto the porch boards. The shock on his face reminded Joel of the time he slapped a seal that tried climbing into his boat at the mouth of the Columbia River.

The seal clung to the side of the boat and stared blankly at him before falling back into the water.

Joel continued, "Well, the good news is she didn't kiss him on the porch. That's good news, Morton. But unless I'm wrong, it looked like she might've been smooching on him pretty good once they reached the buggy. I think she was trying to hide from me."

Morton felt numb. He was crushed, and his eyes began to mist as a hollowness expanded within his chest, "Uh…"

Audrey's laughter was heard from inside as she came down the stairs. "Go eat your dinner, you big clown," she laughed. She had washed her face and changed into a plain light blue dress.

Joel laughed heartily as Morton pointed a finger at him with a relieved half-grin. "You got me good, Joel."

"You kids have fun," Joel said as he returned to the dining room to finish his meal.

Audrey looked at Morton, and her smile faded while she peered at him strangely. "You…your eyes look different."

Morton's lips curled upwards slowly. "I accepted Jesus as my savior today."

"You did?" Her smile widened with excitement.

"Yes. A man in the jail named John Painter talked with me, and I prayed with him. And all of a sudden, I felt it! I was renewed and forgiven. All that shame and guilt I felt was gone."

Audrey's eyes began to water. She sniffled and hugged him. "Praise, Jesus! I am so excited for you!"

She released him and looked at him as if studying his face. "You look joyful. Morton, I am so excited."

He smiled easily. "I never realized how alive I could feel... until Joel almost ruined it!" He shouted past her towards the dining room.

Joel laughed as he took a bite of his dinner.

He paused to gaze into her eyes. "Audrey, thank you. If it wasn't for you coming into my life, I don't know where I would be. Probably running away with my cousin to rob a bank or something. But I would never be as happy and thankful as I am right now."

She held his hands in hers as they kissed softly. "Congratulations, Morton. You are now part of God's family. The creator of heaven and earth will now lean down from heaven to hear you whisper a prayer. He loves his children so much that you can approach his throne in prayer anytime. God wants, no, God longs to hear your prayers. God came to earth as Jesus and died on the cross just so we can have a relationship with him. A close and personal relationship. Oh, Morton, the Lord wants to hear your prayers about anything and everything. And he will never leave you. He is so close to us that he can see his own reflection in our eyes. And that closeness will never leave you because you now belong to him. Always remember that, because someday, it will feel like God has left you, but during those times, just remember he is right here so close that he can see his own reflection in our tears."

Morton took a deep breath and exhaled. "I have a lot to learn, but I will remember that. Audrey, now that I have committed my life to the Lord, can we move forward in our relationship?"

She lifted her lips, revealing her bright smile as her eyes narrowed. "I don't know what you're asking me."

"How about… will you marry me? Because I would like to spend the rest of my life with you."

"Yes, Morton Sperry, I will marry you," she said with tears of joy building. She had come to Jessup County under false pretenses to marry a man that would have made her life a living hell. But somehow, the Lord, in his greatness, led her to the man that she was excited to marry.

Morton laughed with exuberance, lifted her in the air, and he spun slowly in a circle while kissing her. "We're going to do it. We're going to be married, and I know we're going to be alright. Thank you, Jesus! Thank you." He held her tightly in his arms, fighting the moisture in his eyes before she could see them.

Chapter 15

The poisoned water hole of the Long T Ranch had riled the cattlemen to the point where massacring the entire sheep population was only a stone's throw away. Gunther had his ranch hands drill a hole through the handles of garden rakes and tie twine to them to toss the rakes into the pond in an effort to retrieve any evidence of poison or an explanation as to what was in the water. Fearing the possibility of strychnine contamination in the water and penetrating through the men's skin, extra precautions were being taken. Gunther made it very clear to stay out of the water first and foremost. He bought several pairs of extra leather gloves and had the men coat the gloves in axel grease to create a water barrier, but he also bought several oilcloth canvasses to be cut into one-foot square pieces to be pressed into the grease of the glove's palms of the men while they pulled the wet twine out of the water. They were to pull the rakes slowly, carefully,

and take their time, switch out the old square pieces of canvas and gloves when needed, and throw
the old ones in a barrel. The barrel of collected wet
square patches and grease-covered gloves would
later be taken to a ravine where the dead cattle were
disposed of and rolled over the edge. It didn't take
too long, with four rakes being thrown into the
pond, for the men to drag out two opened brown
bottles with their paper labels intact stating it was
soluble cyanide powder. With the evidence in hand,
Gunther approached Matt Bannister for whatever
good he might do. The facts were simple though,
with or without the U.S. Marshal, the sin could not
be tolerated and demanded immediate justice.

Matt understood Gunther's fury, but he pointed
out that there was no proof that Robert Fairchild
had anything to do with it. Matt had gone to the
Fairchild Estate and spoken with Robert, Ed Bostwick, and Ira Kelly. All three men denied any involvement and brought up the point that they had
gained everything they wanted and had no reason
to start a war with the cattlemen, which such an act
would certainly do. Robert suggested that perhaps
the Thomas family poisoned their own waterhole,
which Matt dismissed immediately. Fairchild then
reasoned that the only motivation there might be is
if the Hollister Sheep Shooters poisoned the water
to end the agreement with the cattle association
and continue their reign of terror. Robert Fairchild
adamantly denied having any involvement.

Matt had gone back to the Long T Ranch and

spoke with Gunther, who thought the accusation of the Hollister Sheep Shooters being responsible was absurd. The meeting did not end well, and Matt and Truet left the ranch knowing there was a great amount of hostility building and one wrong word or another dead cow could spark a war between the sheep and cattle men that Matt would not be able to control. Being caught between the two warring parties was never a safe place to be; a bullet could come from either direction.

Matt and Truet tried to relax over dinner at Mel's Good Food restaurant after a stressful day of heated emotions. As they entered the hotel, the desk clerk handed a plain envelope to Matt and said, "Marshal Bannister, this message was left for you."

"Thank you. Who left it?" Matt asked as he took the envelope with his name written across the front.

The desk clerk shrugged. "I do not know. It was left on the counter when I was upstairs cleaning."

Matt could see the man was sincere. He pulled out a single sheet of paper with a message that stated:

> *Marshal Bannister, meet me in the Hollister Cattlemen's Association meeting room at 11:00 p.m. if you want to know who is responsible for the sheepherder's and the Blackburn's deaths.*

Matt handed the note to Truet. "It seems we might be getting to the bottom of things after all."

***

Shortly before eleven, Matt and Truet found the cattle association building's door unlocked. They entered the meeting room, lit by multiple lanterns hanging from the ceiling. A large red envelope was set upright against a small easel in the center of the curved desk that faced the many rows of seats. It had Matt's name written in large bold letters across the envelope.

Matt stepped past the rows of seats, the silence in the building was broken by his echoing booth-eels against the wood floor as he approached the envelope. He ripped it open to find the envelope was empty.

"You got my message," Gunther Thomas said as he stepped out of a side room to the right of the curved table. He was followed by six men carrying rifles and wearing black dusters and burlap bags over their faces. A door on the left side of the curved table opened, and six more men came out dressed like the others and likewise spread out. The main door that Matt and Truet entered through opened, and a long line of men dressed precisely as the others filled the meeting room. All carried rifles or had revolvers in their hands.

Matt glanced around him as thirty to forty armed men encircled him and Truet. There was no way to identify them other than Gunther, who was in plain clothes. The sheriff's clean black boots, slightly covered by the day's dust, was one of the six that followed Gunther out the side door.

"What's this?" Matt asked. He was suddenly feeling quite uneasy. He knew if the Hollister Sheep Shooters wanted to, he and Truet could both be gunned down like sheep and disappear into history.

Gunther walked behind the curved desk, sat in his rightful chair as president of the Hollister Cattlemen's Association, and leaned back unconcerned. "You wanted to know who killed the sheep and murdered the Mexican. Now you know, the Hollister Sheep Shooters did. You might be able to identify and arrest me, but I didn't leave town, and all these men can attest to that. The same could be said for every man in here. There is nothing for you to do here, Marshal, so you might as well leave town and let us be."

Matt scanned the room, looking for anything that would betray any of the men, but nothing stood out as recognizable above any others, except for the freshly cleaned black boots of the sheriff.

"Marshal," Gunther spoke pointedly to get his attention. "Did you hear me? I said you must leave town and leave well enough alone what happens here."

"And if I don't?"

Gunther tilted his head slightly while pausing. He spoke slowly, "You might end up missing and buried under forty-seven dead cows in a gully. This is our town, Marshal Bannister. We control it, and we don't need or want you here."

Matt was bewildered. "You've made your point. Last night there was an agreement about where Fairchild could graze his sheep, and as long as you all stick to it, I have no reason to be here. So why was I invited here with all of you? I'm guessing it has something to do with what you're planning and don't want me in the way. Am I right?"

Gunther raised his hands innocently. "Well, let me begin by saying, as far as we know and will testify, your brother Adam killed Wes Wasson. In fact, if you pursue the death of Wes any further, I'm confident a few fellas here and Dora from the restaurant will testify that they witnessed your brother murder Wes Wasson in cold blood. In your official court of law, that might sentence your brother Adam to death, if not prison. However, in our court of law, settled here in the Hollister Cattlemen's Association, we acquit Adam of any crime and praise him for his contribution to keeping this a cattle town rather than a Woolley town. How about we end it here, Marshal? Go home and forget about us and let bygones be bygones."

Matt sighed. "It doesn't sound like I have much choice, do I?"

"No, young man, you don't. I appreciate you and your efforts to clean this county of villains, as we are law-abiding men, but you're not welcome here. We have some payback to do, and I don't want you in the way."

"Payback?" Matt asked. As he suspected, there was a further motivation beyond the dead shepherd, sheep, and Wes's killer for the meeting. It was to get Matt out of town so the sheep shooters could massacre the Fairchild Estate.

Gunther spoke frankly, "Don't be stupid. My water was poisoned, and I lost thousands of dollars today with dead cattle. That water will take a long time before it is usable again. Two bottles of cyanide powder were thrown in there, maybe more that haven't been pulled out with the rakes." He paused with a twisted grimace. "That's an act of war, and I'm declaring it. Now Matt, unless you think you can outgun all these men, I suggest you and your deputy pack your saddlebags and get out of town tonight."

"And if I don't?"

Gunther chuckled. "Look around you. There are thirty-seven men that you cannot identify. Any one of them could shoot you and your deputy down in cold blood tomorrow at any given time, and no one in this town will see or hear a thing if they want to live."

Matt nodded. "I see." He turned around to face the largest number of masked men. "Is that what you all want too? You outnumber the Blackburn Marshals, sure as daylight, that's made clear, but are you all killers? I ask because they are, and they won't hesitate to pull the trigger, and they aim well. Your numbers will drop soon enough. Some by death, some by injury, and others quitting because they're scared to death once the shooting starts. If you want me to leave town, I will. But when the killing is over, ask yourselves if it was worth it.

I don't think it will be when the graveyard holds your friends and family members. Might I suggest you forget about this war and go home and live in peace, knowing the sheep are far to the east and not grazing on your land?" Matt shrugged. "Ask yourselves, what motivation would Fairchild have to do such a heinous act and start a war knowing he is outnumbered?" Matt pointed at Gunther, "Instead of following that man like a flock of sheep to your own graves, think! I don't know how the poison got into the pond, but the Blackburn Marshals and Robert Fairchild deny doing it. I have to believe them because there is no reasonable motivation for it when considering the consequences that would come from it. Fairchild is as happy as a loon with the agreement made last night. Why would he risk losing everything he has by poisoning the Thomas pond? That makes no sense."

Gunther chuckled. "Marshal, you're full of bull. Thanks for coming to Hollister, but we'll take it from here. Disperse, gentlemen."

Matt and Truet watched as the men left the room without saying a single word. They were left alone in complete silence within two minutes.

Truet sighed heavily and then said, "You like to keep my life exciting, don't you?"

Matt chuckled uneasily as he exhaled to calm his nerves. "I do, yeah. It keeps you young."

Chapter 16

Matt and Truet's arrival at the Fairchild's home at midnight was most unexpected. Robert and his wife were woken up by the news that Matt and Truet had arrived and he was needed downstairs.

Robert entered the family room wearing a blue silk robe with black trim and black slippers with a golden leaf design on the top. "Gentlemen, it's a bit late for a social visit, isn't it?"

Matt answered frankly, "I'm sorry to disturb you, but this isn't a social call."

Robert yawned, "Can I get you two anything to drink?"

"No."

"Robert, is everything okay?" his wife, Holly, asked from the doorway. She wore a colorful silk robe over her nightdress and red slippers with an intricate needlepoint design. She may have been woken up from a deep sleep, but she was just as elegant and lovely as she was at the strike of noon.

"Yes, dear. Everything is fine. Go on back to bed." He motioned Matt and Truet towards the cushioned chairs and davenports, "Have a seat, gentlemen and tell me what is so urgent." He sat down in his favorite leatherback cushioned chair.

Ed Bostwick and Ira Kelley walked into the room after being awakened by Raul, one of the two male caretakers of the property. Ira was in a foul mood from having been woken up in the middle of the night. "What the hell is the purpose of this? What can't wait until the morning?" he griped as he entered.

Ed answered calmly, "Matt must have a reason to be here."

"Maybe he should spit it out then!" Ira snapped with a cold glare at Matt.

Matt spoke, "I had a meeting with the sheep shooters tonight. Truet and I were surrounded by thirty to forty men holding weapons to tell me to leave town. I believe they intend to come here and kill all of you. They blame you for poisoning Thomas's water, and I can't change their mind."

Ira was quick to exclaim, "You should leave! If they come, we'll take care of it."

Robert held up a hand to quiet Ira with concern. "Marshal Bannister, when do they plan on coming?"

"I don't know. I was told to leave town, so maybe tomorrow. Gunther Thomas is furious, as you might expect."

Robert spoke quietly, "I can understand that; I would be too if someone poisoned my water. But what if I am innocent? Is there no way to avoid a violent confrontation?"

"I think Gunther wants a confrontation, and if he wants it bad enough, then no. You will have to fight whether you want to or not."

"I think it was the sheep shooters that poisoned the waterhole to blame me." Robert sighed pointedly. "As you pointed out, I am intent on building a sheep empire in the center of cattle country. It is a conflict of business ideologies, but it is a conflict that I intend to win. If they want to bring out the guns, I hired the right men for the job. The question, Marshal Bannister, is; which side will you and Truet fight for? Mine or the cattlemen?"

Matt answered thoughtfully, "It's not my job to take sides. My job is to try to stop any violence before it begins. At this point, that seems unlikely."

"So, your answer is what?" Robert asked, pressing him.

"It isn't as easy as taking sides. I have to do what I think is right and that is defend against the aggressors in this case. You have the right to be here and seek your fortune, the same as they do. Unfortunately, you are greatly outnumbered and in danger. My advice, Mister Fairchild, is for you and your wife to leave town until tempers cool down and this is settled."

Robert was quickly agitated. "You want me to leave my home so they can come in here and steal everything I have or burn my home down and kill all my sheep? Absolutely not!" Robert refused to hear of it. "No. If they come onto my property, these men I hired will kill as many of them as it takes for the cattlemen to run away with their tails tucked between their legs. I will not run away, but I will hire a hundred more gunmen if necessary. I hired three more tonight. Wes was a loss, but it wasn't such a loss that I can't hire more men." Robert stood and approached a small bar and poured himself a rare drink. "I feel sorry for the ranchers that come against us. But if they come, we will fight!"

"I don't think it would be safe for your wife to be here. Let me take her someplace safe," Matt suggested.

"Safe?" Robert laughed. "Where would she be safe around here? In town?" Robert asked scornfully. "She is safest right here. Our home is secure."

"I would take her to the Monarch Hotel in Branson," Matt answered.

Robert scoffed with a disgusted laugh. "So, you're leaving like the cowpokes told you to? I expected a lot more, I don't know how to say it, but I expected more *oomph* from a man of your reputation. It's funny, Marshal Bannister, in the big cities back east, these neighborhood gangs roam the alleys and streets in their sector of town. To become part of this gang of thugs, one must prove their worth; the value of that worth is their reputation as a tough roughian. They must fight to do so, but usually, the victim is weaker and safe for them to beat to a pulp. In doing so, they win the fight, and their reputation grows even though they still might be cowardly and weak. You see, it isn't how tough or courageous they are that's important. It's the reputation of being so—the *mirage* of being so.

"You, sir, have the reputation, but I haven't seen anything to convince me that it wasn't made from weaker victims to create a mirage. As these cowboys say, I may be an eastern dandy, but I know people. The police in big cities let the gangs fight each other in hopes that they kill each other off. It's just fewer thugs and more food in the supply chain for someone else. No, Marshal Bannister, my wife, will stay with me. Ed and the boys will protect us." He looked at Ed Bostwick, "By the time the sun rises, we should be on high alert and prepared for a battle. I suggest we discuss that further after the good marshal leaves."

"We'll do," Ed said. He knew better than anyone how dangerous Matt could be, but he did not dare to correct Mister Fairchild. His future dreams were dependent upon Robert's financial backing and knowledge.

Ira Kelly asked Matt, "Did those sheep shooters say they killed Wes?"

Matt was insulted by Robert's accusation of his character. The implication of it stunned him. He shook his head in answer to Ira's question. "Not in so many words."

Ira sneered, "He'd still be alive if Wes wasn't tied up and left like wolf bait. Tell your brother to enjoy his days because I'll be coming for him when this is over. You don't treat a Blackburn Marshal like that and get away with it. Ever!"

"I'll let him know." Matt put his attention on Robert feeling a need to defend his honor. He wanted to tell Robert where he could stick his opinion of comparing him to some teenage city street hood. Pausing before reacting gave him a moment of clarity, and he knew it would only further enhance Robert's impression of him if he responded aggressively. "I'll talk with Gunther in the morning to try to reason with him. Have a good night. I'll see myself out," he said coldly.

Ira chuckled bitterly, "Talk doesn't solve anything."

Robert waved a hand to dismiss Matt and Truet as they stepped towards the hallway to leave the room. "Tough talk is key to keeping a reputation. The weakest kids in New York City probably couldn't fight their way through a paper fence, but they sure put on a show. They need to because if they actually fought a worthy opponent, everyone would know how weak they were. It's just a verbal dance; gentlemen, let the famous marshal do his dance."

Matt turned around as Ira laughed. He was both insulted and humiliated by the words that were directed at him. There was a time to talk, and there was a time to act, but there was also a time when silence was the wisest choice. If he yanked Robert Fairchild up by the collar and tossed him across the floor to prove his toughness, it only proved his reputation was a farce by manhandling a much older and weaker man. If he vented his frustration in a loud, angry stream of rhetoric, it only further proved to be a verbal dance, as Robert had called it. The best thing he could do was walk away without a word. That might have been the best thing to do, but Matt refused to leave without having the last word.

"Yes, Marshal?" Robert asked before taking a sip of his drink. He watched Matt with a sly little smirk on his lips.

Matt smiled slightly. "Have a good night. I'll let you know if I can reason with Gunther or not."

"Well, thank you!" Robert said sarcastically in a loud voice. "Ed and Ira, we can rest assured the good marshal will talk to those vicious ranchers for us."

Matt and Truet left the family room and walked up the corridor of the large home towards the front door. As they passed the grand staircase, Matt's wrist was grabbed by Holly Fairchild, who had been sitting at the bottom of the stairs listening to the conversation.

"Are they really planning to come here to attack our home and kill Robert?" she asked. Holly Fairchild's large blue eyes blinked several times as they filled with anxious tears. It was easy to recognize that she was scared.

Matt was slightly red-faced from the humiliation of Robert's words. "That's the impression that I got. I suggest you pack a bag and let me take you to Branson to be safe."

"I don't want to leave Robert. Is there no way to stop them?" she asked.

"I'm going to try reasoning with Mister Thomas in the morning. He seems to be the one in charge and the voice the others listen to. Somebody poisoned his water, and he's rightfully furious about it."

"Poisoned? With what?" she asked.

"Cyanide."

"Oh, my goodness," she said with a glance toward the family room, where the three men continued discussing the matter.

Something in her expression made Matt curious. "Do you know anything about that?"

"No. No. It's just terrible that someone would do that. Marshal Bannister, we just want to live peacefully. We never wanted any trouble with our neighbors."

"Missus Fairchild, I'll let you know tomorrow if I succeeded at keeping the peace. Mister Thomas lost a lot of cattle and the water supply for his livestock. Messing with a man's livelihood is playing with fire, and you never know how a man will react."

"You're talking about Gunther Thomas, right?"

"Yes, Ma'am. Lord willing, he'll listen to reason and realize he can't assume someone is guilty without proof. What happened to his water is a very malicious crime, but without proof, assumptions can get the wrong people killed. Your husband and the Blackburn Marshals swear they didn't do it. But I can tell you with certainty that the sheep shooters did not poison his water, nor will a rancher poison his own. So there you have it; they blame your husband."

When Matt and Truet left, Holly stepped quietly into the family room to overhear Robert saying,

"There are enough extra boards in the barn to build shields below and around the windows to offer extra protection from bullets. The house can be repaired, the windows can be replaced, but you fighting men stand between them and me. Ed, I need more gunmen. We always intended to make the Blackburn Marshals a corporation. Now is a good time to expand." His attention went to Holly. "Oh, my dear, I thought you were sleeping?"

Holly asked, "Did you poison that man's water?"

Chapter 17

Holly Fairchild had not slept well as the first rays of sunlight broke over the eastern sky. She lay in the dim light, watching her husband sleep soundly beside her. He had stayed up late with Ira Kelly and Ed Bostwick discussing how to defend the property and keep her and the servants safe if the Hollister Sheep Shooters did attack their home. Holly could overhear them speaking, and although she could appreciate Robert's concern for her and the servants, she knew very well that Robert was worried for his safety as well. He had crawled into bed a few hours before and would sleep in later than he usually did.

Quietly, she slipped out of bed and freshened up for the day. She put on a peach-colored dress and covered her wavy blonde hair with a tan wide-brimmed felt hat with a peacock feather on one side. She ate a plum for breakfast and told the servants not to disturb Mister Fairchild before stepping into the morning sunshine and making her way towards the stable. Holly saddled her red roan mare and led her out of the stable. Holly was met by Kent Kruse, one of the Blackburn Marshals. Beside him was one of the three newly hired Blackburn Marshals that showed up last night.

"Missus Fairchild," Kent Kruse said gently, "you shouldn't be riding off today; from what I understand, there could be some trouble coming our way." Kent's concern was sincere. Of all the Blackburn Marshals Holly had spoken to over the past month that were living on their estate, Ed Bostwick and Kent were the only two that made her feel comfortable.

She smiled generously, but a touch of unease penetrated through her pretty smile. "I'm just going for a short ride. I'll be back soon enough."

"Missus Fairchild," Kent repeated, "I don't think your husband would want you riding off today. There could be trouble, and you don't want to be caught out there alone with them. How about I ride along with you?"

"No, thanks. I want to be alone." She gracefully took her seat on her lady's sidesaddle. "I'll be fine. I'm a lady, after all."

"Ma'am," Cass Travers said, "can you tell us where you'll be riding so we know."

Her large blue eyes fell on him, and then she blinked rapidly to remove a speck of dust with a wipe of her finger. She didn't know the newly hired man, but from his rough unkempt exterior and claw-like scars on his cheek, she had no doubt he was a tough man with a sordid past. Like all of the Blackburn Marshals, he undoubtedly could become violent when needed. With her eye clear of debris, she smiled as bright as the morning sun. It wasn't that she found the new hire handsome or charming in the least; it just amazed her how a newly hired man, whom she had not even met, was already questioning her. It made her feel like a captive in her own home, and she wasn't going to allow that. "I'll be riding around. Have a good day, boys." She rode away without another word.

Cass Travers watched her leave, slack-jawed. The morning sun on her face had given her an angelic appearance that revealed the depth of blue in her eyes. She was the most beautiful woman he had ever seen. "Huh!" he exclaimed. "She's absolutely glorious. I've heard people say that some woman is as pretty as an angel before, but with the sun shining in her eyes like that. I can't imagine angels are prettier. So that's the old man's wife? How does that happen?"

Kent grinned. It was the same question that all of the Blackburn Marshals had asked themselves. He answered, "It's not his money. She is as dedicated to him as any young couple in love."

Cass watched her ride further up the long driveway. "Should I get on my horse and ride along with her to keep her safe? Maybe steal her away from that old man while I'm at it."

Kent offered a short chuckle. "Good luck with that. Trust me, Cass, we've all thought about it, and I have gotten to know her some; but she is happily in love with Robert Fairchild. We'll let Ira know she went for a ride and see what he says. She goes for morning rides sometimes, but she'll stay on the property. If Mister Fairchild isn't too worried about her riding today, then maybe we shouldn't be either."

"Are you sure she just isn't after his money?" Cass asked. "Because if she was, then that's my kind of woman."

Kent shook his head with a laugh. "I'm sure that's not her motivation. Holly is an amazing lady, and trust me when I say; you better keep it professional with her because she will quickly put you in your place."

***

Holly didn't consider herself overly brave, but when she was determined to do something, she did it. She had a blank check in her pocket and a silver fountain pen to write it with. Holly had been hesitant to move to the wilds of Oregon from their estate in New York City, but now she loved living under the shadow of the majestic mountains on the shore of Gibbons Lake. She loved rowing the boat out to the middle of the lake with a bottle of wine and sharing a midnight conversation with Robert under the stars. She loved riding her horse across the hills and discovering new places to picnic. She loved the Fairchild Estate in Hollister as much as she loved their home back east. She wasn't willing to see it destroyed or risk her life with Robert coming to an abrupt end. Something had to be done aside from planning for a war. Sometimes, it was a lady's prerogative to take matters in hand and settle the storm before it came blowing in.

Matt Bannister had told her the proverbial straw that broke the camel's back was the poisoning of the water and the accumulative loss of livestock. It only stood to reason that an honest conversation, along with an offer to compensate the Long T Ranch's losses as a peace offering, would alleviate the anger and mend their relationship. With that in mind, Holly rode off the Fairchild Estate towards the Long T Ranch six miles away. She had never been there before, but she heard it was easy to find as the headgate was a prominent landmark on the northbound road.

On the way, she ran into a buggy driven by eighteen-year-old Jake Thomas, who was taking his older sister, Darra Lee, to town. Holly had met them both at church in the past and even had Darra Lee at her home for a church ladies' tea party a couple of times. That was when Holly first arrived and attended the church and made friends with several ladies, Darra Lee, being one. That changed when it became known that Robert intended to build a large woolen mill along the river and change the town forever into the wool capital of Oregon. The idea of bringing fifty thousand sheep into cattle country was not well accepted, and the tensions rose to the point that she was made to feel unwelcomed at church by the cattlemen and their wives.

The short meeting on the road with Jake and

Darra Lee was encouraging and sweet as they both assured her that their father was at the house and would be interested in talking with her. The large headgate to the Long T Ranch was as noticeable on the road as a red barn was in the snow. It had two thick vertical logs and a horizontal log crossing over the driveway. The front face of the log had been planed, stained, and the ranch's brand, a T with an extended cross bar along the top, was engraved in the center.

The driveway was long, but after a few turns along a hillside, the Thomas family homestead came into view. Their home was a large two-story log cabin with cedar roofing and a wide front porch that faced south so they could watch the sun rise or fall. A large barn was about seventy yards away from the house and several other buildings clustered near the main homestead, including the bunkhouse and cookhouse. Two men were talking in front of the barn doors, and three more rode their horses across a field to meet Holly as she reached the house.

Bode Thomas, Monty Saunders, and Fallon MacArthur saw her riding towards the house and turned back to meet her as they were curious why she was there. Bode jumped from his saddle and gently took hold of Holly's red roan's bridle. "Well, if it isn't Missus Fairchild coming out to see us. What can we do for you, Holly?"

She did not like how Bode held the bridle's cheek strap, which stopped her from leaving if she intended to. Her horse didn't like it either, as his knuckles pressed uncomfortably against the mare's cheek. The other two cowboys, Monty and Fallon, dismounted and stood close with lustful intent burning in their eyes. The three men made her feel uncomfortable.

She spoke with all the confidence that a lady who meant business could, "I came out to speak with your father. Is he in the house?"

Bode nodded. "I believe so. Do you want to come inside?"

Holly had carefully considered her decision to ride to the Long T Ranch. She had pictured a sit-down discussion with Gunther Thomas, where they could speak as equals and agree to her paying for the lost cattle as a peace offering while making it clear that the check was not an admission of guilt. She was merely a neighbor willing to help a new friend.

However, she had not considered that Bode might grab the bridle's cheek strap, ensuring she couldn't leave as he now controlled the mare. She began to think she had made an unwise decision by coming all this way alone, and worse, no one knew where she was going. Holly had been raised in an upper-class home in Philadelphia, the daughter of a District Court Judge, the Honorable Harry Gilles. She was raised to be a proper lady, and although she knew there were crimes and criminals, she had never been exposed to them or was ever threatened by them until now. Her stomach turned and twisted with an anxiousness swelling within her that was uncommon and frightening. The cold and predatory stare in Monty and Fallon's expressions made her most uneasy. To go inside the house was to separate her from her only means of escape, and once inside, she would be behind closed doors and at their mercy. Her gut instincts screamed with condemnation for her own foolishness to put herself in such a situation and the stupidity of not letting anyone know her intentions. She was presently at their mercy and becoming warier of it by the second.

"No," she answered as her throat tightened. "Could you ask your father to come out here, please?"

"Fallon, go ask my father to come out here. Miss Holly Fairchild would like to speak with him."

"Sure," Fallon said and went inside the house.

Bode pet the mare's neck as he continued, "Can I ask you a question? I don't mean to be disrespectful, but why are you married to that old man? He can't be that spry."

"Robert is a wonderful man if you get to know him," she answered uneasily. She glanced at Monty wearily as he removed his hat and rubbed his hand over his thinning brown hair.

Monty asked her, "Was it an arranged marriage, or did he buy you from your parents? I know he's rich. Is that why you married him?" Monty was the older of the three cowboys in his mid-thirties. He was a short and stocky man with broad shoulders, a round face, balding with short brown hair, and a thick mustache.

"No," Holly answered with an offended scowl.

The questions were rude and didn't deserve an answer. Holly had gotten to know Monty's fiancé, a middle-aged widow named Nancy Fortner, at the tea parties Holly hosted, and she introduced Holly to Monty one Sunday at church. That was before the community discovered Robert and her wanted to build a woolen mill and raise thousands of sheep.

Bode chuckled. "Monty, that's ancient British royalty. Americans don't prearrange marriages."

Monty was offended by how Holly dismissed him with her arrogant grimace, like he wasn't worthy enough to ask her a question. A part of him wanted to yank her off that horse and press her face into the dirt to show her she wasn't so high and mighty.

Monty scowled. "He's rich enough to buy a young wife if he wants one."

Bode chuckled lightly. "I suppose he is." He let his eyes fall on Holly. "Have you ever been asked if you married him for his money?"

"Of course," she answered shortly, "And quite frankly, I'm getting tired of it. I married my husband because I love him. There is no other reason."

Monty asked, "So how much will you inherit when the old man dies? A hundred thousand, two? Or more?"

She rolled her eyes, frustrated. She ignored Monty and spoke to Bode, "If you wouldn't mind, I'd like to speak to your father alone. So please, let go of my horse."

"Sure," Bode said, removing his grasp from the cheek strap. "I mean no disrespect, Miss Holly. I'm just curious about what made you marry your husband. I mean, he's as old or older than my father. Your husband's old enough to be your father or grandfather. We're about the same age, you and I."

She looked at him frankly. "I just said I married Robert because I love him."

Monty scoffed doubtfully. "Right. I don't believe that for a minute. You're a money-grubbing swindler just waiting for him to die. Cut me in, and I'll make that happen."

"Monty," Bode said while shaking his head.

"Maybe," Gunther Thomas gruffly said as he crossed the porch approaching her, "that's why she has bottles of cyanide? Do you want to poison the old eastern dandy and take over his property? If so, let me know, and I'll help you do it free of charge." He walked down the few porch steps to approach her.

"No, Mister Thomas, I do not. And I do not have cyanide anywhere on our property…"

"Not anymore. It's in my pond!" Gunther snapped, interrupting her. "What do you want?"

Holly swallowed dryly and cleared her throat. "I hoped we could talk reasonably. The marshal mentioned that you might intend to attack my home. My husband nor anyone on our estate had anything to do with poisoning your water. But in the name of neighborly love and keeping the peace, I came to compensate you for your losses and make everything right to end this feud between you and my husband. I could write a check for any amount you think is fair."

Gunther gasped while he glared at her with disdain. "Does the pompous dandy think sending his pretty wife out here to write me a check will compensate for poisoning my pond? Is he too much of a coward to speak to me himself?" he snapped angrily. "Do you understand the pond is ruined? I don't want your damn money; I want your husband's life! This will never be sheep country. And you know, I despise you for coming out here and trying to buy my mercy! If your husband wants to send you out here like a peace offering, fine! We'll accept it and send you back with a Long T Ranch baby inside you. Take her to the barn and ensure she's pregnant before leaving here. Share her with all the boys. That's my peace offering to your husband," he spat out bitterly. He shoved her backward forcefully over the sidesaddle with both his hands, right into the waiting arms of Monty.

Monty slammed her to the ground face down and grabbed one wrist while Fallon grabbed the other to drag her to the barn.

Holly screamed helplessly as Monty and Fallon dragged her along the dirt road toward the barn well over fifty yards away. Her dress ripped on a rock as its sharp edge scrapped across her skin. She looked up and saw the barn drawing nearer and two other men watching from the door with interest.

Monty shouted, "Call in all the boys! The big boss gave us an order, and I'm going first."

"Second!" called Fallon.

Her instincts had warned her to kick the horse

and get away while she could, but she waited to continue a conversation that ended abruptly, and now terror seized her like an evil nightmare she could not wake from. She was dragged face down along a rough road toward certain torment and pain. She never imagined she would be treated with such disregard by Gunther and thrown to the wolves to be brutalized. The terror was unimaginable; she sobbed, pleaded, and begged them to let her go. "Let me go. Get your filthy hands off me and let me go! Help! Lord, stop them. Help me!" her cries echoed across the valley.

Prayer took time, but time stood still as the seconds felt like minutes as every inch of road dug into her skin, ripping the peach dress as her nightmare was just beginning. "God, help me," she pleaded as the last resort. Her face was carried inches above the ground when a black beetle scurrying across the road caught her attention. For a moment, her face hovered above the beetle as their lives crossed paths, and she realized in that brief second that to the men dragging her, the life of that beetle and hers were equally worthless.

"What did the boss say?" one of the cowboys at the barn asked, walking forward.

Monty answered through his heavy breaths, "The sheepman's pretty wife is childless because he is old and withered. Gunther ordered us to get her pregnant for the old sheepman as a favor and send her home. I'm going first; there's a good chance the baby will be mine. If we have a baby girl, she'll be as cute as a baby lamb between her mama's blonde hair and my good looks." He chuckled mercilessly.

"Well, we gotta follow orders," A ranch hand named KC said with a chuckle and picked up her dragging feet to carry her.

The touch of a third man's hands on her ankles raised her panic, surpassing any fear she had ever known. Her heart pounded, and her throat tightened. She tried to jerk her wrists from the men's grasp and kick the third man free of her ankles, but everything she tried made them laugh at her struggling all the more. She could not look up and see their faces, but she did not doubt that they were smiling like the devil himself with such evil vileness in their hearts and minds. Her screaming had done no good so far, but a wave of fierce anger sparked within, and Holly screamed louder and more profoundly than ever before. Her bladder released, dripping a stream of urine from her dress while she was carried quickly toward the barn.

The sound of the urine flow hitting the dirt road left a wet trail that KC stepped in. "She's pissing herself!" he exclaimed.

"Fellas, that ain't right," an older man standing at the door said. "You need to let her go."

"Shut up, Dusty!"

In desperation, Holly shouted at Monty, "Nancy! I'll tell Nancy!"

Monty ordered the other two men to put her down. He flipped her over to her back and knelt to place a strong left hand over her throat and began choking her. He hissed between his clenched teeth, "Nancy's my wife! We just got married two weeks ago, and if you say a word to her, I swear it will be the last time you ever speak! Don't you ever say her name again!" His right fist curled into a tight fist and fell like a hammer into her fragile face. He called her several foul names and struck her repeatedly with his fist until her face was swelling, bleeding, and blood painted his knuckles red.

Fallon and the other cowboy, KC, pulled Monty away from her to stop him from beating her to death. "What are you doing?" Fallen shouted. "No one said to kill her or to hit her! Now look, she's all bloody! I don't want to be kissing on a bloody face. What's wrong with you?" He pushed Monty irritably.

A gunshot sounded, and the dirt beside the men shattered with the penetration of a .45 caliber bullet.

"Drop your gun belts and step away from her!" Matt Bannister's eyes were as hard as a cold block of granite and offered no other alternative than to do as he demanded. His Colt .45 was pointed at them with the hammer pulled back and his finger on the trigger. Matt stood near his buckskin gelding with no trace of grace on his face.

Fallon MacArthur raised his hands and stepped back before slowly releasing his gun belt and letting it fall into the dust. KC Owens followed the orders nervously. His chest heaved quickly with fear of being shot or arrested by the marshal.

"Now!" Matt yelled at Monty, who had turned to face Matt with his right hand slowly drawing closer to his revolver. His chest heaved in and out with fury. An angry snarl twisted his lips. He was not willing to let Holly go without a fight. He hated the woman and wanted to make her hurt. "Make me!" he challenged.

Matt pulled the trigger and drove a bullet into Monty's left shoulder, forcing him to spin backward and take two steps back before turning back to face Matt. An enraged snarl twisted his lips with a deep guttural roar while he tried to draw his revolver. "I'll kill y—"

Matt pulled the trigger again, placing a .45 caliber slug into the center of Monty's chest, forcing him to the ground to breathe his last few breaths.

The rage Monty had known a moment before vanished as thoughts of his wife filled his mind. He was dying and had not kissed her goodbye that morning. Monty would never kiss her again. Hate, why did he hate Holly Fairchild? It seemed unimportant now. There was no reason other than envy. Time was running out, and the bright morning sunlight was fading fast. If only he could hold his wife one last time and tell her... "Sorry," he said to no one as he breathed his last breath.

Screaming uncontrollably, Holly scrambled to her feet and ran from the men blindly towards Matt. She ran into him abruptly as her arms clung around him while she wailed uncontrollably. Matt held her with his left arm while ordering the other two men ferociously, "Start walking across that field, and don't stop for half an hour. Go!"

At the house, chaos took over as Gunther and Bode Thomas shouted at Matt for killing their friend and faithful employee. Truet Davis held his revolver on the father and son in case they became a threat. Matt's attention was on trying to calm Holly's loud, uncontrollable sobbing by reassuring her that she was safe. Her panicked cries and sobbing were loud and pierced Matt's ears. He was infuriated to see her face beaten and knowing what the men were about to do to her.

Holly's strength gave out and she slipped to the ground sobbing. Matt knelt beside her to comfort her. At the touch of his hand on her shoulder, she swung her arms and scrambled away from him, screaming in a terrified state of mind.

Matt caught her and held her shoulders firmly. "Holly, It's me. You're safe. You're safe now, and I'll get you home. It's okay, I got you." He watched as her panic-stricken wild eyes seemed to take root, recognize him, and settle into sobbing. She wrapped her arms around him again in a tight hug and sobbed on his shoulder. He held her while she began to calm down and regain control of herself. His chest tightened with emotion that brought a glaze of moisture to his eyes. "Let's get you home."

"Gunther," a weak and concerned aging woman's voice asked from the porch. "Why is that lady crying? Who is that?" his wife demanded to know. She was in a wheelchair and had deformed joints with severe arthritis along with fading eyesight.

Gunther ignored his wife and pointed a finger at Matt. He shouted, "You drew first blood, Marshal! Monty's been working for me all his life."

Matt helped Holly onto her horse and then

walked around her horse to stand face-to-face with Gunther and lifted his hand to show Gunther Holly's blood smeared on his hand. "He drew first blood. Innocent blood." He shook his finger at Gunther, fighting the temptation to hit the old man. "What happened here is unforgivable."

Gunther spat, "Nothing happened."

Bode volunteered, "I told my father to stop it. He's the one that ordered them to do it."

Matt pointed a finger at Bode and spoke heatedly, "Then *you* should have stopped it! Quit asking for daddy's permission to do what's right!" He took a deep breath and spoke to Gunther, "I came out here to try to stop you from declaring war, but now I won't be able to stop the Blackburn Marshals from declaring war on you! You just made the stupidest decision you have ever made!"

"Tell them to come on out," Gunther invited. "In fact, you can tell Fairchild that I'm going to burn his place to the ground," he threatened.

Matt grabbed Holly's reins and stepped into the saddle to lead her horse back home. He looked and Gunther and said, "I won't need to tell them anything."

Chapter 18

Matt and Truet took Holly Fairchild home but rode around the town of Hollister to spare her the humiliation of the citizens seeing her bloody and swollen face. When they arrived at the Fairchild home, they discovered that Robert had been frantic to find his missing bride and sent the Blackburn Marshals out to search for her. Kent Kruse had told Robert and the others what Holly had said earlier that morning, but she had been gone too long for a quick ride around the property.

When Robert saw Holly's beaten face, he wept with her as he took her inside to comfort her and clean the wounds on her face. There was a cut above her eye; even though it was a superficial wound, it bled severely and covered her face with blood. Her eye was swollen nearly closed, and her cheek swelled, promising to be bruised and discolored for a week or two.

Matt answered questions that Ed Bostwick and

Ira Kelly asked, but he could not answer why Holly was alone at the Long T Ranch. She had not said a word on the way back to the Fairchild Estate. Matt and Truet stayed downstairs, talking to the two leaders of the Blackburn Marshals, while Robert stayed with his wife upstairs.

Kent Kruse came inside after searching the perimeter of the lake for Holly. "I understand Holly came home?" he asked Ira.

Ira nodded. "Marshal Bannister and Truet found her on the Long T Ranch in the clutches of some men. She's a bit beat up, but nothing serious happened to her."

"She wasn't..." Kent asked Matt with growing fury.

"No," Matt said.

Kent's fondness for Holly was apparent. "I hope you killed the men that put a hand on her."

"I killed the one that beat her," Matt answered.

"I haven't met you. I'm Kent Kruse." He reached a hand out to shake. Kent had short reddish-brown hair and a groomed short beard and mustache. His dark blue eyes showed sincere concern for Holly.

"I'm Matt. This is my deputy Truet Davis. You must have been one of the Blackburn Marshals that took the gold to San Francisco when the strike happened at the Branson silver mine?"

Kent nodded. "Yes. Ira, Ellis McKenna, and I took that trip to California. It was quite a shock to come back to Branson and find out Jeff Blackburn was dead. We weren't expecting any of that. Luckily, Ed signed us up here and we still have a job."

Ira Kelly sounded irritated as he said, "Kent, go out and let everyone know Holly is back."

Ed Bostwick stepped past Matt, tapped him on the belly, and nodded towards the front door. Matt and Truet followed him onto the front porch. Ed turned to Matt and spoke quietly, "Listen, you know, we can't let this attack on Missus Fairchild ride free. Do you know the names of the man you killed and who else held her?"

Matt shook his head. "Monty is the one I shot. I didn't ask for any other names. Truet, do you know?"

He shook his head. "No. I had my attention on Gunther and his son. By the way, Bode was trying to get his father to stop those men. Gunther ordered them to take her to the barn."

Ed clicked his tongue. "Well, I was hoping they wouldn't come here. Now I hope they do."

Two other Blackburn Marshals rounded the side of the house and one took off his hat to wipe his brow with his shirtsleeve as he glanced up on the porch. "Marshal Bannister, I heard you were here. I don't suppose Morton is here by chance. We just saw him yesterday at your office," Jesse Helms said. He was with Jimmy Abbot.

"You are a Blackburn Marshal now?" Matt asked curiously. He was surprised to see Jesse wearing a silver star with the word *Marshal* engraved in black. It was the standard Blackburn Marshal's badge that they all wore.

"Yes. Cass Travers, Elliot Zook, and I gave up crime to find a more legitimate job. I figured if

Morton could do it, so could we. But, this is about as close to the law as I come." He grinned.

"Hmm," Matt said, sounding unconvinced. "Well, good luck to you."

Jesse's cold eyes never changed as his lips rose a touch as if he knew something Matt didn't, "You, too."

"You know those three?" Ed asked. "They showed up late last night looking to join us. They were friends with Wes and said he invited them. They were surprised to hear he was dead. Jesse said he knew your brother Adam and where he lived. That convinced Ira to want to hire them."

Matt watched Jesse and Jimmy walk towards a flower garden while talking together. "That might've got him in the door, but Jesse knows better than to think he can go onto the Big Z Ranch and cause trouble. To answer your question, yes, I know them. Members of the Sperry-Helms Gang, all three of them. But it sounds like they are now your problem and not mine." Matt didn't trust the Blackburn Marshals to begin with, but now with those three joining them, Matt was even more uncomfortable.

Ed leaned against the porch railing. "You can feel a fight coming in the air, can't you?"

"Yes, I can."

"I'm nervous," Ed admitted. "I don't know what it is about this place, but it makes me uneasy."

Matt took a deep breath and exhaled. "I hoped to avoid a battle, but I don't know if it can be stopped. And now, to be honest, Ed, I don't know who I can trust less, the cattlemen or your men. Truet and I are kind of stuck in the middle. And those three aren't friendly with me either," he said, pointing towards Jesse Helms.

"Matt, you have nothing to fear from any of our marshals. I'll give you my word on that, and I'll make sure they all know it. It might be worth knowing that Jimmy Abbot and Henry Dodds are convinced your brother killed Wes and aren't likely to let it go. Ira is like-minded in that."

Matt glanced back at Jesse Helms talking to Jimmy Abbot in the garden. "Yeah, that might be worth knowing." He sighed. "Ed, if you have a bad feeling about this place, quit while you can. I don't need any more deputies, but the Branson sheriff will hire you."

Ed laughed. "No. Mister Fairchild is going to take the Blackburn Marshal name and make it nationwide, and I'll be on top. Someday, maybe you'll be asking me for a job."

***

Holly soaked in the warm water of a bathtub filled with perfumed bubbles and a glass of white wine. Her husband sat on a chair near her and quietly watched her relax with her eyes closed. Her cheek and eye throbbed.

"Holly, you haven't told me why you went out there yet," Robert spoke softly.

Her eyes opened slowly and then closed. "I thought if I offered to pay for Gunther's lost cattle, he'd be more reasonable."

A cold chill worked slowly up Robert's spine. "Ohh..." he groaned, "that's only going to convince him that we poisoned his water, Holly. I wish you wouldn't have done that. It's going to turn the entire cattle industry against us."

Her eyes opened with a hardened edge. "Then you shouldn't have done it." she said accusingly.

"Who said we did?" he shrugged innocently.

"I know you did. I know when you're lying. You don't let anyone have the last word, Robert. Not ever."

He sighed. "Well, you're right. I did it. But I know Gunther is the head of the sheep shooters and is responsible for everything that's happened. He's responsible for Juan's death and for branding my shepherds like cattle. That cannot be forgiven, Holly. Poisoning his waterhole was meant to show him what it is like to lose livestock. He needs to know that I'll fight just as dirty as he can. I can be just as brutal, too; I'm just smarter about it. And sweetheart, what they did to you, won't be forgiven either. I'm going to hit them a lot harder."

She closed her eyes and groaned. "I went there to save your life, Robert." She began to weep as she said, "He told his men to send me home with a baby inside of me." She gazed at him with a perplexed expression. "I don't understand how a man could do that. I was so scared, Robert." Her eyes closed tightly as she wept.

He left his chair to kneel next to the tub and gently embraced her head against his chest. "You're safe now, my love. I have no answer for men like that, Sweetheart."

She broke free from the gentle hug and glared at him. "You're no better. You'll keep pushing back and fighting until none of us have anything or anyone." She sniffled and shook her head. "Why do we need sheep and a woolen mill? We have more money than we need, and all this dream of yours is doing is causing trouble that could get us both killed. Look at my face!" she shouted. "They don't care that I'm a lady! What's next, Robert? You getting killed and me carrying some cowboy's baby? That is what is going to happen!"

Robert moved back in his chair. "Sweetheart, we agreed to do this. I don't have an heir to pass my name to. The Fairchild Woolen Mill will stand for generations and produce the best wool in the nation. That is my namesake, and I won't let go of that. This land is perfect for sheep, and I will make Hollister the sheep capital of Oregon. To me, that's worth fighting for."

Holly grimaced before speaking softly, "I love our home here. But if you must have sheep, I'm willing to give this place up to move somewhere else where sheep are more welcome. We don't need the trouble."

Robert's expression was emotionless. "I'm not leaving. We have everything we need right here, including a great view of a beautiful lake. This is paradise, Holly. We just have to fight the little fights to keep it. Someday, all of this will be yours, and I want to make it perfect so that the wool industry lasts for the rest of your life."

Holly sighed. "This is your dream, Robert. It's

not even your dream. It's just a business. I think sheep are cute, but we don't need this business. We have enough money to last a lifetime already. We could live here and enjoy our life without sheep."

Robert ran a frustrated hand over his gray hair. "Holly, you don't get it. I don't need the money. What I need is a purpose. I need to have something to build. Something I can create and make my own." He offered a sad hint of a smile. "I won't live forever, and when I'm gone, you'll own everything I have and can choose to sell them or not. You're young enough that sooner or later, you'll marry again, and my name will be forgotten. But if I build a large woolen mill and have the bricklayers write the Fairchild name with bricks above the door and on the sides, it will remain long after I am gone. We live our whole lives, and towards the end, you realize all my success means nothing without leaving a legacy to be remembered. Holly, you will remarry, and the Fairchild name will disappear once you do. This woolen mill is my last big project, and the Fairchild name will always be a part of the building. That's what I'm willing to fight them for. To be immortal, my name at least. I don't want to be forgotten."

Holly asked softly, "If the marshal wasn't there this morning and I was...raped. Would your name in bricks still be worth it?" Her blue eyes slowly gathered a thick puddle of tears as she waited for an answer.

Robert answered defensively, "You shouldn't have been there to begin with."

"That's not an answer."

He remained silent while staring at her refusing to answer.

A tear slipped down Holly's cheek. The dullness of her voice revealed the depth of her broken heart, "I guess that was your answer."

Robert sat quietly for a moment, growing uncomfortable under her gaze. "I don't know what you want me to say."

She gasped. "Nothing. I want Matt Bannister to take me to Branson. I want to leave today right after I get packed and dressed."

"There is no need for that, Holly. We can protect you as long as you don't run off alone as you did."

She splashed him with water irritably. She shouted, "I don't want to live like a prisoner in my own home! We have a handful of guards, and if those cowboys fought their way in here, you already know what they would do to me. I'm not taking that chance. I'm scared, and you don't care. I want to leave!" Her bottom lip quivered as she glared angrily at him.

Robert sighed and blinked away a thin layer of moisture. He nodded. "I'll arrange it with Matt immediately," he said softly.

***

Two hours later, Matt and Truet were packed, checked out of the hotel, and waiting for Robert Fairchild to say goodbye to his bride. She was on her red roan mare, and Truet was leading a pack horse with her luggage. Matt had told her it would

174

be a long ride and they wouldn't arrive in Branson until close to midnight, but she was determined to leave.

Robert was emotional as he released a firm hug with Holly and approached Matt and Truet. He looked at Matt with sad, watery eyes, "Promise me, you'll watch over her."

"I promise. She's in good hands."

He nodded and walked Holly to her horse. "I wish you would stay with me," he said.

"I can't do it. I won't be a prisoner in my own home. Make things right, Robert, and I'll come home. But I won't until then."

He took a deep breath and sniffled. "I say it a lot, and I've meant it every time, but I've never meant it more than now. I love you, Holly. You are my life."

A thick film of water clouded her vision. "Then forget about the sheep, and let's just live our life together here. We don't need it. I'll stay if you will."

He twisted his lips distastefully. "I can't do that."

She closed her eyes as any hope of staying left her. "Give me a kiss, and then I'm leaving."

Robert kissed her and helped her into the saddle. He would have insisted they take his carriage, but the town blacksmith was taking his time replacing a cracked axel. Her lady's sidesaddle was replaced with Robert's for a more comfortable and safe ride over the many miles of rough ground and steep hills.

"I love you, Holly."

She nodded irritably. "I love you too. Let's go, Matt."

Robert stood on his lawn and watched Holly ride away with the two lawmen until they were no longer in sight. He looked at Ed Bostwick as his expression transformed into stone. "Take a bottle of cyanide and drop it into the Long T Ranch's drinking well tonight. Let's end this now so my wife will come back home."

Ed's eyes widened with alarm. Poisoning cattle was one thing but poisoning the drinking water of a home that would murder innocent people wasn't something he was comfortable with. "Ah, I think we should talk about that."

Robert jabbed a finger into Ed's chest abruptly. "You heard me! Would you still be hesitant if Holly was molested and beaten half to death? If so, maybe you're not the man I thought you were! Their *intent* was to do just that! Throw a bottle in the well, or you can get off my property and forget about leading these men. Ira will do it, won't you?" he asked.

"I always have led these men," Ira answered.

Robert looked back at Ed. "I made a contract with you. You're the man I talk to and the leader of the Blackburn Marshals while employed by me. But if you can't do this, then you will leave, and the future President of the Blackburn Marshals corporation belongs to Ira. You have until dinner to let me know how you plan to do it!" He stormed into the house and slammed the door behind him.

Ira looked at Ed and spoke, "You do know there are innocent women and children that will be drinking from that well. I don't think you have it in you to murder them, Ed. You might want to let me

176

do it. I was in charge under Jeff anyway, not you."

Ed scowled at Ira. "You heard Robert. I won't lose my future position to you." He walked away to be alone.

Ira hollered after Ed, "Walk away and let me do it. You know you haven't got the guts."

Chapter 19

There were four Thomas children that lived to adulthood; Bode, Teddy, Darra Lee, and Jake. Bode Thomas was twenty-nine years old and the oldest of the Thomas children. Teddy was twenty-five and married Marie Almond from the Double Tall Tree Ranch. Teddy and Marie built a nice home on the border between the two ranches and already had their first child.

Darra Lee Thomas was twenty-two years old. She wanted to attend Willamette University in Salem in order to become a teacher, but her days were spent caring for her mother, who had severe arthritis in her joints and could barely get around without help. Darra Lee was a very attractive dark-haired young lady. Several cowboys wanted to court her, but Darra Lee didn't want to marry young and live as a rancher's wife. She wanted to graduate from the university with a diploma to show her brothers that women could be more educated than men.

Jake Thomas was eighteen and worked the ranch with his brothers. Jake, like Teddy, was already in love with a young lady named Laura Whitehead. She was the daughter of Mitch and Hellen Whitehead, owners of the hardware store in town. Unfortunately, she was too young for her parents to agree to Jake courting her.

Dinner at the Thomas home had become quieter over the years. Gunther, who had always been strict, had become more imbittered by his beloved wife's medical condition, which handicapped her and put her in a wheelchair. Arthritis ravaged her joints throughout her body, twisting her fingers into knots. Her shoulders, neck, back, hips, knees, particularly her ankles and feet, were all areas of severe pain and aching. She needed help daily, and Darra Lee was her daily attendant.

Sasha Thomas was once a beautiful young lady with long black hair, but after thirty-two years of marriage to Gunther, six kids, and a lifetime of hardness and arthritis, she was a gray-haired old woman long before her time. Sasha could no longer be self-reliant, as even a hairbrush was too difficult to hold in her clenched hands, but Sasha was still Gunther's wife, and she still spoke her mind. Sasha's head was lowered by an arthritic curved neck, but she glared at her husband with an angry scowl. "You did what?"

The news of Monty being killed by Matt Bannister outside of their home was shocking, but the full story had not been told to the ladies of the house until now. Bode told them at the dinner table what their father had told the ranch hands to do to Holly.

Gunther, sitting at the head of their dining table, was enjoying another dinner with his family, in fact, he had just scooped another helping of mashed potatoes onto his plate when Bode volunteered that information. Gunther cast a condemning glare at Bode as his beloved wife's temper rose.

He remained silent while he scratched his cheek lightly. In hindsight, what had happened that morning with Holly Fairchild was a foolish decision on his part. Gunther had not considered what he had told his ranch hands to do would get back to his wife and daughter.

"Father, how could you do that?" Darra Lee asked, appalled. "Holly is a wonderful lady. Jake and I saw her this morning and told her you'd want to talk to her. How could you do that to her?"

"Gunther," Sasha said with a scolding tone, "answer the question."

Gunther was irritated at Bode for telling the ladies. What was said between the men on the ranch was ranch business and was not a woman's prerogative to know about. He knew Bode was upset about what had happened, but it never should have been brought up at the dinner table.

Gunther spoke sharply, "I was angry."

Sasha reached a deformed hand over to his and spoke gently, "Gunther, you are a better man than that. Thank the Good Lord that the marshal was here to stop those men. I want those men fired. If they are willing to do such wrong to that fine lady, then our daughter is fair game to them too. I won't

180

have it—shame on you, Gunther. I am disappointed in you. I thank the Lord that our son was not involved in that and had the common decency to tell you that it was wrong." She furrowed her brow with great sincerity. "Where are you, Gunther? When did you become such a wicked man?"

The pork loin, mashed potatoes, and buttered vegetables on his dinner plate did not taste quite as good now that Sasha had spoken to him. Despite her deformities, he loved her as much as he always had and valued her opinion and words. She was the only one who could get away with speaking to him the way she often did. His head lowered as he laid his fork and steak knife down. His chest rose and fell noticeably. "I don't know, Sweetheart."

"You have always been a good father to these children and a wonderful husband, but since the Fairchilds bought that land and built their home, you have grown more bitter by the day. He has sheep, and I understand your concern. But the agreement you made with Mister Fairchild the other night is good. That wasteland out by the canyon is perfect for him and all of us."

Gunther's expression hardened. "Then they poisoned our water! All the spring calves and cows are lost—forty-seven in all. My dog is dead. Two horses, one of Darra Lee's goats, and seven chickens are dead. Two raccoons that we found and all the fish in that pond are dead. Sasha, I'm not bitter; I'm mad as hell! Without a clean water supply, that whole section of land is worthless."

Sasha raised her right arm and tried to point at

her husband, but her finger could only straighten enough to point at Bode sitting across the table next to Gunther. "I don't care how mad you are. You never have a right to harm a lady, and you know that! What kind of example is that for our boys or your own daughter? What if Fairchild's hired men did that to our daughter? Would that be acceptable to you?"

He exhaled heavily as his voice lowered, "No, it would not."

"Then why is it with Mister Fairchild's wife? She is a sweet lady, Gunther, and you did the ugliest thing you could have ever done." She looked at her son, Bode. "Thank you, Bodey-Joe, for being a righteous man when your father crawled in the dirt."

Bode hated to be called Bodey-Joe, but his mother had a right to call him whatever she chose; she did name him, after all. "You taught me to treat ladies well, Mother. And Holly is a lady."

Darra Lee added, "An educated lady too. She went to a university back east and graduated." Darra Lee paused to give her father a disappointed glance. "We need to apologize to her for our father. We should all ride out there and do it in person."

Bode spoke forcefully, "No one is going out there, and neither are you. Those Blackburn Marshals would hurt you, Sis, to get even for what almost happened to Holly."

"That's right," Gunther agreed. He spoke in a gentle, repentive voice, "I was wrong to do what I did, and it got Monty killed." He nodded and patted the top of his wife's hand affectionately. "You're right. I was in the wrong."

There was a knock on the door. "I'll get it," Bode said and went to the door. "Oh, hello, Sheriff."

"Bode, is Gunther in?"

"Yeah, come in."

"Gunther," Sheriff Pat Emerson said, holding an envelope in his hand. He nodded to Sasha and Darra Lee with a pleasant smile. "Ladies. Gunther, I was handed this envelope by one of the Blackburn Marshals who doesn't like the tactics one of his leaders uses. He agreed to work with us to run Fairchild out of town, but I can't share his identity. You need to read this and prepare."

"What is it, Patrick?" Sasha asked.

Gunther opened the note and read it. His facial muscles tightened as he read. He took a slow deep breath as he read the letter:

> *Mister Gunther Thomas,*
>
> *I wish to remain anonymous for my safety, but I am a Blackburn Marshal hired by Robert Fairchild to protect his persons and interest. I must inform you that Mister Fairchild did not poison your watering hole. That act was done without Mister Fairchild's knowledge or permission. It was done wholly by the leadership and direction of Ed Bostwick, one of the leaders of the Blackburn Marshals. Ed took matters into his own hands to prolong the battle and fight with the cattlemen once an agreement was made to settle land disputes. The agreement made*

the other night promised to end our contract with Mister Fairchild, and we would leave. Ed Bostwick does not want to leave and is now even more set on revenge after the roughing up of Holly Fairchild, with whom Ed has a romantic interest in.

Mister Thomas, as a whole, we want to end this hostility between the cattlemen and sheepmen. We hope there will be lasting peace once the sheep flocks are moved east along the canyon. That agreement is suitable for all parties, and Mister Fairchild is very pleased with that arrangement. However, he is most angry about the sabotaging of your water and wants to know who did it. I fear for my life as Ed is a brutal and dangerous man. I'm ashamed to say, I cannot tell Mister Fairchild who poisoned your water until Ed is dead. And so, I leave that in your capable hands. Tonight, late tonight, around midnight, you can expect Ed Bostwick and two others to encroach upon your property and throw another bottle of cyanide into your drinking well by your home.

I cannot let this happen as your family is just important to you as my own is to me, or Mister Fairchild's is to him. I do not believe in murdering innocent people and cannot sit back and allow this evil to continue. I leave Ed Bostwick in your hands to stop once and for all. Please, throw this letter in the fire and do not let it get back to my men, or I will

*be shunned and possibly killed. I will work
behind the scenes with you to bring a quick
and profitable ending to this so-called feud,
and I hope to leave your fair township soon.*
   Signed,
   I'll let you know sometime.

Gunther handed the note to Bode. "We'll be ready, but just in case, we'll rig up something to make sure nothing can penetrate that well. It's better to be safe than sorry. Pat, we have enough men here that I don't think we're going to need your help. Too many men makes it easier to be spotted, and I want them coming close to the well."

Bode laid the paper down. "I'll hitch up the carriage and take Mother and Darra Lee to Aunt Carolyn's. You two don't want to be here tonight."

Chapter 20

Ira Kelley entered Robert's office and closed the door behind him before setting a dark brown 12-ounce bottle of soluble powdered cyanide on the desk. "Here you go, Ed. Just pull the cork, drop it in the well, and get out of there. The powder will do the rest."

Ed Bostwick was a former U.S. Deputy Marshal who worked in Wyoming with Matt Bannister for a few years. The badge Ed wore back then drew a line between right and wrong that he believed in and risked his life to enforce. Ed had hunted many outlaws over the years, but he could not think of one that had done anything quite as heinous as what he was about to do. He had squared off against robbers who had not harmed a single person, robbers who killed in necessity, and others who killed cruelly. He tracked murderers of many kinds, including a wife who had poisoned her husband. But he had never gone after someone who poisoned a well to murder a whole family.

He had turned his U.S. Deputy Marshal badge in and left the business to pin on a Blackburn Marshal badge. He willingly joined a brotherhood of men who were cold-blooded killers and ex-criminals hardened to life and willing to kill at any given time by any means that paid them. The money was good, but a man's soul carried the weight of his guilt. There were some men that Ed doubted had a soul, as their conscience was not bothered what-soever. Ed had a soul and knew right from wrong, but unfortunately, in a world turned upside down, wrong paid much more than fighting for what's right. The fight within him debated if the murder of a family was worth making him wealthy. He could own a home anywhere in the United States that rivaled Robert Fairchild's or William Slater's mansion on a hill. He could travel the world and become a powerful friend to politicians and other men of the caliber of Robert Fairchild. In the back of his mind, the thought occurred to him that if he was successful, he could also wait for Robert to pass away and make Holly his bride. They had already become friends, and the future could be bright if he simply dropped a bottle down a well. He could own the world, and it would be paradise on earth if he had Holly at his side.

Robert Fairchild pushed the bottle across the table to Ed. He spoke softly, "Ed, have you ever heard of a man named Niccolò Machiavelli?"

Ed shook his head. "No. Does he live here in town?"

"No." Robert smiled. "Niccolò Machiavelli was a Florentine Statesman, philosopher and author in the sixteenth century. He wrote a book titled, *The Prince*, which is still in print today. It is a book about how to manipulate power in political leadership. He believed people in power should be feared rather than liked and should do whatever it took to win or keep power. He was not a moral man nor looked out for the little man. Luckily the founders of this great country did not follow his beliefs, and we have a Republic where we, the people, have a voice and a vote. Machiavelli was what you might call a tyrant, or his ideas would lead to a tyrannical government. Niccolò is where we get the word: Machiavellianism or Machiavellians, which means somebody who believes that the means, however evil, can justifiably be used in achieving political power."

Ed stared at him blankly.

Robert continued, "I'm not a politician, I am a businessman. However, I hold the same beliefs in my business dealings. I get what I want, as you will get what you want when the Blackburn Marshals become a nationwide corporation and you battle other private police and detective forces for high-revenue contracts.

"My wife was attacked. My life was threatened, and in the defense of self-preservation, we must attack and do so harshly to end any further hostilities and to let the other ranchers know we do not play games. I hit, and I hit hard. I have a woolen mill to build here, and mere cowboys will not thwart it. Ed, you have a dream too. We've talked about it, and I agreed to fund such a large-scale operation with you in charge. I know you are not a heartless man, and doing this horrible deed may compromise your personal beliefs." He paused to allow the empathetic words to resonate with Ed's conscience. "But I want you to remember that this is just a job you are being paid to do. Consider it an investment in saving Holly's life and, in doing so, assuring your future stability to live as you may dream."

Ed held a hesitant hand out towards the brown bottle. "It's poison...it would kill everyone."

Robert grimaced slowly, uncaringly. He sputtered, "This is not the first time anyone has used poison as a deathly means. During the Siege of Kirrha in 590 BC, the water supply was poisoned with hellebore, a toxic plant. In the Siege of Hatra in 198 AD, the Roman army tried to scale the walls of Hatra, and the men on the walls dropped fragile pots filled with deadly scorpions. The scorpions stung many Roman soldiers, ensuring they would die, and the Roman army fled. In the Siege of Kaffa in 1346, the Mongols flung dead bodies infected with Bubonic Plague over the wall to infect the inhabitants, who then surrendered to the Mongols. And finally, right here in America in 1763, the British army at Fort Pitt gave smallpox-ridden blankets to the local tribes, who spread the disease far and wide, killing thousands of Indians with smallpox.

"What you are about to do, has been done since the beginning of time. Ed, it is nothing new. What is new is how it will secure your future. I know you respect and think highly of my wife, as she does you, and by committing this so-called crime, you will be saving her life. And now I must ask, are you up for the task? Because if not, Ira assured me he is. And he would be the one to benefit in the future."

Ed Bostwick could only think of one combination of things that raised the rewards above the guilt that may or may not haunt his soul. The promise of financial success with a respected position at the helm of a corporation and the hope of someday having Holly as his bride. He nodded. "I can do it. I want Kent and Ellis to back me up, though."

"No," Ira argued, "Kent and Ellis are too valuable to risk in case you're spotted. Take any of the newbies, but Kent and Ellis are mine. They hired on here under me."

"Fine. I'll take Jimmy and the new fellow Elliot that showed up yesterday."

"Sounds good to me," Ira said. "Listen, Ed, be careful and good luck. I'd sneak in a back way if you can."

Robert added, "Ed, the best way to win a war is to win it without fighting; and in this way, we are."

Chapter 21

The night was clear with a bright moon that lit up the countryside enough to find the Long T Ranch, but it also made it possible to see a person approaching the drinking well in the dark. Ed had been at the Long T Ranch homestead once before and remembered the large log cabin house, outbuildings, and large barn were all tucked into a grove of mature hemlock and pine trees while younger fruit trees were planted in an orchard along the road. It was easy to spot the homestead, but the shadows cast by the trees and buildings darkened the area around the house just enough to make Ed feel uneasy. He lay on the crest of a small hill looking at the ranch a few hundred yards away. From his vantage point, Ed could see the entire homestead, including the large house, smaller outbuildings around it, and the barn and beyond to the bunkhouse. He was watching and waiting for any sign of movement, but except for the crickets, all was still.

He could see the abandoned pond and a few dead cows that still needed to be removed from the fenced-off pasture. A long lean-to was built to protect the young calves from the sun or foul weather, and now it stood empty and silent like a ghost in a field of rotting flesh. They had tethered their horses to a small tree and approached on foot, hands and knees, and belly crawling through the grass to approach silently and unnoticed. It was late enough that most of the ranch hands would be sleeping, but a light in the upstairs window of the ranch house made Ed nervous. It was quiet and still, except for the high-pitched yipping of a coyote a ways off. They had spotted a coyote prancing across the open grass earlier, but the one yipping was further away. Ed knew what he was about to do was deathly wrong, and it troubled him. But the fact was that he figured he could forgive himself over the next thirty or forty years that he lived in luxury.

Ed knew Jimmy Abbot very well and knew he was not a capable shot with a rifle. Elliot Zook claimed to be good with a rifle and was set on the hilltop to watch for any threats and cover their escape if, by chance, Ed and Jimmy were spotted and needed to run. Ed did not know Elliot Zook but liked what he knew of him and took him at his word.

Ed and Jimmy crawled down the short hill and maneuvered across the pasture towards the edge of the shadows of the buildings and trees surrounding the house. Ed had no idea where the well was, but he figured it would be near the main house and not too hard to find. The question gnawing at the back of his mind was wondering if it was an open well like some people had or if it was a closed well with a hand pump like the Fairchild's. Older homes with established wells often had open wells with a bucket and pulley system of various kinds, while newer wells were becoming more commonly closed at ground level with hand pumps.

The two men entered the shadows and carefully made their way toward the large log cabin with a wide porch. There was no dog to bark or sound except the crickets on the prairie.

Ed and Jimmy moved closer and recognized the vertical three-foot circle of bricks extending out of the ground of a brick-lined well and the short dog-house roof over it. A hand pump was centered on a board covering laid across the bricks. Knowing he could either lift the wood covering enough to drop the poison in or pour the powder between the board slats, Ed moved forward unwaveringly. Six feet from the well, Ed pulled the cork from the neck of the bottle.

"Don't move!" Bode Thomas's voice boomed as he stepped out of the shadows of a newly constructed three-sided lean-to facing the opposite direction ten feet from the well. Four other men came out of the structure to surround them with shotguns, rifles, and handguns.

Suddenly surrounded by five men, Ed took notice of the two carefully drilled-out knotholes in the wall of what he assumed was a small shed to use as peepholes. He knew immediately that he had been set up and fell into the trap like a stupid wolf blindly rushing in for the bait.

"Put the cork in that bottle slowly, or I'll kill you now," Bode ordered. The other men with him urged Bode to open fire, but Bode was more concerned about the poison. Cyanide could be bought over the counter as a common practice of killing pests such as yellow jacket nests, gophers, moles, rats, and mice. Even the Thomas family had a bottle or two to put on dead cattle to kill coyotes and wolves. The powder had a practical purpose, but it became a lethal weapon in some people's hands.

Ed's heart pounded as the blood flowed, turning his ears red while his chest tightened like the hand of death had gripped it and squeezed. His throat closed, and his mouth went dry, making it hard to utter a sound. Although he had heard the order to seal the bottle, his arms didn't move. He was frozen in a state of horror unlike any he had encountered. Unlike when he was in danger and at a disadvantage when he was a lawman, this time was different; he was guilty, and there was no way to beat the crime.

His palms began sweating, and the bottle slipped free and hit the hardened ground. The sound of the bottle being dropped was all Jimmy needed to hear to assume Ed was drawing his gun to begin fighting their way out. Jimmy drew his revolver halfway out of the holster with a quick jerk when four shots from various guns filled Jimmy's torso with invasive lead. Jimmy dropped to the ground writhing in pain and slowly turned toward his stomach before going limp.

Ed couldn't get a breath as he watched his friend die. Petrified, he gazed at a prominent figure who lit a cigar with a strike of a match before stepping out of the shadows and standing before him. It was the patriarch, Gunther Thomas. He grinned like a victorious general over a defeated army. "You're stupid to come back here, but I'm glad you did. Take him to the barn and hoist him up."

Ed was quickly grabbed by two of the men. "No, no. I ah…" A rifle butt was driven into his face, mercilessly knocking out three teeth.

"Shut up!" Bode snarled, pulling the rifle back. "Hang him by his hands." Bode grabbed Ed's jaw and shouted into his face, "It's going to be a long night for you."

***

Elliot Zook could not see the well or know what was happening when he heard several gunshots, but he knew by the heavy sound of a shotgun that it wasn't his new friends doing the shooting. All he could do was watch as a group of men escorted Ed Bostwick towards the large barn and took him inside, where a lantern or two were turned up and cast a yellow light out of the doorway. Elliot's heart pounded, and he knew instinctively that Ed would either be hung in the barn or beaten to death if he didn't do anything to help him. Elliot wished he could get some help from his fellow Blackburn Marshals, but Ed needed help now.

Elliot moved towards the light of the barn door and knelt in the short grass of a pasture to watch two men strip Jimmy Abbot's gun belt from his body and go through his pockets for whatever they could find. The two men then picked up Ed's gun belt and admired their newly found weapons, comparing them to their own to see if they could upgrade weapons as they walked into the barn's light.

Elliot moved closer and could hear the sound of Ed grunting and the men shouting in the barn. Hidden behind a pine tree, Elliot could see Ed hanging in the air from his bound wrists and the ranch hands taking turns beating him. Ed was already bleeding and halfway unconscious by the look of him.

Elliot was tempted to raise his rifle and shoot the man hitting Ed, but he knew doing so would bring a firefight he could not win. His best option was to catch them unexpectedly and have them disarm themselves before he began killing them.

"Hey, Jason, here's a new toy for you. It's better than the one you carry." The cowboy tossed Elliot's gun belt to a young cowboy named Jason, who had Ed Bostwick's fresh blood on his knuckles.

"Thanks." Jason pulled the .44-40 single-action Remington out of the holster to admire it. "Hess, you carry a Remington. What model is this?" He held it up to show from across the barn.

John Hess made a hard uppercut to Ed's jaw, snapping his head back like a loosened cork from a bottle. He looked back at the young man. "I'd say

1875. Mine's a bit newer. There's nothing wrong with that one, though."

Elliot Zook glanced towards the house and, not seeing anyone, ran to the barn door where he could see all the men at once and raised his rifle. "Cut him down!"

Jason, already holding his new revolver in his hand, pulled the hammer back and spun towards Elliot. Elliot turned the barrel of his Winchester just slightly to his left and pulled the trigger with a single shot dead center in Jason's chest. The young man fell for his final few breaths.

Elliot set the rifle's sight on Hess, who was closest to Ed. "Cut him down! The rest of you loosen your weapons or die! Hurry up, or I'll kill you all and cut him down myself!"

"Okay, calm down. I'll cut him down," Hess said as he unbuckled his gun belt and let it fall. He pulled a three-inch folding knife from his pocket and reached up toward Ed's hands to cut the rough rope. Ed's wrists were already seeping drops of blood.

"Fella, you're on private property, you know." Bode Thomas said. He could see his father approaching the barn with a revolver in his hand. "We have no intention of killing your friend. We just wanted to beat him up before sending him home. Your other friend, we had no choice," he spoke nervously but tried to sound calm. Having the barrel of a loaded gun pointed at him brought a strong sense of anxiety.

Elliot shifted his attention to Bode with the barrel of his rifle. "Well, I did come to kill you all. I'm going to start with…"

"Elliot…" Ed gasped, watching Gunther approach with a raised revolver.

Gunther pulled the trigger, firing a bullet into the back of Elliot's head, dropping him quicker than Ed could say another word. Blood splattered forward, spraying a fine mist over a few men, all of whom had casually stepped out of the way without Elliot noticing.

Ed squeezed his eyes closed with every ounce of hope leaving him. He knew his life would soon end as he was now helpless and alone.

Gunther cursed angrily, "I wasn't fast enough to save Jason! You boys always need to cover your backside, especially at night. Luckily, I saw this snake slithering across the lawn. KC, take a couple of the boys and scout the property. There may be more out there." He pointed at Ed hanging by his wrists. "I don't want him killed." He gazed at the body of the young cowhand. He spoke sadly, "Get Jason covered up. I tried, but I just didn't get here fast enough."

Chapter 22

By morning, Ed Bostwick, Jimmy Abbot, and Elliot Zook had not returned, and concern was starting to show on the faces of Robert Fairchild and the Blackburn Marshals who waited for their friends. A few of the men departed to look for them and came back with startling news. Now in the fresh morning sun, Robert Fairchild and the Blackburn Marshals sat on horseback, staring in disbelief at the three bodies hanging from the Fairchild Estate headgate.

Jimmy Abbot was hanging by his feet with his fingertips about a foot off the ground. He had been dragged by his feet over the six miles that separated the Long T Ranch from the Fairchild headgate. His clothing was shredded and torn, exposing many abrasions and cuts from the road. His cause of death was easily identified as he had been shot several times along with a shotgun blast that left his torso a blood-soaked mess that dripped slowly to the ground. To the horror of them all, Jimmy's Blackburn Marshal badge was pinned to his eyebrow over his left eye.

Ed Bostwick was hanging by his neck. His clothing was not dusty or torn but was saturated by his blood from being beaten so severely that his face was hardly recognizable. His hands were bound behind his back, indicating that he was alive and alert when he was hung. His Blackburn Marshal badge was cruelly pinned to his left ear.

Elliot Zook, like Jimmy, was dangling by his feet. He had been dragged over the six miles of hardened ground, which showed by the dirt-filled abrasions and cuts on his body. His cause of death was a single shot to the back of his head that exited above his right eye. Elliot's newly given Blackburn Marshal badge was wedged into his mouth between his teeth and lips.

Robert Fairchild stood with the other marshals, quietly gazing at their friends. No one said a word as the blow of seeing such hardened men hanging in such appalling conditions was no less than shocking. No one expected the night to end with their deaths, let alone the grotesque conditions and where they were left to be found.

"I'd say Ed failed if it wasn't so obvious," Ira Kelly offered. He had to hide the joyous smile that beamed brightly within him to see his rival for control of the Blackburn Marshals hanging dead. Elliot Zook meant nothing to him, and Jimmy Abbot was a sacrifice he could replace soon enough.

Jesse Helms turned his head toward Cass Travers. "I say we kill them for doing this to Elliot."

Cass nodded slowly. "Agreed."

Robert Fairchild rubbed the goatee on his chin thoughtfully. "The message they sent is intriguing."

"Intriguing?" Jesse asked bitterly. "I'd say it's a death warrant! Tell me who is responsible and where they are, and we'll finish this." His fierce eyes glared at Robert dangerously.

Robert's eyebrows raised curiously as he gazed at the fiery young man. "And who are the *we* that you refer to?"

"Cass and me if no one else will join us. None of you knew Elliot, but he was our friend. Cass and I are not going to turn our backs and walk away. Someone will pay for this with or without you fellas or the badges."

Robert remained quiet but nodded gently.

Henry Dodds asked, "Why would they pin Ed's badge to his ear? That seems strange."

Kent Kruse was a close friend of Ed Bostwick and was quickly angered by Henry's question. He snapped bitterly, "Maybe his nose was too thin. I don't know why they would do that, Henry!"

Robert pointed at the bodies one by one as he explained, "See no evil, hear no evil, and speak no evil. It is an intriguing riddle that I can only translate to mean they don't want any lawmen involved in our dispute from this point on." He continued to rub his goatee thoughtfully as he peered back and forth over each hanging man.

Ellis Mckenna spoke, "I say we wait until they have a meeting in the cattle association building, blow it up, and gun them down like turkeys as they come out! We can't let them get away with killing three of our brothers."

"We won't let them get away with it," Ira said pointedly.

Jesse Helms challenged, "What are you going to do about it other than sit on your butt and talk? I haven't got time to talk. We need to kill every one of them we find right now. We'll hang them up by their feet like dead game." He pulled his hunting knife and rode his horse to Elliot's body. "I'm cutting my friend down. I don't want to see him hanging like this. I knew I should have gone with him."

Robert Fairchild watched Jesse with a slight hint of a smile. "Kent, bring a wagon and take these men down. We'll send them back to their families for burial. Jesse Helms, why don't you and Cass come with Ira and me to speak with the sheriff, and then we'll come back and have lunch."

Ira spoke, "I thought you just said they didn't want the law involved?"

Robert shrugged his shoulders. "That is the only message I can decipher from their riddle. Trust me, the good sheriff, Patrick Emerson, is not on our side. But if we take these bodies and display them for the honest people in town to see the brutality of the cattlemen, then we may sway the public opinion of the cattlemen. That is why I have always preached to you, Blackburn Marshals, that it is essential for you never to cause any trouble in town and be on your best behavior. In this case, we will not be the instigators but the victims. Being a victim wins hearts, and that can be a great benefit to us. Kent, bring a wagon."

***

Sheriff Pat Emerson looked at the three bodies in the back of the wagon with interest. To Robert's instructions, the badges were left where they were discovered. The sheriff raised his eyebrows with surprise. He knew the men were coming to poison the well and had planned on helping stop the rogue Blackburn Marshals, but too many men trying to hide at once would become a hazard. The Thomas family decided to build a fake three-sided shed near the well, and the sheriff was not needed. He had heard the three men were killed, but he did not know they had been strung up on the headgate.

"I don't know what you want me to do. You don't know who did it, do you? I haven't heard a gnat's wing or whisper about this," Sheriff Emerson said as convincingly as he could.

Robert explained so the growing crowd could hear, "I don't know. The three gentlemen went for an evening ride and did not return. We found them this morning hanging, as I told you." Robert spoke louder to draw more townspeople closer, "And these were fine gentlemen. Have they caused a single ruckus in town since they have been here? No. These are not hired killers or thugs. These are specially trained professional private police officers hired by me to protect my home from the vicious animals that did this to these fine gentlemen."

Robert turned to the crowd with opened arms and spoke loudly and clearly, "Ladies and gentlemen, my beloved wife, Holly, whom some of you ladies know, was attacked yesterday morning on the Long T Ranch. If not for the luck of U.S. Marshal Matt Bannister going there at the right time, Holly would have been savagely molested, as Mister Thomas told his ranch hands to send her home with a child."

A gasp rose within the crowd. He continued, "Why was Holly there, you ask? She was merely trying to empathize with Mister Thomas for his losses due to someone poisoning his water. She offered him full reimbursement for his losses because she was afraid. I'm sure you all have heard that I am to blame for contaminating his water. I assure you, I have never been motivated to do so. We had settled our differences before his water was poisoned, and I've agreed to graze my sheep where the cattle don't roam. What motivation would I have to start a war with Gunther Thomas? I may own sheep, but I'm not that stupid. I don't have a reason under the sun for why I would want to cause Mister Thomas or his family any harm."

A man from the crowd asked doubtingly, "Maybe because the sheep shooters keep killing your sheep?"

Robert caught a glimpse of Gunther and a few other cowboys approaching them from the cattlemen's association building. He answered loudly, "There is no evidence that Gunther is part of that group. What I am suggesting is that maybe someone poisoned his water to blame me and continue this fight to run me out of town. Probably the same people that murdered one of my shepherds and branded two more, scarring those two young men for life. Not excluding, of course, that poor soul with his head bashed in just the other morning. There is a war against me, and the only reason is that I own sheep."

Edith Richards was an elderly woman and the local reverend's wife. She and the Reverend Len Richards were returning home from a late breakfast at the restaurant when the wagon stopped outside the sheriff's office. The news about Holly aggravated her. Holly had attended their church and was kind enough to invite all the ladies of the church to her home once a week for a time of socializing, Bible study, and a good meal. It was a shame when Holly quit coming due to the growing hostility with the cattlemen.

Edith's brow lowered when she saw Gunther Thomas approaching. She had known him for many years and was not pleased by what she had heard. "Gunther! Did you tell your cowboys to molest Missus Fairchild?"

"Please tell me we live in a better community than that?" Reverend Richards stated with a sound of discouragement.

Robert spoke, "Oh, Mister Thomas, I didn't see you there. Would you know anything about my three dead hired policemen?"

"Hired policemen?" Gunther questioned with a scowl. "The Blackburn Marshals are anything but policemen." He held up a hand to quiet the crowd demanding an answer to Edith's question. "Listen up," he demanded in a firm voice. "Yes, I did do that to Missus Fairchild."

"How could you do that?" Edith snapped. "The sheriff should take you into that jail right now and leave you there!"

"Good heavens, Gunther!" Reverend Richards snapped.

"She's so nice," another lady said with a sigh. "Shame on you."

A young cowboy who did not work for Gunther said, "No one ever said women were part of the deal. That ain't right."

"Agreed."

Gunther nodded his head as the rebukes came. He spoke louder, "I know! I was wrong to do that. Quiet!" he shouted. He looked at Robert. "I owe you and your lady a very sincere apology…"

Edith quipped, "You better believe you do! I swear…"

"Edith…" the reverend warned.

She continued with a pointed finger at Gunther, "Your mother would be spinning in her grave if she knew about this. Thank goodness she's in heaven, where you won't be if you don't start behaving as she raised you to behave!"

"Robert," Gunther said, ignoring Edith, "I made a big mistake, and I am sorry for what I did to your missus. I blamed you for my water, and come to find out; it wasn't you at all. Your wife came out with good intentions, and I mistreated her. Please tell her I would like to apologize to her myself, but I am also sincerely sorry to you. I hope you'll accept my apology, and our agreement stands about where to graze your woolies." He put out a hand to shake.

Robert was taken by surprise. He had no idea what trickery Gunther was up to, but with the crowd watching, he reluctantly shook hands. "I'll let her know. What about those men?" he nodded toward the three dead bodies in the wagon.

Gunther lifted a finger and reached into his vest pocket to pull out an envelope. He pulled the letter out and handed it to Robert. "It seems these men were responsible without your knowledge. They came out to my place last night to poison my drinking well. I killed them to protect my family. That letter was given to the sheriff yesterday. When you find the man of yours that warned me, let me know. I owe him."

The surprise on Robert's face was genuine as he read the letter. His jaw dropped, and his breath was taken away for a moment as his brain tried to comprehend what he was reading. His obvious shock wasn't what Gunther thought it might be. Robert was shocked that someone had betrayed the three men and set them up to be killed. "I...I...don't know what to say," Robert said quite honestly.

"What's the letter say?" Ira Kelly asked and reached for it.

Robert handed the letter to Ira. He spoke awkwardly, "Mister Thomas, I feel responsible for your loss of livestock none the less now that I know who did it. I never had a clue. Please, send me a bill, and I will reimburse you as my wife had the wisdom to think of doing." The surprise was wearing off, and anger was beginning to boil within. "Does this mean it's water under the bridge? We can move forward in peace?"

Gunther nodded. "As far as I'm concerned."

Ira finished reading the letter he had written. "We were betrayed."

Jesse Helms snarled. "Betrayed by who? Is this the man that killed my friend?" he pointed at Gunther. "Did you kill my friend?" he shouted and tried to reach Gunther, but he was pushed back by Ira Kelly and Robert Fairchild. Cass, knowing his friend, took Jesse's gun as a precaution.

"You'll get it back when you calm down," Cass said as Jesse turned on him.

"Jesse Helms!" Robert shouted angrily, "Not another word, or you can return that badge and go home. Cass, take him back to the house now," he warned with a harsh glare.

"Jesse Helms? Of the Sperry-Helms Gang?" Gunther asked, looking Jesse over.

Jesse widened his cold glare. "Yes. And your…"

"Not a word, Jesse!" Robert said with authority. "Leave now!"

Robert explained to Gunther, "Jesse and his friends were hired two days ago. This poor soul lying here is a friend of theirs named Elliot Zook. Have you heard of him too? He was a member of their little gang."

Gunther watched Jesse begrudgingly step into the saddle to leave. "I've heard of them, never met them. Nice policemen," he said mockingly.

"They are trying to change their lives and use their learned skills for good to make an honest living. I cannot fault them for that." Robert paused. "Nor can I fault you for protecting your family last night or having these wretches hung on my head-gate. All is well between us. And I hope it stays that way. If you have any say or knowledge of the sheep shooters, perhaps, you could ask them to leave my shepherds and sheep alone from now on?"

Gunther tilted his head questionably. "I can only try to pass that word on. But I'll do my best."

Chapter 23

Gunther Thomas was not willing to let Robert keep the warning letter, but Robert had read it three times to study the handwriting, phrasing, spelling, overused words, and punctuation along with any unique angles or tells on a particular letter of the alphabet. Robert did not consider himself a gifted writer, but he was experienced enough to know every individual had their own handwriting and ways of shaping letters, habits of phrasing, vocabulary, and so on to make handwriting as individually unique to a person as their face and personality.

He and Ira had taken the three bodies to the Hollister Livery Stable for the town's only undertaker. Robert arranged for the carpenter, who acted as the undertaker, to transfer Elliot Zook's body to Branson to be embalmed and given to his family for burial. According to Ira, Ed Bostwick and Jimmy Abbot didn't have family and would be buried in the Hollister Cemetery.

The ride back towards the Fairchild Estate was quiet. Robert didn't feel like conversing as his mind was on the letter and what had transpired.

Ira spoke with a cheerful disposition, "Now you can wire Matt and have him bring Holly back. It was a wasted trip. If she had only waited one day, that old man could have apologized to her himself."

Robert responded slowly. "Yes. I suppose so." He was riding on the uncomfortable wooden bench seat of the wagon while Ira drove the team of horses. Ira was right; he could send for his bride and have her brought home.

Suddenly, as if a storm cloud had dissipated and a beam of bright sunlight warmed his skin, Robert realized the sheep killing and worrying about his shepherds was actually over. Peace had come to the valley between him and the ranchers. It was a joyful sensation to hope that the battles had reached their end and the violence was over. He could bring Holly home and start planning the construction of the woolen mill. Slowly his grin widened, and Robert chuckled.

"What's so funny?" Ira asked.

"Nothing. I was merely pondering that the fighting is over. I need to move my flocks east to the canyon as agreed, and we'll have no more trouble." He paused and then added slowly, "Whoever wrote that note got three good men killed, but it probably saved many more lives and ended a potential feud simultaneously. I want you to find the man who wrote that note and thank him for me. I may even give him a bonus."

Ira took a deep breath. "You won't have to go far to do that. I wrote the note." He offered a small, proud smile.

"Well," Robert said slowly. He suddenly felt sickened to his stomach. "I should thank you for solving all my problems with one swift move. That was a smart move. What made you do it?" Robert questioned.

"I just figured if they got what they wanted and knew you were innocent, everyone would be happy," Ira answered simply enough. "Holly was almost hurt. And when she left here, I knew enough was enough."

Robert narrowed his brow thoughtfully. "I appreciate that. But what would you get out of it?"

Ira shrugged questionably. "The satisfaction of doing my job and ensuring she is safe. Like we were hired to do."

His answer sounded hollow and lacked sincerity. Robert shook his head, not believing a word of it. "No. There must have been a stronger motivation. What was it?" The truth was as clear as day, but he wanted to hear Ira say it.

"Honestly?" Ira asked.

"It's what I expect from you."

"Alright, I'll tell you. I figured if everyone was happy, Holly could come home and know she had nothing to fear."

"That sounds very similar to what you already said. So, in other words, you did it for me?" Robert asked.

"Yes, of course."

212

"Huh," Robert grunted. "I'm disappointed. I thought you did it to take full control of the Blackburn Marshals with Ed suddenly gone."

Ira exhaled with a relieved grin. "That too." He pointed his thumb toward himself as he explained, "Jeff Blackburn was my best friend, and although he started the Blackburn Marshals, I have always been the second in command. I was there from the beginning, and we made the Blackburn Marshals what we are today. Ed was too new to be a leader, and I won't be second fiddle to him. This is my company to lead, not his."

"I can understand that," Robert said softly with a nod.

Ira continued, "I was listening to you tell Ed about that man Mathenhoney or whatever his name was, the one that said, do whatever it takes to gain power, and the idea came to me. So I did."

"Machiavelli," Robert corrected. "Yes, I was angry and pushing Ed to do something he would normally not do. Machiavelli said many other things too, which were more honorable and wiser. I just didn't reflect that at the time." He turned his shoulders to observe Ira. "So having your friends ambushed and slaughtered didn't bother you?"

"I didn't let Ed take Kent if that answers your question. Now that Jeff is gone, I did what I needed to do to get what I want and what is rightfully mine. I am tired of traveling around the country and being shot at just to move to a new town and do it again. I want to own a business and make money while others do the work. You're an inspiration to me, and now that I see what life can be like, I want more. I want what you have. And I'll do whatever it takes to get it."

"Yes. I know. Well, we have a lot of work to do. But for now, it seems our business is winding down, so you should seek other contracts as you normally would to keep you and the boys working."

"What? I thought you were going to help us grow?" Ira asked sharply.

"I am. But it takes time, and I don't feel it is my responsibility to house and feed you all while that transition is being organized. Certainly, you can understand that. You must have someone interested in hiring the Blackburn Marshals for something. I'll contact you in January and let you know where we are as far as taking over goes."

"Taking over? What do you mean by that?"

"In short, I use the Blackburn Marshals name and create a national force of private detectives and police force. It takes time to set up and find the right people to run it."

"I thought I was running it. I am the rightful leader," Ira's voice was becoming more hostile.

"Ira, you are a fine leader, but this will be a professional business and not a...how should I say, it will no longer be a criminal element wearing a fake badge. Of course, you will still be employed, but I will need to hire experienced men from similar businesses to get it off the ground."

"That's not what you told Ed and me before."

"Ira, would you hire a man who has never ridden a horse or shot a gun as one of your marshals?"

"No."

"It's the same principle. You know your business, I know mine. We need men in the middle that know both ends of the business. You can learn and work your way to the top, but until then, let me get it started."

Chapter 24

Learning that John Painter had led Morton to accept Jesus as his savior was exciting news. Morton was excited to share that news with Matt and that he had proposed to Audrey. They were engaged to be married in less than seven days. The wedding would be small as Audrey didn't know many people in town, and Morton didn't want to invite anyone from his past. There would only be a handful of friends and a quiet dinner afterward at Joel Fasana's home. The wedding was going to be small, quick, and informal.

Matt spent the day in his office writing a report on what had transpired in Hollister. It was essential to write the details down as best that he could so that he would not forget anything in his official report when it was completed. When Matt was going to leave the marshal's office to take his fiancé out for dinner at the Monarch Restaurant, a delivery boy entered the office with an urgent wire.

Matt opened it and read the words sent by Robert Fairchild:

Bring Holly back home. The fight is over.
Peace has come, and all is well.

Matt doubted the hostilities from either party had dissipated overnight. He took the message along with him as he walked arm-in-arm with Christine toward Main Street. He had not seen her for a few days, and holding her hand as they walked was a rejuvenating reminder of what was good in his life.

Matt and Christine went upstairs at the Monarch Hotel and knocked on the door to Holly's room.

Holly's wavy blonde hair seemed flat as it settled on her shoulders. She smiled slightly as she said, "Matt, come in. I was hoping you would come by today."

Matt stepped inside the room, holding Christine's hand. "We were wondering if you would like to join us for dinner. This is my fiancé, Christine Knapp."

"Christine?" Holly asked as she gazed at the beautiful lady with long dark hair weaved together in a perfect braid and a flawless oval face with large brown eyes. Holly had assumed Matt's fiancé would be attractive, but she had not expected to meet such a beautiful woman. Holly's hand moved unconsciously to cover the swollen and discolored area of her cheek and around her eye. The eye, itself, was blood-red from broken veins.

"My-oh-my, you are lovely," Holly continued. "Please, come inside. Forgive my appearance. Matt may have told you I was attacked and left looking like this. I am forever in Matt's debt for saving me, as I am sure you can understand. Matt told me what you went through when you were kidnapped. Having been victimized yourself and given a black eye such as mine, I'm sure you can understand how I feel."

Christine smiled warmly. "My eye looked a lot like yours. It is just temporary, though. Would you like to come downstairs and join us for dinner?"

Holly wrinkled her nose and shook her head. "I don't want to sound vain, but I'd rather not sit in public looking like I do. Matt arranged for my meals to be brought up here. Matt could go down and order our dinners, and you two can join me for dinner here. I want to speak with Christine alone anyway."

When Matt left the room to order three dinners, Holly waved towards the sitting room's davenport and two padded chairs, "Please, have a seat. I have a question for you, Christine. I'm Holly Fairchild, by the way."

Christine sat down on the davenport and eyed a cluster of purple grapes in a bowl. Her stomach growled. "May I have some of your grapes?"

"Yes, please. What about wine? Would you care for a glass?" Holly asked.

"No, thank you. I have to work this evening," Christine explained as she pulled a vine of seven grapes off the cluster.

Holly poured herself a half glass of wine before sitting in a padded chair. She sipped the wine and set the glass on a side table. "Matt told me you were kidnapped and nearly froze to death. You've been shot and so many things. I guess I look at you and think you might be the only person who would understand what I went through. You have been through so much more, and you seem fine. I was grabbed by two men and dragged towards a barn to be molested by who knows how many men." She wiped a tear away. "I was terrified. I have never been more terrified. Thank you, Jesus, for bringing Matt in time to save me. I have never witnessed such evil or the sound of a man being killed. Matt shot the man that hit me." She wiped the tears with her palms. "I'm scared, Christine. And I don't know how to put it behind me and move on as you have."

Christine spoke gently, "It's only been a day. It takes time to relax and come to terms with what happened to you. For me, it's a little bit different because I'm marrying Matt, which means I could become the target of anyone wanting to hurt him anytime. Because hurting me, would hurt him. There are brutal people in this world, but I also have learned that I need to be wiser and aware of where I am and who is around me. I was kidnapped because I was naive enough to trust a stranger who said Matt was hurt. That will never happen again, though it could be tried."

"Doesn't it scare you?"

"It could if I let it. Fear is a paralyzing wall that

will freeze a person into making their life into a prison of its own making. If I let fear have its way, I would not marry Matt. My relationship with him has cost me a lot, and he could be killed on any given day. That's a fear too. But we are both Christians, and I know the Lord tells me three hundred and sixty-five times in the Bible to *fear not*. I trust the Lord to guide our lives and keep us safe. Now, I could be dumb and wander into the saloon where half the men hate Matt, and I might just find myself being attacked and hurt. I don't go to places where I would be at a greater risk, and I am not as I about trusting people as I was before. All I can do is protect myself and trust the Lord for the rest. I refuse to let fear intimidate me so much that I throw away the best thing in my life. Fear will do that if you change directions every time it shows its ugly head."

"Are you calling me dumb for going out to the Long T Ranch alone?" Holly asked with raised eyebrows.

Christine nodded slightly. "It wasn't wise."

Holly nodded in agreement. "You're right; it wasn't. I'm a Christian too. I honestly thought Mister Thomas and I could sit down and talk like you and I are, but that couldn't be further from what happened. Do you think I'm too trusting?"

"I think trusting people is a wonderful way to be, as I'm that way too. However, you and I are in positions where we love men with enemies, and that should raise a sense of caution when we are forced to recognize that not everyone has our best interest at heart. We never want to stop trusting people, but we do need to listen carefully to our intuition if it raises a red flag. And when it does, get away from the situation as quickly as possible."

Holly frowned, "I had that feeling like I should leave as I rode onto their ranch, and I ignored it."

"You're blessed Matt showed up when he did. I'd say the Lord was looking out for you. Now you know from experience to follow that intuition immediately. I do. I believe it is the Lord saying, leave now because if you stay, it can turn bad."

Matt returned to the room and pulled a paper out of his pocket. "Dinner is ordered and will be brought up here. Before I forget, I got this wire today. It appears Mister Fairchild wants me to bring you home."

Holly read it and looked at Christine as she spoke, "Christine, I must ask your advice, and please be honest. Would Matt put his dream of building a woolen mill before your safety?"

Christine furrowed her brow. "Matt doesn't have a dream of a woolen mill that I'm aware of, but he would never put anything before my safety. He never has."

Holly's sad smile spoke louder than her solemn voice, "I love my husband, but he refused to give up his dream even when he knew my life was in danger. A fight is brewing between my husband and the cattlemen over sheep. I say we should get rid of the sheep and just enjoy our home, but Robert insists his dream is worth fighting for, even if it risks my life. Christine, I have no friends here. In truth, I probably have very few friends at all. But I need to ask, what would you do in my situation?"

Christine shook her head slightly, not knowing what to say. "I don't know if I could answer that. I just know Matt would never put me in danger or do whatever he could to keep me from it. A man's livelihood is how he survives, so I can understand fighting for your means of survival, but at what cost? I don't know where to draw that line."

"My husband, Robert, is retired and very wealthy. He doesn't need the sheep, nor is it his livelihood. It is a mere hobby and an idea to keep him busy."

"Oh." Christine's brow rose with a shrug of her shoulders. "He won't get rid of the sheep even with all the trouble going on up there?"

"No," Holly answered sadly. "Would you make him choose between you and the sheep?"

Christine chuckled despite the seriousness of the question. "I'd hope Matt would choose me over a sheep."

Holly sighed heavily, not feeling any humor. She waved the paper message in the air as she said plainly, "This message is from Robert wanting Matt to take me home. But I don't feel safe there anymore. Yesterday morning I was attacked, and today everything is fine?" she questioned. "I don't know that I should believe him."

Christine leaned towards Holly and grabbed her hand affectionately. "Then do what is right for you. Stay here until you do feel safe."

Holly smiled slowly. "Thank you. I just need-ed someone to tell me that." Her large blue eyes welled up with moisture. She turned her head to look at Matt. "Robert did poison Thomas's water hole, Matt. My husband does not quit a fight, and he always finds a way to win. So that message you received today, I don't know what he did, but if that message is true, he must have hit the Thomas's hard for what they did to me."

The confirmation of Robert's guilt for poisoning the water proved Robert Fairchild wasn't nearly as innocent as he liked to proclaim, and it muddied the waters of who was harassing who. "I suggest we go back in the morning and find out what he did because I'm curious about that too," Matt said.

"No." Holly picked up her glass of wine and took a sip. "I am staying here for a while. I will write Robert a letter to explain myself to him, so you do not need to. Christine and I have a lifetime of catching up and a lot of shopping to do in your absence. I hope you don't mind, Christine?"

Christine laughed lightly. "No. I don't mind."

"Good. I don't have any friends, and I hate to admit it, but I'm lonely."

Christine placed the last of the grapes she had plucked off the cluster into her mouth. "I'm sure we will become good friends," she said as someone knocked on the hotel room door.

Holly questioned, "Would dinner be here this soon?"

"No. I'll answer it," Matt said and opened the door. He twisted his hands upwards as he questioned, "What are you two doing here?"

William Fasana's loud and deep voice answered,

"Pamela said you and Christine came up here, and you didn't stop by the beast's room and say hello to us. So, the beast sniffed you out with his canine nose. We thought we'd join the party."

"It's not much of a party," Matt said, reluctant to let his cousin, William Fasana, and his friend, David Chatfield, inside the room.

"I know," William said as he stepped into the room uninvited, "but now it is. Come in, Dave." He ignored Matt and spoke to Holly, "Hello, Miss, I am William Fasana. I'm not just Matt's cousin but also the hotel security. I always make it a point to meet every guest we have, but I've not yet met you." He reached his hand out to shake hers.

"Holly Fairchild," she answered with an awkward expression. She was intrigued but also a bit horrified to see David Chatfield standing behind William.

William continued, "This is my pet friend, David. Now Miss, if you have lice or fleas, we'd appreciate it if you told us now. We just shampooed Dave, and he's pest free. You could smell his coat if you want. He smells like lilacs, I think."

She shook her head awkwardly, not knowing how to respond.

Christine laughed and stood to hug David. "I can't believe you are walking around. You walked up all those steps?"

He smiled. "I did. Doctor Ryland told me to start walking around a bit more. William wanted to come here. Thank you for the pie the other day. It was sure good."

"It was," William agreed.

"You're welcome." Christine could see that Holly was uncomfortable and perhaps afraid of David's werewolf-like appearance. He was a sixteen-year-old freak from the Chatfield & Bowry Circus and Sideshow known as the Tasmanian Wolf Boy. David had a rare disease called hypertrichosis that covered his entire body and face with long silky hair.

Christine took hold of David's hand and led him three steps closer to Holly. "Holly, this is David. He is living here temporarily as he recovers from being stabbed. The doctor was fortunate to be able to save David's life. His family owns a traveling circus that he is a part of. He is one of the most amazing young men you'll ever meet. David, this is Holly."

"Miss, it's nice to meet you, Ma'am. I know I look different, but I don't bite, and the full moon doesn't make me howl, so you'll be okay," David said with a growing smile. He could tell she was skeptical of shaking his hand, although she reluctantly did.

"I'm sorry to stare. I have never..." Holly said lightly.

David feigned excitement in his voice, "I know what you mean. You should have seen me when William first handed me a mirror. I was stunned! I had no idea I was so handsome."

"Your hair is so soft," she said, letting go of his hand with a slowly gaining smile.

"Thank you," David said.

William piped in, "That's because I just bathed him, Miss. I wanted to welcome you to our hotel and introduce ourselves. David is my beastly soul brother, and we roam these halls together now that he can walk. I can't help but notice your black eye. If the fellow who gave that to you shows up here, rest assured I will make both sides of his face look like that if not put him in the ground for blemishing such a beautiful lady as you."

"Your cousin already did, but thank you," she replied slowly.

William looked at Matt. "Why do you get to have all the fun?"

Matt shrugged. "Perks of the job."

"So, how long will we have the pleasure of your company?" William asked Holly.

"I don't know. For as long as I want to stay."

"Great. We'll try to make your stay so enjoyable you'll never want to leave. How would you feel about joining Dave and me for lunch tomorrow?"

"I take my meals in here until this," she pointed at her black eye, "is healed."

"That's fine. We'll move lunch up here and bring Dave's water bowl if he wants a drink."

Holly lowered her brow at the insensitive comment. "That's mean, isn't it?"

William paused as if he was stunned by the comment. "Miss, if I was nice to him, he'd think I liked him." He nudged David. "Huh?"

David nodded. "I've learned not to beg during dinner since being here."

William laughed. "He doesn't whine anymore, either. No, we are pals, and we joke around a lot."

"It's kind of harsh with his condition, isn't it?"

Holly asked.

"Condition?" William asked with surprise. He looked at David curiously. "Do you have a condition?"

David shook his head. "Not that I know of. What kind of a condition, Ma'am?"

Holly grinned. "Maybe it would be nice to have lunch with you two tomorrow. Certainly, it would be better than eating alone."

***

After spending the day together, Matt walked Christine to the dance hall and kissed her goodnight. She had to get ready for work, and Matt wanted to get a good night's sleep before riding back to Hollister in the morning. He wished he could spend more time with Christine, but it wasn't possible. He would have liked to come back at midnight to sit on the dance hall roof with her and talk as they watched for shooting stars, but he needed to sleep.

On the way back to his house, he stopped by his office and unlocked the steel door that led into the jail cells. A lantern burned to illuminate the main room. A smaller lantern's light reflected off the wall in the second cell, which was hidden from view by the granite block wall that separated it from the first cell.

"Evening, John," Matt said as he sat down on a visitor's bench against the wall.

John Painter sat on the edge of his bed, glad to

have some company. "Matt. Isn't it a little late for you to come by?"

"I didn't think you'd be asleep yet. How do you like working at the granite quarry?"

"I didn't, at first, but now I do. Why?" John was arrested some time back and agreed to live in jail and work at the granite quarry to pay off the debts for his crime rather than go to prison.

"I was just curious. Have you thought about what you are going to do when you are free to leave here?"

"Yes and no. I'll live with my parents and keep working at the quarry until I am called to do something else. Who knows, maybe I'll go back to seminary, and if I'm told I'll never be a reverend again, I'll have the confidence to tell the professor to shove that opinion right down his throat. If that's what I'm called to do, then I can do it no matter what anyone else believes about me. The one thing I have learned that I didn't know back then is my life is between the Lord and myself. Other people's opinions of who I am don't matter as long as I walk in the Lord's word and stay within Biblical truth. We are all made to be different and have different gifts, talents, and purposes. Thank heavens we are not all the same. Because I still wouldn't fit in." He laughed.

Matt smiled appreciatively. "Praise the Lord for that. I have been trying to get Morton to receive the Lord for a while now. Somewhere, someone planted a seed of the gospel in his ears, and maybe I watered that seed from time to time, but it took you to break through that hardened soil to lead him to Jesus. I am excited about that. I'm excited for him and his life, but I'm also excited to see how the Lord uses you in your life.

"You're right, John. Not everyone fits into the standard Christian mold that most Christians and non-believers form in their minds of what we should be. I remind people that John the Baptist would not fit into the modern mold of what a Christian is supposed to be as far as external appearances go. People care more about external appearances than the internal work that the Lord is doing. Take you, for example, a failure as a Christian, turned into a drunk and womanizer, and what did the church community do? Well, they almost fired your father from his pastorship because of your external appearance and actions. Little did they know that this failure would be restored and, while in jail, would lead the county's most feared villain to Jesus. That is the beauty of Jesus. It took you, John, the good reverend's failure of a son to reach Morton Sperry."

"It was just the Lord's timing," John said softly.

"Yes, but it took someone who knew where Morton was and could empathize with him. That professor at the college who said you'd never make a good reverend could not have reached Morton, nor would he even try, I bet. You tell me who is the better minister, he who judges by the external appearance or the one who sees people for the failures that they are? We all fail, John. But we can all be restored and used in great ways too. You are the proof of that."

"Thank you. But I can't take any credit."

Matt stood, pulled the cell door's key out of his pocket, and unlocked the cell door as the sound of the extra keys clanged against the steel frame of the lock. He opened the door. "Grab your stuff and get out of here. Your debt is paid in full, and you are free to go."

"Seriously? I figured I had another month or two to go."

Matt nodded with a smile. "John, you've been fully restored by the Lord and used in a great way in your relationship with Morton in such a short time. The world is desperate for hope and something unchanging and unchangeable to cling to. You are ready to leave this cell and walk outside these doors to share with the world the one hope that can bring light into the lives of millions. You may not be a licensed reverend from a college, but you know the secret of salvation and how to share it. You can leave this jail and let the world know that Jesus is the only answer for a dark world and a failed life. There is hope, and it is everlasting, ever willing, and ever forgiving. Let the people know so they don't miss it. You can go now, John. You can go show this city what a changed life looks like."

Chapter 25

Robert Fairchild sat outside in his silk robe, enjoying the simple pleasure of a bright moon casting its silvery light over the lake, surrounding hills, and jagged mountains towering above the valley to the north. Thousands upon thousands of people in the eastern cities would never know what it is like to sit in the wild country without another human being in sight. Robert would also know what it was like if it wasn't for the loud voices and occasional bothersome Blackburn Marshals.

Robert was on his second-story deck connected to his bedroom, gazing out over the lake and eastern skyline. He watched a red fox pounce in the grass near thick cattails patch on the lake's shore to snatch a mouse. He smiled as the fox trotted proudly along the bank with the night's meal in its mouth. Crickets and frogs sang a beautiful harmonious tune that pleased his ears. It was a delightful evening and would have been all the sweeter if his bride had been with him. The towel thrown over the empty chair beside him was left by Holly the last time they had sat outside together. She had gotten irritated because a couple of the Blackburn Marshals were staring at her. There was a time when Robert and Holly could stand on their deck naked, if they wanted to, without being seen by anyone, but since hiring the marshals, there was no more privacy. It was frustrating for Holly, and after that night, she had given up trying to enjoy her deck overlooking the lake.

Maybe it was that memory and Holly's absence that annoyed Robert at the sound of loud voices, banging, and the stable door opening, followed by Jesse Helms, Cass Travers, and Henry Dodds bringing their horses out of the stable. They waved and said hello as they rode past the house.

Robert lifted his hand holding his drink. The three men had disrupted his peace and quiet. To aggravate him further, they left the stable door open. He had a comfortable bunkhouse built to house the Blackburn Marshals at a certain distance from the house for his and Holly's privacy. However, hiring a group of hardened men to protect them came with certain frustrating interactions, such as Holly now sharing her stable and corral space with the Blackburn Marshal's horses and often their company. They had a place to sleep but ate in the main house, causing more work for the Fairchild Estate's servants. It didn't take more than a day to lay down the rules, and the first rule was there would be no tolerance for the marshals pursuing the servant ladies. The house servants, two married couples, and one couple had two teenage daughters that worked as servants as well. They were all of South American descent and spoke English well enough to be understood. They lived in three nice rooms in the attic and were more like family than employees. Robert expected the Blackburn Marshals to treat the servants with respect and kindness.

The Blackburn Marshals were temporarily hired hands that were paid to do a job, and Robert was looking forward to cutting ties now that the job was completed. Robert supposed he had spent a handsome fee, and the Blackburn Marshals had done little to earn their money other than being present, which is sometimes just enough.

Robert had liked Ed Bostwick a great deal. Ed was a man with integrity and had a human kindness that could be both gentle and dangerous. He was a man with honor and loyalty. He was just the kind of man that Robert wanted to work with to recreate what the Blackburn Marshals could be. Robert envisioned Ed as the face of the new Blackburn Marshals. There were a few others in the group that Robert would recommend keeping, but ignorant thugs like Ira Kelly would have no part in the new business.

But now that Ed Bostwick was dead, so was the idea of expanding the Blackburn Marshals. Ira Kelly had played his hand at treachery and accomplished it like a professional, as all he planned had worked out beautifully. Ira's competition was gone; more importantly, the client was in the clear of blame and proven innocent. Robert could sit on his upper back deck and drink a glass of fine wine while relaxing in the moonlight. He had no worries about the sheep shooters killing his sheep or coming after him. He could sit peacefully for the first time in months. It was over. And despite his personal opinions of the man, Robert had Ira to thank for it. However, seeing Ira walk across the grass towards the house brought a ball of aggravation to Robert's chest.

"Hey, boss," Ira Kelly called from the yard. "I saw that you weren't sleeping. I was thinking about what we were talking about earlier today, and I have an idea. Instead of leaving here to find work elsewhere, how about we just work for you, tending the sheep or whatever? You're going to be building a wool mill, and we might as well help with that, right? We all have building and carpentry skills. Heck, Kent's father was a stonemason. And while we're building that, you and I can plan on how to make the Blackburn Marshals bigger than Jeff Blackburn and I ever dreamed. What do you think?"

Every ounce of available energy left Robert with a heavy sigh. "We'll talk about it tomorrow."

"Yeah, that's fine. I just stepped outside to pee and saw you sitting there. Your missus should be coming back, yeah? I'll bet you'll be glad to have her home." He stepped nearer and lowered his voice, "She'll be surprised to learn Ed is dead. They were getting kind of close, you know. I probably did you a favor there too."

Robert's bottom lip tucked between his teeth. "If

you are suggesting Holly would be interested in another man, you might choose to start backtracking your words."

"Of course not!" Ira scoffed. "No, sir. I never intended it to be taken in such a way. Ed was the one falling for Holly, not the other way around. That's the honest truth, Mister Fairchild."

"Ed was a good man. He was not the only man infatuated with my wife, nor will he be the last. But don't ever suggest Holly is interested in another man or somehow I owe you for eliminating a friend of ours."

"No sir, I would never do that. Well, maybe I should hit the hay and get some sleep."

"Perhaps so. Where did Jesse Helms ride off to? I like him, don't you?"

Ira snorted. "I tend to like Cass Travers better. Jesse is too quiet and hard to read what's going on in that big head of his. I don't know about him yet," Ira answered. "They got bored and decided to go for a night ride around the lake or somewhere."

"Keep him and his friend on a short leash. I don't need any more trouble. Goodnight, Ira."

"Goodnight, boss." He waited in the yard for Robert to go inside, but he remained in his chair. "I thought you were going to bed?"

Robert couldn't help but smile with a shake of his head. "I said goodnight so that you would leave me alone."

"Oh." Ira laughed. "Goodnight."

Chapter 26

Jesse Helms sat in the corner of the 1878 Saloon with his predator eyes scanning the room for an unsuspecting victim. His fingers held a shot glass that he tilted back and forth but not yet lifted towards his mouth.

"Do you see anyone?" he asked quietly.

Henry Dodds shook his head in reply. He had been a Blackburn Marshal long enough to know there was a variety of dangerous men. Most people were like sheep and wanted to avoid violence and live peacefully in a safe environment. Every town in America was full of good people who were kind and loving while working hard to raise their families as best they could. They were very good people, and being so, they were the perfect victims for a predator.

The most common predators to a flock of sheep were wolves and coyotes. Wolves would attack a full-grown sheep and tear it to shreds, while coyotes were a little more cautious and preferred to attack lambs. It was a common theme to compare outlaws and other criminals to wolves, and certainly, Jesse Helms and Cass Travers were of the wolf caliber. They were blunt, vicious, straightforward, and deadly. They were like starving wolves that saw what they wanted and attacked suddenly, unexpectedly, and brutally.

There were coyotes in the human race too, but Henry Dodds didn't know many of them because men that harmed women and children did not survive long around the Blackburn Marshals. Jeff Blackburn, who had founded the organization, had made it clear that they may be hired to do anything, but they would never harm women or children.

Both types of predators attack without mercy and have no empathy for tears or pleading. The predator cares nothing for the sheep; its concern is getting its needs met, whatever that need may be. However, before any predator makes its presence known, it falls into a group that Henry likened to venomous snakes. There are many types of venomous snakes in the world, and all have their unique camouflage to blend in with their environment. In the same way, predators put on camouflage to fit into the environment where they can isolate and attack a victim.

Coyotes always seek weaker people than themselves to victimize. Such criminals do not want to risk being hurt in a fight, so they seek victims that won't fight back and surrender to their fear in the moment of attack. It is a brutal world, and sheep have no understanding of the criminal mindset or how to defend against it when it strikes other than freezing in terror and becoming a victim. Mister Fairchild's sheep have one defense, to flee, blindly, foolishly, panic-stricken, and sometimes right into more trouble than they were fleeing from. Human beings can flee as well, but they can also fight back when there is no other option. Jabbing a finger forcefully through a predator's eye and blinding him to create the space to escape is one thing a human victim can and should be prepared to do when necessary. Predators care absolutely nothing about the victim's life, and the same measure should be taken while defending one's life. Fleeing is a great first defense, but when caught, a decision has to be made, submit in fear and be at the mercy of a merciless predator or fight.

Thankfully, there are guard dogs in the human population. Sheepdogs are loyal protectors, and the sheep can lie in comfort knowing the sheepdog is watching over the flock. At the first sign of a threat, the sheepdog is there to meet the threat head-on and will fight a wolf to the death to protect the sheep. The sheepdogs are the lawmen, military, fathers, mothers, and other such brave souls willing to defend their homes, neighborhoods, churches, and other organizations from the slithering parasites of a predator. Sheepdogs stand in the way and protect those who cannot protect themselves. A watchful sheepdog will quite often scare a predator looking for easy prey away, assuring their flock remains safe.

Henry Dodds liked to consider himself a sheepdog that would guard against a coyote, but in truth, he was a criminal too, a wolf. He just got paid to be one.

"Is that one of them?" Jesse asked as three men came into the saloon.

Henry knew right away that Jesse Helms and Cass Travers were the wolves to society. What started as a night ride to get out of the bunkhouse and enjoy the cooler temperature had become a situation that Henry was uncomfortable with.

Jesse turned his sharp eyes to Henry. "Well?" he demanded.

Henry pointed at each man as they crossed the room, greeting others they knew. "That's Barry McCracken and KC Owens. KC works on the Long T Ranch, Barry doesn't. That kid is a Thomas, but I don't know his first name. He's Bode's little brother."

"I don't know who Bode is," Jesse snapped quietly. He was in a foul mood.

Henry was annoyed by Jesse's impatience. "Bode is Gunther Thomas's son. They own the Long T Ranch. That kid is Gunther's youngest boy. I know that much, but I don't know his name."

Jesse watched the three men sit at a table and holler for drinks. "Well, that much will do. Yeah, he is the one I want. He's the softest. You agree, Cass?"

"Yep," Cass said as he took a drink. "He'll squeal

quicker than a pinched piglet."

Henry leaned over the table and spoke softly, "Fellas, when we went for a ride, you didn't say anything about this. I know Elliot was your friend, just like Jimmy and Ed were mine, but we can't seek revenge without asking Mister Fairchild," Henry reminded them.

Jesse lifted his shirt lapel to be noticed by Henry. "I'm not wearing a Blackburn badge, and neither is Cass. We're on our own time, and if anyone has a problem with that, we'll quit outright. You're free to leave if you don't want to be involved. I don't care about Fairchild or the Blackburn Marshals; I care about finding the man that put a bullet in my friend's head."

Henry shook his head. "I can't let you two do that without Fairchild's permission, and I know he will not give that. You're Blackburn Marshals now, and we don't have the luxury to act independently. So, let's get going back home before we get in trouble."

Cass spoke, "Jesse just told you we're not wearing badges. We're on our own tonight, and we'll make that known."

Henry lowered his voice and warned candidly, "If you two hurt any of those men, don't come back to the bunkhouse again. I don't want to lose my life because you two want to get even, and I lost more friends than you did. We have a job to do. Personal feelings have nothing to do with it!" His eyes burned warningly into Jesse's.

Jesse looked at Cass and smiled. "Then, I guess

we quit. I didn't like the feeling of a badge much, anyway. Did you?" he asked Cass.

Henry stood and finished his drink. "You fellas are on your own."

Cass grinned, "We're always on our own, and we've done just fine."

"So be it," Henry said.

Jesse stood abruptly and drove a fist into Henry's face, sending Henry crashing into another table where some older men were seated. They were not pleased to have their drinks spilled and started to raise a ruckus until Jesse grabbed the whiskey bottle the men were sharing and slammed it mercilessly against Henry's head. The bottle shattered, and a shard of glass entered Henry's eye.

Henry was not expecting to be attacked and could not defend himself in time, as the damage was already being done. Dazed, bewildered, bleeding, in pain, and blinded by a searing pain in his eye, Henry was desperate to get to a source of water to rinse his eye. He knew he was seriously injured, and he needed help.

Still holding the bottle's neck in his palm, Jesse drove the jagged glass into Henry's ribs and ripped it forward to slice Henry open as he stumbled towards the door as fast as he could while holding his hand over his eye. Jesse kicked Henry in the buttocks and then pushed him out of the bat doors to the street with a laugh.

Jesse turned towards the table where KC Owens, Jake Thomas, and Barry McCracken were sitting and grinned. "My pal and I hired on as Blackburn Marshals two days ago and I can't stand them. My name's Jesse Helms, and this is my pal, Cass Travers. We're suddenly unemployed, but if you know if we can get a job killing sheep or marshals, let me know."

KC Owens peered at Jesse curiously. "I've heard of you. Working a job isn't what you're known for, is it?"

"No," Jesse answered honestly. "But a man can change his life, can't he?" He noticed the youngest Thomas boy looking at his pocket watch.

KC didn't like the way Jesse's eyes glared at him. They were cold and ruthless. "Why did you cut that man up?"

Jesse's lips rose slightly. "The reason is none of your business. I don't even know your names."

"I'm KC Owens, that's my pal, Barry McCracken, and Jake Thomas is the boy still wet behind the ears. I work for his Pa on the Long T Ranch. We got a sudden opening that you might have heard about when Matt Bannister came to the ranch and took your boss's wife away from us."

"That happened the day before we hired on, I think." Jesse asked, "Tell me, who shot that Blackburn Marshal in the back of the head before you all hung him up by his feet? You know, the one with his badge shoved in his mouth?"

"A friend of yours?" Barry asked cautiously. He didn't like the rage buried in Jesse's expression. It also seemed an odd question since three men were hung on the headgate.

Jesse's eyes darted towards Barry with an icy glare. "Friend? No. Maybe I wanted to do it and feel robbed. I want to shake the man's hand that did it."

Jake offered, "It was my father."

Jesse reached a hand over to shake Jake's hand. "Tell your father I wish I could shake his hand, but yours will do. Nice to meet you, young man."

***

Jake Thomas left the saloon, walked towards the edge of town, and went behind the white church where he met his beloved Laura Whitehead. Laura lived in town, just a block away, above the hardware store that her parents owned. Jake and Laura had been courting for some time, but it had to be done secretly. The secrecy was needed as she was fourteen years old and the daughter of a God-fearing Christian couple who would never support their daughter being courted by Jake Thomas. Her parents caught the two of them hiding in the hardware store long after closing hours, heavily engaged in kissing in a way that was very inappropriate for older unmarried courting couples to do, let alone their child.

Laura's parents, Mitch and Helen Whitehead, were well aware that Jake Thomas had inclinations to court their daughter. Unfortunately, since his mother had taken ill, Jake had long since quit attending church and took up drinking in the saloons with the ranch hands and fornicating with the painted ladies at the Pink House bordello. The experience he had learned from going there, Mitch and Helen feared he was trying to share with Laura long before she was of marrying age.

Mitch and Helen had no idea what their daughter found attractive about Jake, but her eyes shined like diamonds, and her smile glowed when she saw the young man. There were two serious seekers of Laura's hand when she came of age, and Jake's only competition was another young man named Aaron Longley. Aaron was a rancher's son as well, but he was a Godly young man with strong morals that promised to be a fitting husband and provider for Laura's future.

In the daylight, Laura was courted by Aaron as a respectable young lady should be, and her affections for him were convincing. But it was a trick mirror as her affections turned to Jake late at night when her parents and siblings were asleep. She would sneak out of the house as quietly as a mouse to spend time with Jake, where no one would find them.

There was a connection between Jake and Laura that could not be tamed. There was a fire burning bright that consumed them when they were together. Jake loved her with all his heart, and she was in love with him. They met every night at eleven o'clock in the underground cellar behind the church. Jake kept a small lantern and blanket on a shelf for them to sit on while they visited for an hour or two.

Jake walked down the eight concrete stairs to

the door and pushed it open. Inside, he could see the faint light of the lantern's wick and turned it up before setting it back on the shelf. He was always excited to see Laura and hold her in his arms. He planned on marrying her once she turned sixteen and moving her to the Long T Ranch.

He grinned when the door opened. Laura entered and closed the door before leaping into his arms to press her lips against his in a firm kiss. She broke the kiss and said, "I have been waiting for this all day! I saw you ride by the store earlier today and my heart melted like butter on a griddle. You, Jake Thomas, make my heart melt. I love you so much." She kissed him again.

He chuckled contently with a large grin. "I'm glad to hear that because I can hardly stand the hours away from you. I swear, as soon as your father says you're of marrying age, I'm asking him if I can have your hand in marriage. I know he'll refuse, so we're eloping! I don't need his permission to love you."

"Apparently, you don't need to ask my permission either because I did not hear a marriage proposal in there," she teased.

He kissed her gently. "I assumed you would agree. That is unless you drop me like a rotten apple and take up with Aaron Longley."

"I would never do that to you."

The door burst open with a bang that made the pair of lovers jolt in fright. Jesse Helms asked, "Well, what are you two kids doing all alone in here?"

Cass Travers closed the door behind them. "My-oh-my," he said, taking a look at Laura.

Laura clung tighter to Jake as he moved in front of her protectively. "What are you doing here? You're not supposed to be here," Jake said nervously. Jake didn't wear a gun belt nor had a weapon of any kind.

Jesse put his finger to his lips. "Shhh. I came to talk to you because I have a message for your father."

Jake's hands shook visibly as he could not hide the fear overtaking him. Laura was frightened as well, and it showed in their nervous expressions. "W…w…what do you want me to tell him?"

Jesse exhaled as he tightened his lips and nodded slowly. "You can tell him…."

"What?" Jake asked with concern.

Jesse hit Jake in the stomach with a hard right fist that knocked the wind out of him and doubled Jake over. Jesse grabbed the back of Jake's hair and rammed his face into a rising knee. He kneed his face again and let the boy fall to the blanket Jake had spread out on the concrete floor. Jesse dropped down on the young man's chest, pulled his knife from the sheath on his belt, and set the sharp blade against Jake's throat.

Laura screamed when Jesse hit Jake and tried to run, but she was grabbed by the throat and slammed against the shelves by Cass. His revolver was quickly pressed against her head. "Hush!" Cass snarled. "I don't want to hurt a pretty jewel like you." He jerked her body forward and slipped around behind her, keeping an arm over her breast to hold her tight. "You just be quiet and watch, or you'll never leave this cellar alive." He warned with the barrel of his gun gently caressing her cheek.

Jake was on his back with a knife blade pressed against his throat. Despite his defenseless position, his eyes and concern were on the fierce stranger holding Laura. "Please, don't hurt her. I'll do anything you want. Just please, don't hurt her," he pleaded.

Jesse tapped the side of the blade against Jake's cheek to get his attention. "Your father killed Elliot?" Jesse asked plainly.

Tears ran down Jake's face as he stated truthfully, "I don't know who Elliot is! I don't know. Please, let her go," Jake begged.

"Elliot was my friend that your father shot in the back of the head before he was hung up by his feet!" Jesse snarled.

"It wasn't me! I swear I had nothing to do with it," Jake said as he broke into frightened sobs.

Jesse narrowed his brow. "You already told me who did it. I'm only here to send a message to your father. Do you know what my message is?"

"No," Jake wept with his eyes watching Cass. "Please stop it. Let her go."

Jesse looked back to see Cass had holstered his revolver and was allowing his hands to roam over her body. Jesse moved the knife blade from Jake's throat to the inside of Jake's mouth and pressed the blade against his left cheek. "Here is my message to your father. Listen carefully; tell your father Jesse Helms will be seeing him soon. This is for shoving that badge into Elliot's mouth." Jesse ripped the knife sideways, slicing through Jake's cheek from the corner of the lips to nearly the joint of the jaw.

Jake cried out and turned to his stomach to not choke on the blood that was pouring out.

Laura screamed, but Cass quickly covered her mouth. He drew his mouth close to her ear and chuckled wickedly. "Now it's our turn."

Chapter 27

Jake Thomas half stumbled and half ran while trying to press his hand against two halves of a split-open cheek to stop the bleeding, but the blood flowed between his fingers and out of his mouth like trying to grasp water from the hand pump. He sobbed loudly as he stumbled towards the 1878 Saloon and burst through the bat doors reaching out for his friends, Barry McCracken and KC Owens, before falling to the floor, exposing his slashed open cheek.

"Jake!" Barry exclaimed, horrified. "What happened?"

"Get him a towel!" KC shouted to the barkeeper as he and Barry helped Jake into a chair. "Let's get you to the doctor."

Jake shook his head and stood. He grabbed Barry's wrist and tried to say, "Come on," but the flapping cheek and mouth full of blood muffled the pronunciation. He pulled at Barry, urging him and the others to follow.

"Alright. I'm coming," Barry said as he was dragged outside. KC caught a thrown towel and helped Jake hold it over the wound. They were followed out by the other twelve men inside the saloon that were equally concerned. They all worked on different ranches, but they all knew Jake and were curious to learn what happened to their young friend and what trouble he was anxious to show them. By the tears and desperation in Jake's eyes and his quick stumbling pace to lead them somewhere, they all knew what they would find was bad.

The night had turned into a nightmare. Jake had been held down and forced to watch the two animals rape Laura. He was helpless to intervene, and the prayers he prayed seemed to bounce off the cellar walls. Jake would never be able to get the anguished expressions on her face or her muffled screaming out of his memory. It was an unimaginable and excruciating nightmare made worse by the wicked laughter of the two men who were as vicious as wolves. When the two beasts finally left, Jake touched her shoulder, and she screamed in blind terror as if she didn't know him. That was when he went to get help.

"Jake, where are we going?" Barry asked as Jake led him behind the church. Jake fell to his knees sobbing while motioning frantically towards the stairway to the cellar. KC Owens and two other men went down and opened the door.

KC quickly ascended the stairs and shouted, "Get the Whiteheads and tell them Laura is hurt!

Joey, get the sheriff and the doctor! Hurry up!" KC was not a sensitive man, but the sight of Laura lying nude in a fetal position shaking uncontrollably in pain and weeping while listening to Jake sob simultaneously, was enough to shake a solid stone to tears. "Tell her parents to bring a blanket! Get the doctor and her parents here now!"

***

Laura had been taken home by her parents, where the town doctor, Wayne Anderson, was summoned to treat her wounds and give her something to calm her down, ease the physical pain, and let her sleep. Laura was traumatized, in shock, and would need to heal physically and emotionally from such a horrific experience. Doctor Anderson was gentle with her and tried to reassure her that she would be okay, but she was incoherent and needed to rest.

The doctor then went to the 1878 Saloon, where the cattlemen had taken Jake to wait as they had some drinks to calm their nerves. What had happened to two of the communities finest young people was enough to rock the strongest man's countenance. Doctor Anderson took Jake to his doctor's office to disinfect and suture the young man's cheek.

Gunther Thomas stepped into the office with his son Bode. They had been told what had happened when they were summoned and came to check on Jake. "How is he, Doc?" Gunther asked.

"He'll be okay. He'll have a heck of a scar to live

with, but he'll be good as new in a few weeks."

"And the girl?" Gunther asked.

Doctor Anderson frowned noticeably. "She's in a bad way. She's been violated and is traumatized. I don't know how well she'll recover. She will heal physically, but her personality may never be the same."

Jake groaned and began to weep.

"Who did it?" Gunther asked his son.

Doctor Anderson spoke, "I'm trying to suture his cheek; Jake can't talk right now."

Gunther waved a hand towards the door as he explained, "All these men outside and in the saloon have been asking who did it, but Jake couldn't answer. Let him write it down so we can start looking for the man responsible." Gunther ordered.

Jake motioned for a piece of paper and a pencil. The doctor stopped what he was doing, found the writing materials, and watched Jake write frantically. Jake's body began to quiver as he broke down into sobs while handing the paper to his father.

Gunther took the letter and read the writing smeared with blood from Jake's fingers. Gunther's eyes may have misted for a quick moment as they left the note and gazed at his son. "Get home to your mother when you're done here. She's worried about you. Do you hear?"

Jake gave a thumbs-up as he fought to control the tears.

The doctor's office door burst open, and Mitch Whitehead stormed into the office. Mitch's usual gentle countenance burned with the fire of hell's rage. He yelled, "I heard you were here, Gunther! Keep your damn son away from my daughter!" Mitch pointed at Jake, "I told you to stay away from Laura, and now look what you've done! Don't ever come around my daughter again! It's your fault my daughter is..." He fought from sobbing as his lips trembled uncontrollably. "It's your fault! Some man hurt my baby girl..." He no longer had the strength to fight the sobs.

Gunther put a hand on Mitch's shoulder to guide him out of the office. "Let's go, old friend. If you want to help us get the men responsible, I know who they are."

"Men?" Mitch asked as the word doubled his agony. "How many men?"

"Two."

Mitch stumbled as the answer hit him in the gut harder than a bullet could. His princess was just a child, and the idea that two men would do such a horrible thing to her didn't just break his heart. It crushed him deeper than being caught between two speeding trains could.

"Who was it?" Bode Thomas asked, taking the note from his father. He read it aloud to the men on the street waiting for any news.

"This is what my little brother wrote: *It was Jesse Helms and his friend. I don't know his name. Tell Laura I'm sorry. Tell her I love her, please.*" Bode's heart skipped a beat as the final words choked him for a moment.

"Blackburns!" Pat Emerson exclaimed with a twisted mouth.

"Gunther, do you want me to gather the boys for one final ride?" Joe Bookman asked. He was a cowboy employed for another ranch and a Hollister Sheep Shooter. "It's your call, but just a day ago, they were going to murder your family by poisoning your well, and now this. I say that's enough! Let's go wipe them all out while we can."

"Yes! It's about time!" one of the men exclaimed.

"What's next if we don't exterminate them?" A deep voice asked.

"A better question is, *who* is next after your family, Gunther? Mine?" a man named Mick Olsen asked. "We've given them everything they wanted, and this is what we get! That young lady deserves justice, and I'm mad as hell! We should've run them out of town a long time ago."

"Agreed!"

"I couldn't agree more, Mick."

The Sheriff, Pat Emerson, spoke loudly, "Jake will be scarred for life, and Laura, she may never get over this. The doctor told me there was a good chance she could become pregnant after what happened to her tonight. What if that beautiful young lady we all love was given a whore's disease? I agree with Mick, I'm mad as hell, and I say we burn that whole damn place to the ground and piss on the ashes of those men!"

Gunther Thomas stood on the steps of the doctor's office and raised a hand to quiet the group of men. He spoke loudly, "Didn't Matt Bannister say this is what would happen if we fought the Blackburn Marshals? Well, we made peace, and then

254

they tried to murder my family, and look at what they did tonight. I want all of you to split up and wake up every sheep shooter and let's wipe the entire Fairchild Estate and the Blackburn Marshals off the face of the earth tonight! Get everyone here by sunup and let's finish this. We're going to protect our community once and for all."

"And don't you try to stop us, Mitch!" Sheriff Pat Emerson exclaimed at the mayor of Hollister, Mitch Whitehead.

"Stop you?" Mitch asked in disbelief. "All I have to say is if you need weapons, dynamite or black powder, rope to hang them with, or anything else, I have it at the store. You're welcome to it all as long as you kill the men that hurt my daughter!"

Chapter 28

Henry Dodds had run to the doctor's office and woken up Doctor Anderson to look at his eye. The pain was severe and he could not open it. The doctor wiped the blood from his face and discovered a shard of glass in Henry's scalp and a sliver of glass lodged in his eye. The damaged eye was beyond saving; there was nothing Doctor Anderson could do about it. He was not skilled enough to remove the eye, so he tied a black eyepatch over his eye, which would remain for the rest of Henry's life.

While his gashes along his ribs were being cared for, the doctor was interrupted by a man urging the doctor to go to the church where Jake Thomas had his cheek sliced open and a girl had been raped. Hearing Jake Thomas's name, Henry knew immediately that Jesse Helms and Cass Travers had committed the crime. Henry kept his mouth shut, and Doctor Anderson quickly sutured Henry's deepest cut and handed him a bottle of morphine before taking his medicine bag and leaving Henry on the street.

Henry followed at a distance and watched the heartbreaking visual of a young girl's devastated parents helping their daughter walk painfully back home. Listening to the young lady weeping filled Henry with rage, and he rode out of town, hoping to run into Jesse and Cass. He rode into the Fairchild Estate stable, unsaddled his horse, and walked into the bunkhouse where Kent Kruse and Ellis McKenna sat at a table with a lantern burning on dim playing cards. Ira Kelly slept soundly in his bunk at the far end of the bunkhouse.

"You boys are finally back, huh?" Ellis asked without raising his head.

"No. I don't think they're coming back, and if they do, I'll kill them myself."

"What's going on?" Kent asked. He took notice of the eyepatch and dried blood on Henry's hairline and shirt.

"What happened to your eye?" Ellis asked with concern.

"We need to wake up, Ira. I think we're in trouble."

"Ira!" Ellis shouted, "Wake up, we need you."

Ira grumbled as he sat up quickly. "What?" he shouted angrily.

"Henry's hurt. He needs to talk to you."

Ira listened with the others as Henry explained what had happened in town. "I don't think they'll come back here. But I know the townspeople are furious."

Kent Kruse had listened and was concerned. "Ira, you should wake up Mister Fairchild and let him know what happened and see what he wants to do about it."

Ellis rubbed his mouth thoughtfully. "I knew I didn't like them two fellas. If they don't come back here, we better go looking for them tomorrow for what they did to Henry, if nothing else."

Ira was hesitant. Robert Fairchild was grumpy earlier, and Ira didn't want to make him more annoyed over nothing that couldn't wait until morning. "If Jesse and Cass come back tonight, we'll tie them up and take them to the sheriff in the morning. But I don't think we need to disturb Robert tonight. It's late, and he needs his sleep. We all do. We'll talk to Robert about this first thing in the morning."

Kent was reluctant to let it go so easily. "Those cowboys can get awfully onery over sheep and Gunther's son being slit open like that along with that girl," he paused to shake his head. "If that doesn't fire those cowboys up, then nothing will. I'm telling you, we need to wake Robert up and prepare for a fight. I know I wouldn't be able to sleep or sit still if that was my daughter."

Ira wanted to sleep and snapped at Kent bitterly, "Well, she's not your daughter. You don't know her, so what difference does it make? If they come out in the morning looking for Jesse and Cass and we'll let them search. We have nothing to do with what happened." Ira yawned. "Get some sleep, fellas. We'll deal with it in the morning."

Kent had an unsettling anxious feeling and wouldn't be able to sleep if he tried. Frustrated with Ira, he walked outside and wandered down to the dock where the rowboat was tied. He removed his boots and socks and sat on the dock to soak his feet in the cool water. The moonlight over the lake was bright and beautiful and brought a sense of peace that calmed his unsettled nerves about what had happened in town. He looked at the boat and then back towards the house. Robert Fairchild was sleeping soundly, most likely, and even if not, Kent doubted Robert would mind him borrowing the boat.

Kent grabbed his boots and socks, stepped into the boat, and rowed out to the middle of the lake. He set the two oars down, leaned back against the bottom of the boat to stare at the stars, and relax to the sound of the water lightly lapping at the boat's sides while enjoying the sensation of floating. Lying as comfortably as he could with his legs over the bench seat was near paradise as a slight breeze blew between his bare toes.

He took a deep breath and closed his eyes. With a slight smile, he drifted slowly with the moon's light towards sleep in the blessed peace he enjoyed.

Chapter 29

It was still dark with a slight hint of orange on the eastern horizon when Gunther Thomas led forty-five members of the Hollister Sheep Shooters through the Fairchild Estate head gate. Three men stopped there to set up a rope for a hanging. Two men rode west with a pair of cutters to cut the telegraph line. The rest followed Gunther as they rode headlong towards the large Victorian home. Some of the men carried unlit torches, dynamite, and kerosene cans to ensure everything was burned to the ground.

They had made a plan, and everyone knew what their job was. Some would attack the house, others the bunkhouse, stable, and even the outhouses needed to be burned down. They all knew there were servants in the house who were to be spared but no one else. It was rumored that Holly Fairchild had left for Branson with the federal marshal, but if not, not even she would be spared. Like the calvary sweeping down upon an Indian camp, the entire Fairchild Estate was to be nothing except dust and ashes.

A sledgehammer swung against the door, burst it open, and a group of men ran into the Fairchild home with lit lanterns and torches. Two other men poured kerosene on the furniture and floor of different rooms.

Robert Fairchild had stayed up later than usual, and for a man who never drank alcohol, he had a few too many drinks in the sorrow of missing his bride's gentle smile. He was woken abruptly by his bedroom door being kicked open and a lantern pushed in front of his face.

"Found him!" a man hollered. Robert was suddenly jerked out of bed and pushed towards the door, where he stumbled and fell to the floor. He was disoriented and in shock, not knowing if it was real or a dream. He was yanked to his feet and held by both arms by two powerful men and moved down the hall.

Upstairs, he could hear other doors being kicked open and the servants screaming as they were ushered out of bed. Outside, guns firing could be heard, but it all seemed too unreal to be happening.

Robert was pushed down the stairs and rolled along the wooden slabs until he landed on the floor, rubbing his elbow, which had been hurt in the fall. He was at the feet of several men dressed in black dusters and had their faces covered with burlap bags.

Robert remained on his hands and knees in his silk undergarments and looked up at the tallest of the men who appeared to have been the leader, or at least one of them. The tumble down the stairs convinced him it wasn't a nightmare after all. "What are you doing? Why are you here?" he asked.

Gunshots roared outside by the bunkhouse, but the frightened cries of the servant girls and their parents as they were taken down the stairs demanded Robert's immediate attention. "Don't hurt them! Everything will be okay, trust me," he said to his servants as they were rushed by him and taken outside.

Robert was confused, and the fresh smell of kerosene in his home confused him even more. He realized they were going to burn his house down. Angered, he stood quickly and yelled, "Leave my home! All of you get off my property. Now!"

The end of an oak club was fiercely driven into Robert's kidney, and he groaned, arched his back, and dropped to his knees before falling forward to his hands. A big black boot kicked Robert in the face and knocked him to his back. "Heel him," the tall man ordered, and two men grabbed his legs while a third slipped a lasso over his feet and pulled the rope to tighten it around his ankles. "Put the servants in the wagon and drop them off way out yonder somewhere. I don't care where."

"What are you doing?" Robert yelled. "We had an agreement! You can't be doing this."

There was no attempt to answer him. The big

man spoke through his burlap hood, "Take him out and stand him up to watch this place burn. Boys, take what you want from here, and then let's burn it to the ground."

Robert recognized the man's voice. "Sheriff Emerson, you won't get away with this! Ira!" He screamed for the leader of his hired gunmen, "Ira!"

The shooting outside had come to an end. Pat Emerson stomped his boot on Robert's chest and slid it over Robert's throat. "Your marshals are dead. No one can stop us now. Take him outside."

The three cowboys pulled the rope and dragged Robert on his back across the foyer and outside the door. He could hear the ecstatic voices of the sheep shooters tearing his house apart and going through his things.

"Everyone get out. I accidentally lit the fire. I can't put it out. It's going to burn!"

"You idiot! Where is his money?"

"Grab my missus one of his wife's dresses!"

"Grab that painting."

"Darn you, Joe! You should've been able to smell the kerosene! Now it's all going to burn."

Bode Thomas kicked the back door open and came inside as he removed the burlap sack from his face. He held a carbine rifle in his hands. "There were only three marshals in the bunkhouse, and they're all dead now. There's no one else around."

Gunther picked up a ceramic music box shaped like a grand piano and turned the key on the back to listen to it play. He looked at his son approvingly.

"Put your hood back on, their servants are outside. Let's go out front and watch the place burn. I'm keeping this music box for little Laura. It might help her feel better."

***

The bunkhouse wasn't made for luxury. It was created to give a place for twelve men to sleep on six bunk beds, three bunks on each side. There was about a ten-foot space between the door and the first set of bunks, where a table and five chairs were and a small woodstove if needed. There were two windows, one on each side of the bunkhouse for ventilation and the entrance door at the front.

The sound of multiple horses awakened Ira Kelly, and he knew immediately they were being attacked before he heard the first gunshot. He rolled out of his bottom bunk to the floor and grabbed his rifle. "Wake up!" he yelled to Ellis McKenna and Henry Dodds, who slept soundly. "Where's Kent? Where the hell is Kent?" Ira shouted. The bunkhouse was dark, but Kent slept in the bunk next to his, and it was empty.

"What's going on?" Ellis asked, hopping down from his top bunk.

The answer came when the door was kicked open and a shotgun fired both barrels into Ellis, blowing him over the bottom bunk onto the floor with his legs draped over the mattress. His blood spread out across the floor.

The man that fired the shotgun stepped aside as

another sheep shooter stepped into the entrance with a shotgun and fired both barrels missing both Henry and Ira.

Ira aimed his rifle over his bunk and fired a shot at the door missing the man as he leaped out of sight. Ira ejected the shell casing and quickly aimed at the side of the door, where a shadow figure of a man aiming a rifle suddenly appeared. Both men shot at the same time. The sheep shooter's aim was off while Ira drove a .44 bullet into the man's forearm. He cried out painfully as he turned from the door, cursing.

Henry Dodds grabbed his revolver and fired as fast as he could towards the opened doorway while quickly approaching the door to slam it shut. With the revolver's cylinder empty, he stood against the door and began to empty the cylinder and then realized he didn't have any bullets on him to reload. "Boss, push a bed over here to block the door!"

A sheep shooter broke out a window to the left and fired a revolver randomly into the room, hitting Ellis's dead body but little else. Ira fired two shots at the window, not knowing if he had hit the man or not.

Suddenly Henry lurched forward, reaching behind him where a bullet pierced his back through the door. Another rifle shot followed it through the door, and Henry dropped to his knees before falling forward.

Knowing he would not survive, Ira grabbed his pocketknife from his pants pocket and cut two small holes in his nightshirt. He fired three shots in quick succession at the door with his rifle and then grabbed his revolver and shot at the windows before quickly diving over the bottom bunk to the body of Ellis. Ira used both hands to scoop up a handful of blood and slapped it over the two holes over his heart and chest. He scooped as much blood off the floor as possible and did it again. And then laid back against the mattress while keeping his knees on the floor. He figured the more uncomfortable he appeared, the greater chance his attackers would think he was dead.

It didn't take long after he had quit shooting for the sheep shooters to carefully peek in the windows and throw in a torch to light the dark room up. Seeing three dead bodies, they pushed the door open, and not finding anyone alive or any valuables except a few guns, the men left.

"Burn it," was the last words Ira heard a man say before leaving with the others to the house.

A sheep shooter carried a can of kerosene into the bunkhouse and emptied it on the floor and the bodies. Ira knew he could not wait for the man to light a match or for the kerosene to reach the burning torch. Opening an eye to peek, he could see he was alone with the unknown sheep shooter, and the man's back was turned to him. Ira gripped his knife and slowly sat up. Aware of the other sheep shooters lurking around, Ira knew he didn't have much time. He darted forward and plunged the small knife blade into the man's neck as he forced the man down to the ground. The knife was plunged into and ripped out of the man's throat frantically while Ira held the man's chin with his left hand and pulled backward with all the force he could until his neck broke and his throat was torn wide open.

Fearing he would be caught, Ira didn't have time to try to change into the man's clothes. He found the stick matches in the sheep shooters coat pocket, poured the remaining kerosene on the floor by the door, and lit it.

He went to the window on the far side of the bunkhouse and found the frame was filled on all four sides with shards of broken glass. He peeked outside, and not seeing anyone, Ira broke as many shards of sharp glass out of the frame as he could and climbed out the window, cutting his belly on the glass that remained, he fell to the ground. He forced the stinging pain of the cuts and scratches of his midsection to the side and quickly went to the back of the bunkhouse. He had a clear path sixty yards or so around the stable and corral down to the lake's shore, where a dense growth of tall cattails invited him to hide.

He waited while the sheep shooters shot and killed every horse in the stable before they lit it on fire. The action infuriated Ira because although he had a revolver in his hand, he was now horseless. Robert Fairchild had a few expensive horses that anyone would love to have, but a horse taken was evidence that would link them to the crime. When Ira could see no other sheep shooters in the immediate area, he began his long and careful run past the corral and down to the lake. Hidden in the tall cattails, he backed into the water and hunkered down.

The large and beautiful home that was the envy of the town was in flames and growing rapidly out of control. A large crowd of sheep shooters celebrated their victory with the pleasure of watching the entire Fairchild Estate burn to the ground.

Robert Fairchild was being held upright by two men and forced to watch his dream home and estate burning. He was in his undergarments and had his hands tied in front of him and his ankles tied together. It appeared that Robert was weeping and begging to be released.

As the sun rose and they readied to leave. One of the sheep shooters spurred his horse with the lasso wrapped around Robert's feet tied to the saddle horn. Without warning, Robert had his feet ripped out from under him, slamming his face against the hard ground, and was quickly dragged behind a galloping horse toward the property's headgate. All the other men stepped into their saddles and followed.

Suddenly, the half an hour of pure hell was over, and all that could be heard was the roar of flames and the crackle of wood burning. Ira stood up and walked through the water toward the dock where he sat.

Chapter 30

Kent Kruse opened his eyes, disoriented. It took only a moment to realize that he had fallen asleep in the rowboat and was woken abruptly by the sound of guns firing. Alarmed, Kent lifted his head and looked towards the shore. He was stunned by what he saw. Everywhere he looked were men wearing long black dusters, burlap bags over their faces with guns, some shooting towards the bunkhouse. Robert Fairchild, in his expensive undergarments, was dragged outside by his feet, and soon the house and bunkhouse were on fire.

There was absolutely nothing Kent could do as he had no weapons, and even if he did, he still could not end the mayhem. There were too many sheep shooters, and if he were noticed in the boat, they'd shoot the boat full of holes and wait for him to either drown or die of bullet holes when he swam to shore. Kent had no choice but to lay low in the bottom of the rowboat and wait for the sheep shooters to leave and hope and pray to a god that Kent didn't ever pray to, that not one of them would decide to sink the boat for some target practice. Hearing the commotion of the sheep shooters cheering, he peeked over the lake to witness Robert being dragged away by his feet with a galloping horse. The other sheep shooters followed with shouts of victory and celebration like it was a twisted game.

Kent knew the sheep shooters would return to watch the property burn eventually; He decided his best chance at survival was to row to the other side of the lake. Kent sat up, grabbed the oars, and then saw Ira Kelly wading through the shallow water toward the dock. Ira had been hiding in the cattails. Thankful to see a friend, Kent rowed quickly towards the dock to save Ira. He was only ten feet away when Ira turned his head slowly and nodded casually. Ira didn't say a word. His shirt was ripped and coated in blood.

"Are you hurt?" Kent asked. "Get in. Let's get across the lake before they come back."

Ira raised his right hand with the revolver and wiped his brow with his forearm. "No. Everyone's dead. Where were you?" he asked accusingly.

"I fell asleep in the boat." He furrowed his brow as the dense smell of smoke drifted over the lake.

Ira's eyes narrowed harshly. "You never slept in the boat before."

"No. I never took it out on the lake before."

"Why did you?" Ira snapped, filling with hostility. "Did you know they were coming?"

"What? No! How could I know that? Ira, we have

to go…"

Ira scowled. "Everyone is dead, and I would be too. That would leave you to inherit the Blackburn Marshals all to yourself. I'd say that's a good enough reason to set us up." Ira pointed the revolver at Kent, who was still sitting in the boat.

"Are you going insane? Put the gun down." He was surprised by the accusation but shocked to have his friend aiming the revolver at him. He could see the anger burning in Ira's eyes and knew that no matter what he said, Ira was convinced he was betrayed by Kent. Ira had every intention of killing him.

Ira spoke loudly despite the threat of being heard by any sheep shooters in the area, "I spared you from going with Ed that night because I thought we were friends! I trusted you with my life. Admit that you set us up to take over the company Robert's going to make. It's the least you could do before I kill you!" he spat out like poison.

"You know me, Ira. I wouldn't do that." Kent knew he was in grave danger of being shot in the boat.

Ira snorted. "They didn't even look your way."

Kent raised a trembling finger. "Wait… did you write that note that got Ed killed?" He already knew Ira had because no one else would have a reason to do so. It was an odd question that, for a moment, would shift the direction of Ira's brain and create an opportunity for Kent to get the upper hand.

Ira tilted his hands innocently. "Of course. But now you're trying to do the same thing to me. You got the others killed, but I'm not easy to kill." He pulled the hammer back until it clicked.

Kent sputtered quickly, "It's going to take two of us to carry the safe out, and I'm the only one that knows the combination."

Ira lowered the gun a bit with interest. "What safe?"

Kent exhaled with a touch of relief. "Mister Fairchild's safe that is in his office. The fire isn't going to penetrate it. All that money inside it could be ours, and no one would ever know. You have to believe me, Ira; I would never betray you and the others. You're all the family I have; I fell asleep. But now, that safe is our only hope. You could start your own company somewhere. But you'll need my help to get it open."

"I'm not stealing from Robert," Ira said, lifting the cocked revolver to aim at Kent. "He's going to make the Blackburn Marshals bigger than we ever imagined, and I'm going to be at the top. I can't believe you tried to steal that from me. Tried to get me killed!" he snarled.

Kent was out of options but needed to act fast. "Robert's dead, Ira. He isn't coming back, and Holly will never miss that money. We'll open the safe, take what's there, and go our separate ways. I did not set you up. Even if you pull that trigger, I want you to know I never did that. I had no idea anything was going to happen. We can still come out ahead with a small fortune. I've seen the cash, Ira. There is thousands of dollars waiting for us. But you'll never get it out alone. I know where the combination is hidden, and the fire won't destroy it."

Ira's gun hand lowered slightly as he considered Kent's words.

Kent slowly kicked his legs over the boat's edge and stood in the water. He handed the rope out to Ira. "Take this and tie it off for me, will you?"

Ira sighed, lowered the hammer expertly, and leaned over the dock to reach for the rope with his left hand.

Kent quickly swung his left hand with a backward swing to hit the revolver out of Ira's loosened grip; the gun bounced off the dock's edge and landed in the water with a splash. Kent's right hand quickly grasped Ira's right wrist with a firm grip and jerked his arm forward, pulling Ira off the dock face-first into the water. Kent trapped Ira's wrist under his armpit while using his left arm to push Ira's shoulder deeper into the water to the muddy bottom three feet down. With Kent standing firmly and pushing down on Ira's back, there was nothing Ira could do except splash his left arm wildly and try to kick his legs. Ira could not get enough traction in the mud to stand or defend himself against the weight and pressure that Kent applied to his shoulder with the armbar. Kent replaced his left arm with his left knee as he knelt in the water for extra weight on Ira, and within two minutes, Ira had stopped flailing. Kent held him there for longer to verify that Ira was dead. He released him, and Ira's body floated lifelessly on the water.

Kent picked the revolver out of the muddy water and paused as he heard approaching horses returning to watch the fire. He ducked under the water, moved under the dock, and scooted along the muddy bottom to wedge himself as tightly as he could between the underside of the dock in the few inches of water at the shore. As he feared, seeing the boat and a floating body had gotten the sheep shooter's attention, and soon, Kent could hear the voices of the men and their boots stepping heavily on the boards above him.

"Who is that?" one of the men asked.

"I don't know, but he doesn't look dead enough." The man unholstered his revolver and placed two bullets into Ira's back.

The other man jumped into the water and turned Ira over to look at his face. "It's a... one of the Blackburn boys."

"He looks too good. Stand back." The man on the dock placed a bullet in the center of Ira's forehead. "That should do him. Why don't you grab that boat and let's row out and watch the fire burn from out on the lake."

Kent lay in the tight corner of the dock for what seemed like hours until the two men rowed the boat back to the dock and left. He would remain where he was hidden in the mud until he was confident that there were no more sheep shooters in the area. His life depended on it. He adjusted himself to lay comfortably in the water and wait.

He had told Ira the truth, there was a safe in Robert's office, he didn't know the combination, but he did know where to find it. Holly had a habit of trusting people and would talk freely if she was

274

allowed to. She had mentioned that her husband had the combinations engraved on the lower back-side of all their safes so he wouldn't forget them.

The burning fires would continue for hours, but by tomorrow he could try to withstand the hot spots, locate the safe, and see what was inside. The sheep shooters showed no mercy on a fragile old man when they dragged him down the rough road. Kent had no doubt that Robert Fairchild was dead. Now that Holly was a widow and inheriting the old man's fortune, Kent figured it would be a good time to go to Branson and comfort her. He had every advantage to win her heart now that she would be mourning, lonely, and looking for a tower of strength to lean on. Kent was just that kind of man.

Chapter 31

Matt Bannister was stunned. The body of Robert Fairchild hung by the neck from the Fairchild Estate headgate. By the rope burns around his ankles, badly chaffed skin, and broken arm, it was clear that he had been dragged by his feet to the head gate. His body dangling by the neck was a terrible sight, but worse was knowing that Robert Fairchild's neck was not broken. He had slowly strangled to death, and the gouges at his neck from his fingernails trying to loosen the rope told the story. Matt twisted Robert's wrist to look at the chaffed skin from a rope.

"They cut his hands free to watch him struggle," Matt said to his deputies Truet Davis and Morton Sperry. They had just arrived from Branson and came to speak with Robert Fairchild about the wire he had sent the day before. In Matt's pocket was the letter Holly had written to her husband explaining why she wasn't coming home with Matt.

They could smell the aroma of burnt wood and the slight plume of smoke rising toward the sky.

Matt was perplexed, shocked, and numb. "I'm thankful Holly stayed in Branson because this would have been a horrible sight to come home to."

"Where are all the marshals?" Truet Davis asked.

Matt shook his head. "I have a bad feeling. Let's go see what's burning."

They followed the long driveway to the house and found three charred remains of the house, stable, and bunkhouse collapsed into heaps of rubble. The blackened debris still smoked and popped as the coals continued to burn. There were no signs of life other than the ducks quacking in the lake.

Truet slowly rode past the house to the stable to look at the charred remains of several horses visible in the debris.

"Well, if you're hungry, the horses ought to be done by now," Truet tried his hand at a bit of bad humor with a disgusted grin. His body shivered with the memory of having to dig the charred body of Roger Lavigne out of his cabin after Wu-Pen Tseng had burned the cabin down with Roger inside.

"Where is my cousin?" Morton Sperry asked, glancing around the lakefront property.

Matt shook his head slowly as he considered the same thought. He caught sight of the charred remains of a man's legs partly visible under the rubble of the bunkhouse. "There's a body in the debris. I'm guessing there might be more in there too."

Morton Sperry's face lost its color as he feared

finding his cousin Jesse's body under a pile of burned rubble. He spoke to Matt, "I know you don't like my cousin, but I don't want to find him in there. We're not digging them out of there, are we?"

Truet's face drained of color. "I'm not. I did it once, I don't know if I want to do it again. The skin and flesh just comes right off in your hands." He quivered with the memory.

"Tru, you will if we need to," Matt answered his friend quickly. He looked at Morton pointedly. "I wouldn't be happy to find your cousin in there either. Let's talk to the sheriff and figure out what happened and who is responsible for this."

"I can tell you," a man's voice said from behind them.

Matt, Truet, and Morton spun around to see who had spoken to them.

Kent Kruse held his hands in the air and walked uphill from the lake's dock. He was soaking wet, covered with mud, but showed an attempt at a broad grin. "Thank goodness, it's you, Marshal Bannister. I've been hiding under the dock all day. We met the other day; I'm Kent Kruse."

"What happened?" Matt asked.

Kent bent over, placing his hands on his knees as he exhaled. "The sheep shooters rode in before the sun came up. They took Mister Fairchild prisoner and attacked the bunkhouse at the same time. They killed my friends and burned it all down. The only one that survived was Ira Kelly, and I had to kill him down at the lake. He was acting insane and tried to kill me. I don't know what happened to Mister Fairchild, but I watched them drag him away." He pointed up the driveway.

"They hung him on the headgate," Matt replied. "I got a wire yesterday from Robert stating everything was fine and to bring Holly back." Matt paused to shrug his shoulders questionably.

Kent nodded. "It was fine, yesterday."

"I don't understand," Matt answered, becoming impatient and annoyed. "What happened?"

Kent explained how Ed Bostwick and two other men went to the Long T Ranch to poison the water well but were betrayed by a letter Ira sent and were killed. The letter laid the guilt and responsibility on Ed alone. Having killed the man responsible for poisoning the water on the Long T Ranch, the cattlemen were ready to call it even and compromise with Mister Fairchild to live peacefully. Robert was happy and wired Matt to bring his wife home now that the threat was over.

Unfortunately, the cattlemen hung the three bodies of the men they killed on the headgate, and one of the three men killed was Elliot Zook. His two friends, Jesse Helms and Cass Travers, went to town last night and brutally attacked Gunther Thomas's youngest son and the young lady they found with him.

Kent finished, "I was so frustrated when I heard that, that I took the boat out and fell asleep on the lake. I was woken by gunshots, and you can see the rest."

Morton asked, "Did Jesse and Cass get out?" He pointed a thumb towards the bunkhouse.

"They never came back. Henry was the last one with them, and Jesse told Henry they wanted to find out who killed Elliot and get their revenge. Henry tried to talk them out of it, but Jesse cracked a whiskey bottle over Henry's head and put his eye out. Those two are a couple of mad dogs that need to be put down."

"Were they caught?"

"I don't know. Matt, I'm in a bad way and in hostile territory. I have money in the bank, but not around here. Do you think it's possible you could help get me a horse and saddle so I can get out of here? I'll meet you in Branson to pay you back. I know you don't think much of the Blackburn Marshals, but I'm an honest man."

***

The Hollister Sheriff, Pat Emerson, was surprised to see Matt Bannister burst into his office and was immediately put on the defensive as Matt shouted, "I believe, you, Sheriff Emerson, are responsible for the murder of Robert Fairchild and other men that you and your deputies are going to dig out of that rubble. Where are the house servants? Did you kill them too?"

"W…w…what are you talking about?" The sheriff was startled by the stone-coldness of Matt's expression. Suddenly the marshal's countenance matched his deadly reputation, and Pat knew he was on dangerous ground.

Matt stepped forward and leaned over Pat's desk

with a hard slam of his hand on the desktop. He shouted with a finger pointed in Pat's face. "Don't you dare play stupid with me!" he turned to the sheriff's deputies and yelled, "Take a wagon out to the Fairchild's place, cut Robert's body down, and dig out those other bodies. There's one in the lake too. Go now!"

The Hollister deputy, Lenny Clinton, looked at the sheriff questionably. It was late in the afternoon, and Lenny was tired from a long night and short nap earlier that day. "Pat?" he questioned.

Matt refused to be disobeyed. "Get a wagon and leave, both of you. Do not come back without every human body out there!"

"Do as he says," Pat said. "We had plans of getting those bodies today," he explained to Matt.

"Don't lie to me, Sheriff! Listen, and listen good. I may not be able to name anyone else in the sheep shooters, but I know you are! I recognized your boots from the other night, and I suspect you are also the man that murdered Wes Wasson. I will arrest you right now on several counts of murder and have my deputies take you to Branson to wait for trial if you don't start talking to me right now!" Matt sat in a chair across from Pat's desk. "If I were you, I'd start talking."

Pat chuckled lightly. He watched his two deputies begrudgingly leave the office. "I'm afraid you're wrong, Marshal. You might arrest me, but you have no evidence in which I could be convicted. I'm not a member of the sheep shooters, and a whole town of people will swear in the court of law to that. They will also swear on a Bible that I was with two young victims of the crime that sparked this whole tragedy or at home when Mister Fairchild was murdered. The same can be said for every other man around here. We stick together around here; no one heard, saw, or will say a thing. Guaranteed. Beyond that, I don't know what to tell you. You could arrest me on suspicions, but you'd be wasting both of our time, and I think you know that."

Matt hated to admit the sheriff was speaking the truth. He had no evidence that Pat Emerson had killed Wes Wasson, just speculation from freshly cleaned boots. He had no evidence that the sheriff had anything to do with the massacre at the Fairchild Estate; he only speculated so. Speculation could be the truth, but without proof, some form of evidence, or a witness, it was worthless in a court of law. "What happened? You must know something as the sheriff."

"Of course I do. I know two Blackburn Marshals, Jesse Helms and his pal, Cass Travers, caught Gunther Thomas's son, Jake, and his young love, a fourteen-year-old girl named Laura Whitehead, in the church cellar. They sliced Jake's cheek all the way to his ear and forced that young man to watch them both rape Laura. She's just a child, Matt. She turns fifteen next week. What a happy birthday, huh? Those animals told Jake it was just the beginning and they would be coming after Gunther. Maybe even paying her another visit. She is terrified, as you might imagine.

"Matt, you, of all people, must understand the

outrage in our community, and they took matters into their own hands. I don't like what happened, but enough is enough, and that young lady..." he shook his head sadly. "No one wanted to wait around to see who those men would terrorize next. When a dog attacks a child, you kill it. I see no difference between wild dogs and those men."

Matt spoke in a reasonable tone, "First and foremost, I am very sorry to hear about that girl. And I can understand the fury, but I'm guessing you don't know who those men were that took matters into their own hands?"

Pat shrugged unknowingly. "As I said, I was sleeping. I asked around, and no one knows a thing except that the Blackburn Marshals and the man that brought them here are dead. Sorry, I can't help you."

"And Fairchild's still hanging after how many hours? Nearly twelve?" Matt asked bitterly.

"Yes, he is. As I may have indicated, Mister Fairchild wasn't loved around here. But you have my deputies going out there to cut him down, so all is well. It's all water under the bridge now."

"Speaking of water, did you notice the boat was missing from the dock this morning?" Matt asked quickly.

"What boat? No. What are you talking about?"

Matt chuckled bitterly, having caught Pat in a lie. "A Blackburn Marshal had fallen asleep in the Fairchild's boat last night and witnessed the whole thing from the lake. He stated that Jesse Helms and Cass Travers had quit the marshals before committing that crime. They were no longer staying at the Fairchild Estate. You and the others murdered innocent men and maybe women. Where were the house servants when the house was burned?"

"Jesse and Cass weren't there?" Pat asked with a narrowing of his eyes like a hungry predator.

"Nope. Now, my deputy, Morton Sperry, Jesse's cousin, said he may know where Jesse is hiding. But I'll let him talk to you about that since you know this territory better than I do. I need to know, what happened to the young ladies and other servants belonging to the Fairchild Estates?" he asked with a raised voice.

Pat waved carelessly towards the south. "I understand the servants were hauled out of the area and dropped off. Perhaps you passed them on the way here, I don't know. I also heard a rumor that they were trying to make a lean-to in the grove of trees on the hilltop south of town. I'd like to talk to Morton and find those two men. You should see what they did to those two kids."

"Did you bother to question those servants about what happened today?" Matt asked.

Pat shook his head. "No need. I know what happened, but I don't know who did it, and from past investigations, I can tell you the sheep shooters never remove their hoods. That's all the servants would be able to say. They saw men with black coats and hoods."

"What about Gunther? Did he lead a vigilante group out there?"

Pat took a deep breath. "Gunther was taking care

of his son. If you're looking to make an arrest…" He shrugged. "I don't know what to tell you. Investigate, but you won't learn anything. As I said, the folks around here don't see, hear, or say much. We take care of our own. Now, where can I find Jesse and Cass? Laura and her parents deserve to watch those animals whimper like babies, stagger, piss their pants and cry as they walk up the gallows' steps to hang, and I plan on making the staircase extra long. I have no mercy for them. I suppose the question is will Morton protect his cousin when it comes right down to the blood of it? Blood, they say, is thicker than water."

Matt was frustrated, but he knew he was up against a wall unless he could convince someone to talk. "Pat, I think you're as guilty as hell, but until I can prove it, I want you to join us to find Jesse and Cass. But first, I want Morton to meet that young lady and see what his cousin and old friend did to her for himself. Can you arrange that?"

***

Matt brought Morton and Truet with him as Pat introduced them to Mitch and Helen Whitehead. Their daughter, Laura, remained in her room, traumatized to the point of saying very little but weeping a lot. Sudden sounds startled her, and she was terrified of those two men coming back. She had not dared to look in the mirror at her swollen face that couldn't be blacker and bluer if it was painted with a brush. The swelling deformed her pretty face, and she was nearly unrecognizable. Doctor Anderson believed her cheekbone and eye socket were fractured, along with having two broken ribs. A gash below her eye and a missing tooth were reminders of the two men that attacked her mercilessly.

It was hard to define the emotions of seeing a young lady beaten so severely yet knowing that was the least of her wounds and fears. The innocence with which she saw the world a day before was gone, and she would never be the same little girl again. Matt didn't know her, but he had known ladies like her that had suffered similar attacks and knew the road to recovery would be long. He could feel the wrath that such an attack brings forth, along with the empathy, compassion, and sorrow for what she suffered. He tried to speak to Laura, but she ignored him and stared at the wall without responding. She did not speak once or look at any of the men that invaded the privacy of her room with her parent's permission. Laura would turn the key to a porcelain grand piano music box and listen to it play repeatedly.

Laura's parents were devastated. There was nothing Matt could do or say to ease their pain and brokenness but to do what was expected of him, arrest the men responsible and bring justice to the victim and their family.

When they left the Whitehead's home above the hardware store and reached the street below, Matt stopped and asked Morton in private, "Are you ready to arrest your cousin?"

Morton nodded sadly. "I wouldn't be here if I wasn't."

"You told me earlier that you might know where Jesse and Cass are hiding. Where do you think they are?" Matt asked.

Morton was clearly troubled by what he had witnessed. "The Taylor farm outside of Cold Water."

Chapter 32

Jesse Helms sat in a rickety wooden chair at a dust-covered dining table, glancing up at a swallow that had made its nest on the cross boards of the open truss of the roof. The swallow had found its way inside through one of the two broken windows of the abandoned cabin. It was a small one-room clapboard cabin that had belonged to Isaiah Taylor and his wife, Colleen. Isaiah had ridden with the Sperry-Helms Gang for a year or so before moving his wife to Cold Water to start a farm. Isaiah may have intended to make an honest living farming, but to make ends meet, he teamed up with a group of rustlers who were caught by Pat Emerson and his posse and hung from a tree branch. Jesse had hoped to find Colleen still living there, but the cabin had been long since abandoned, leaving it to the swallows, spiders, and field mice to make their own.

The cabin was neglected and in bad shape, but

it gave them a place to hide and stay in the shade if nothing else. They could not travel in the daylight or show their faces in public since they had committed a brutal crime the night before. There was no doubt the local law would be looking for them, as well as the ranch hands from the Long T Ranch and others. They were the most wanted men in the area, and there was no doubt the Blackburn Marshals would be joining the search for them too. They were safe in the old Taylor home as no one knew there was a link between it and Jesse. They could hide for a little while, but they had no food or water as the old well had been filled in with rocks and dirt. They could see the circled outline of inlaid stones even with the ground.

Cass stood at a window and stared out over the flat valley of grass, wishing he had a cup of coffee. "We need to cut across to more prosperous ground like Montana's gold towns. That might be a good start for us."

Jesse remained quiet as he focused on trimming his fingernails with his knife.

"What do you think, Jesse?"

"About what?" He didn't seem interested in the conversation.

"About Montana?"

"What about Montana?"

"Us going there! What's the matter with you? Am I talking to myself here?" Cass asked irritably.

"No. I was just thinking."

"About what?"

"I was thinking I'm getting hungry enough to

eat that swallow up there. It's just staring at me anyway."

"Well, while you're bellyaching about your belly, I'm trying to plan our future so we can get out of here alive. You slicing that kid's cheek open isn't going to win us any friends."

"They killed Elliot first," Jesse replied simply. "And I'm not done yet. I think we blew our chances at becoming legitimate businessmen just a little too soon, but I'm not finished yet. That old man is going to die."

"Shh!" Cass urgently said as he moved to the side of the window. "Someone's coming." He grabbed his rifle that leaned against the wall and moved near the door. Jesse quickly left the seat and reached for his rifle before taking a position beside a broken window at the front of the house.

"Lawmen?" Jesse asked. "We should have hobbled the horses behind the house instead of out front!" Jesse cursed under his breath.

Two men dressed like poor farmers rode casually towards the cabin, curious about the two horses in front of it with their front legs hobbled together to stop them from wandering off.

"Hello," one of the men called loudly. He appeared to be a friendly man as neither of the men wore a gun belt or held a weapon in their hands. "Hello in there," the man called again.

Cass set his rifle aside and opened the creaking door cautiously. "Hello," he answered with a friendly smile.

The man on the horse looked around forty with

light-brown short hair and a thick mustache. He wore dirty clothing with patched pants with suspenders. He was thin and not overbearing or intimidating, as he spoke with a high-pitched voice, "You know you're trespassing on Ullrich land? This is our ranch. My name's Garner Ullrich, and this is my son Davey. I imagine there are two of you in there?"

Davey Ullrich was dressed like his father and appeared to be in his late teens. His hair was a shade darker than his father's, and he had no facial hair.

Cass answered carefully, "Yes, sir. I'm Jim Garrison, and my pal is Pick Smith. We were just traveling across country and haven't gotten much sleep since we left a few days ago. We saw this abandoned place and took some shelter early this morning. I can't explain why we slept so late, but we did. No trouble was intended, sir. We were just tired and hungry, resting up before we continue on," Cass explained.

Garner listened carefully. "If you're hungry, you're welcome to come to the house and we'll feed you dinner; it's about that time. Then I'd appreciate it if you moved along your way. We've had problems with rustlers in the past. I'm a Christian man, but I'm also suspicious of strangers found on my land."

"That's understandable. I can speak quite honestly when I tell you that we are not cattle rustlers. We're quite the opposite, actually. We're working our way east to apply for work with the Blackburn Marshals over in Hollister to stop the cattle rustling. That's what we heard back in Spokane. Sir, we haven't eaten, and our canteens are near empty, so if we could get a meal before we leave and some water, we'd appreciate it."

Garner grimaced, "Well, you gentlemen heard wrong and came a long way for nothing. All those Blackburn Marshals and their proprietor, the man that pays them, Robert Fairchild, are all dead."

"What?" Jesse asked, stepping into the doorway. "What do you mean they're dead?"

"Just that. The news came today. Last night the sheep shooters swept in, killed all the marshals, and hung Robert Fairchild. They burned his whole place down, all of it, including his horses. It's absolutely shocking," Garner said with a stunned shake of his head. "I knew trouble was brewing, but I never expected that."

"Why did they do it?" Cass asked.

Garner frowned noticeably. "You wouldn't know them, so you wouldn't understand how tragic it is. Last night, two Blackburn Marshals harmed two of our local teens. The sheep shooters thought that was enough and wiped them all out. There were no survivors, I heard."

"What about the men that hurt those kids?" Jesse asked.

Garner shook his head. "The sheep shooters killed every darn one of them and then burned their bodies in one of the buildings. I hear it was quite a mess."

"They burned the bodies?" Jesse asked.

"That's what I hear. They were sleeping when they were shot down like rats. Anyway, I hate to

292

say it, but the two men that tortured those kids deserved it."

Cass questioned, "So the law isn't looking for those two men? There's no search parties or nothing?"

Garner scoffed, "Why would they? They're dead. Anyway, if you two want to follow us home, we'll get you fed before you move on."

"Just out of curiosity, I know some people over in Hollister with teens. Do you happen to know the names of the two teens?" Cass asked.

"I do. Jake Thomas and Laura Whitehead. They are both outstanding families."

"Whitehead? Yeah, they ah...they ah..." He hesitated thoughtfully while shaking a finger momentarily. "They a..."

"They own the hardware store," Davey volunteered. "Laura is a friend of mine."

"Yes!" Cass exclaimed. "It's been a while, but I met her once. Tell her hello for me."

Garner spoke, "Well, if you men want some grub before you leave, you can follow us."

"We'll be right there," Cass said.

Jesse said lightly, "We are free. They think we're dead." He grinned slowly.

***

The Ullrich home was a humble clapboard two-story house with simple furnishings on an eighty-acre ranch with less than a hundred cows. They were not wealthy and struggled to get by, but what they lacked in finances, they made up for in gratitude for what they did have.

Garner's wife, Lizzy Ullrich, was in her late thirties and appeared to be a hard-working woman with darkly tanned skin and calloused hands. Lizzy was not a striking lady but quite plain and appeared older than she was. Lizzy was a tall and thin woman with brown hair kept in a tight bun. She was undoubtedly a busy mother with having five younger children, the oldest being Davey. She was not overly friendly, but she made a fine dinner with fresh sliced bread with butter, thick slabs of ham, and boiled beets with the green stalk and leaves attached to make a fine dish of beet spinach. The meal was served with a glass of fresh warm milk. It was one of the best meals that either Jesse or Cass had eaten in quite some time.

"Thank you, Missus Ullrich. That was a fantastic meal," Cass said. He gave a quick wink to the youngest of the children, five-year-old Augustus, and feigned grabbing the boy's nose with a light whistle. The boy grinned at him shyly. "But we had better get moving before we wear out our welcome."

"You're always welcome to come back," Lizzy said softly while tapping her youngest son's hand when he reached for another piece of bread before finishing his meal. "Finish your piece of crust first."

"I don't like the crust," Augustus whined.

"Little Gus, we go through this all the time. Just because we have guests doesn't mean you can sneak another piece of bread. You know the rule."

Garner raised his eyebrows warningly to his

youngest son before speaking to Cass, "You are most welcome to stay, Mister Garrison. It's only a few hours until sundown, so you might throw your bedrolls in the barn and leave in the morning after breakfast. It's probably the best we could do for you two gentlemen."

"With the news you gave us, I suppose, Jesse... I mean, Pick and I will have to discuss what we might do now." He looked at Jesse. "Any thoughts, Pick?"

Jesse shook his head. "Maybe there is a saloon in Cold Water we could discuss our plans in."

Garner spoke softly, "If you two don't mind, we would appreciate it if you don't come back here if you have alcohol on your breath. We are a Christian home and do not support drinking, as you might understand."

Cass raised his hands in surrender. "Perfectly understandable. Mister and Missus Ullrich, you have my word that we will do nothing to disrespect your wishes and rules. We are just thankful for your hospitality. If we do go to a saloon, we will not return. Speaking of Christian stuff, I admit freely that I am not one. But not long ago, I had the chance to marry a Christian couple. Well, they asked me to marry them, but what do I know about it?" he chuckled. "I had to turn them down. It just didn't seem right."

Jesse yawned.

Davey Ullrich watched Jesse carefully. He asked cautiously, "Mister Smith, what kind of work do you do?"

Jesse looked at the teenager with his cold eyes

and spoke pointedly, "My family owns a dairy."

"You're not interested in working on the family dairy?" Garner asked.

"No."

"What about you, Mister Garrison?" Davey asked.

"Farmer," Cass said, refilling his glass with a pitcher of milk. "Pick and I heard about the Blackburn Marshals and figured it was a way to start new in life. Unfortunately, I think we're heading back to our former occupations if what your Pa told us is true."

"It's true," Garner confirmed.

Jesse stood. "Well, thank you for supper. It was tasty. Are you ready to go?" He asked Cass.

"I suppose so."

Jesse Helms felt naked without his gun belt hitched around his waist; it was hanging over the saddle horn in the barn. Garner Ullrich had asked the two men to leave their guns in the barn if they wanted to eat supper with them. Jesse was anxious to put it on and leave the Ullrich farm. He had a goal in mind, and he wasn't going to leave the area until the old man Thomas was dead and anyone else who got in his way.

Cass took a moment to say goodbye to Lizzy and the children before he followed Jesse, Garner and Davey to the barn.

Davey watched Jesse put his gun belt on and fasten it. "Mister Smith, have you ever shot anyone with that?"

Garner quickly admonished his son, "Davey,

that's none of our business. We don't ask people about their business. Understood?"

"Yes, Pa," Davey resigned.

Jesse ignored the question, satisfied that the boy's father had answered for him. He pulled his saddle from the top board of the stall and set it on his horse. He pulled a five-dollar gold piece from his money purse in his saddlebag and flipped it towards Garner. "For feeding the horses and us. Much appreciated."

Garner missed catching it and picked the gold coin off the ground. "It's not necessary. We're just doing what the good Lord would have us do."

Jesse waved a hand, rejecting the coin as Garner prepared to toss it back. "Keep it. Please."

"Well, if you insist. My gratitude to you."

Cass reached down to pet the family dog named Oscar, a white mongrel with short curly hair. "You have a nice family, Garner. It's been a pleasure getting to know you all. I don't think we'll be back tonight." He put his hand out to shake Garner's.

"Nice to meet you, gentlemen."

They made small talk while Cass saddled his horse. Jesse led his horse out of the barn and hitched it to a rail. Oscar's ears rose as he looked towards the driveway and began to bark.

"Pa, some men are coming," Davey said, squinting in the distance.

Alertly, Jesse glanced at the riders, and a cold chill ran up his spine. "Cass, it's Marshal Bannister, and Morton's with him."

"Cass? I thought your name was Jim?" Davey

asked.

Garner sputtered, "It's not our business, Davey."

"I know, Pa, but he said his name was Jim, not Cass," Davey explained.

Cass looked out the barn door to see his friend Morton Sperry riding beside Matt Bannister. Cass said. "They can see your horse outside!" He grabbed Davey and jerked his thin body in front of him while at the same time pulling his revolver and pressing the barrel against the young man's head.

"Pa!" Davey cried out, alarmed.

"Wait, wait, wait," Garner pleaded quickly as he stepped forward to help his son.

Jesse pulled his revolver and pointed it at Garner's face, stopping him cold. "Stop!" He spun around Garner and wrapped an arm around his neck while pressing the revolver against the father's head. "Shut up!"

Cass stepped out of the barn holding Davey. He shouted, "Stop, or I'll kill him! Go away, Morton!"

Chapter 33

"Pat was right. There is no cover out here whatso-ever at all," Matt said quietly. He continued to ride slowly forward after watching Jesse bring his horse out of the barn and hearing the dog bark, which he knew would ruin any element of surprise.

Morton had told them that Jesse and Cass may have gone to Isaiah Taylor's property to hide, as that was the only safe place they knew of in the imme-diate area. The Sheriff, Pat Emerson, explained that after Isaiah was lynched for cattle rustling, Isaiah's widow, Colleen, sold their ten-acre parcel of land to their neighbor Garner Ullrich for a fair price and left the area. Pat explained that Garner had torn down the barn and outbuildings of the Taylor farm to reuse the lumber for his outbuildings, and the water well had been filled in to save any risk of his livestock or a person falling in.

Matt, Truet, Morton, and the sheriff, Pat Em-erson, reached the Taylor cabin and discovered clear evidence that the men they were hunting had been there just recently; Cass Travers had written his name in the table's dust. Horse tracks going towards the Ullrich's homestead gave Matt and the others a fair idea of where they might find Jesse and Cass.

Pat explained the Ullrich homestead was placed perfectly in the center of a flat area of grassland. No tree was found on the Ullrich homestead or even a slight hill. The few trees that once stood there were cut down for firewood as the winters in the shadow of the mountains could be severely cold.

It was apparent that there would be no sneaking up on the house using foliage or buildings to conceal themselves or any hope of catching them by surprise as the family dog was sure to bark at approaching strangers. They would not know if Jesse and Cass were at the Ullrich home until they approached it. It was that simple, and that dangerous as the open grassland would make a man on horseback impossible not to notice. A steady eye with a good rifle could quickly end a life, and Matt knew it too well not to be concerned. Riding towards the house slowly and easily after being spotted left Matt feeling like a pumpkin set on the log at the Big Z Ranch used for target practice.

Morton pulled the reins to a stop when he saw Cass Travers come out of the barn holding a gun to a young man's head.

Cass shouted over the distance, "Stop, or I'll kill him! Go away, Morton!"

Matt pulled the reins to his horse and watched

Jesse Helms step out of the barn with a hostage. Matt didn't know if Jesse and Cass would be at the Ullrich homestead, but if they were, he sent the sheriff and Truet Davis in a wide circle around the homestead to approach from the rear while he and Morton drew Jesse and Cass's attention to the front. Now, with both men holding hostages, Matt wasn't sure he had made the best choice to approach the homestead because he was now caught in the open, and there was no trace of Truet and Pat Emerson.

The house's front door burst open, and a wiry woman stepped out on the porch, quickly followed by three younger children. "What's going on out here?" she demanded to know.

Garner Ulrich yelled out uncomfortably while in Jesse's powerful grasp, "Get the kids back inside!"

Horrified, Lizzy gazed at the friendly man who, moments before, praised her cooking and played with her children at the dinner table; he was now holding a gun to her son's head. "Let my son go, Mister Garrison," she demanded. "He's just a boy. Now you let him go! He didn't do anything to you!"

"Lizzy, get the kids inside!" Garner yelled. "Pick, please," he said to Jesse, "don't hurt my family. Please," he begged. He was fearful for Davey and the others who were outside and possibly in danger.

"My name's Jesse!" he sneered in Garner's ear. He was angry that Morton had led the marshal to the Taylor residence. He shouted bitterly, "Morton, you son of a—" he cursed. "You have no right to bring the marshal here! We'll kill them all if you come any closer!"

"Matt?" Morton questioned. He had no idea of what to do.

Matt took a deep breath and exhaled to calm his growing nerves. "They think they have us cornered, so we will do the opposite of what they want. Give your horse a kick, and let's run right down their throats. Go!" Matt kicked his gelding with a hard jab of his heels and swung the split reins to the left and right, cracking them over the hind quarters of his gelding to run faster as he hollered, "Yaw!"

Morton, surprised and yet curious of the wisdom of such an abrupt and dangerous action, followed a pace behind.

Not expecting the two lawmen to come charging towards them fearlessly and uncaring of the hostages, Cass panicked and tossed Davey to the ground as he fled towards the house and tried to grab Lizzy on the porch, but as his left arm came around her shoulders, she ducked down and turned away from him to escape his grasp. Desperate to have a hostage in front of him before the marshal and Morton arrived, Cass grabbed the five-year-old boy, Augustus, and knelt on the porch to hold the boy in front of him. He put the gun to the boy's head.

Jesse cursed and pushed Garner to the ground while he fled towards the front porch and tackled Lizzy to the ground as she went after Cass to save her youngest son. Jesse yanked Lizzy to her feet and put his back against the house. Lizzy scratched at his hand while it pressed her against him. She twisted and turned and fought to free herself from him despite the gun pointed at her.

"Knock it off!" Jesse grunted over the noise of the children screaming and pulling at his shirt and legs to let their mother go. He slammed the butt of the revolver over Lizzy's head hard enough to stun her and stop her fighting momentarily. He kicked one of the kids in the stomach, and the eight-year-old boy fell onto the porch, curled up in a fetal position holding his stomach, crying.

Matt pulled the reins of his speeding horse to a sudden stop in front of the house and was quickly out of the saddle pulling his Winchester rifle free from its scabbard and promptly taking aim over the saddle at Cass. He stayed behind his buckskin gelding to use as a shield.

Matt shouted, "Let the child go, Cass! You don't want to be responsible for killing a kid."

Cass cursed at Matt. "Throw your rifle down, or I will kill him!"

Morton had pulled his reins to stop his horse and jumped out of the saddle, but his horse was a bit more agitated from the loud commotion and turned away from the porch as it tried to free itself from Morton's hold of the reins. Morton let the horse run free with his rifle in the scabbard. He pulled his revolver and pointed it at Jesse. "Let her go, Jess. We don't want to do this. You don't want to shoot me, and I don't want to shoot you. Put the gun down, Jesse, please."

Jesse Helms couldn't stand the chaos; the screaming and crying of the frightened smaller children that clawed at his legs and a ten-year-old girl trying to hug her mother, Garner praying to his God, and Davey at the edge of the porch begging him to let his mother go along with the intense shouting between Matt and Cass. To escape the chaotic noise of the annoying children, Jesse dragged Lizzy off the porch towards the open ground between the house and the barn. He couldn't think straight with all the commotion around him. He shouted at Davey, "Shut up! Get all those screaming kids in the house now, or I'll start shooting every one of them!"

"Davey, do as he says," Lizzy ordered. She wasn't crying as one might expect in Jesse's grasp, but fierce and willing to fight to save her family. She glared at Morton Sperry like a badger protecting its den. She shouted at Morton, "Shoot him!"

Garner had no weapons in the barn, but after praying for the safety of his family, he did pull Jesse Helm's rifle from the scabbard on his tethered horse and aimed it at Jesse. "Let my wife go!"

"Shoot him!" Lizzy screamed at Garner.

Jesse turned his body to face Garner placing Lizzy between them. Jesse had faith that his cousin Morton was less likely to shoot him than Garner was. He spoke coldly to Garner, "Put it down. I'm warning you; I'll kill her."

Garner's eyes watered, and his voice quivered, "Just let her go and leave. That's all I'm asking."

Morton Sperry shouted at Garner Ullrich with authority, "Put the gun down!"

Garner answered Morton angrily, "They were leaving until you showed up. Get off my property so they can leave, please."

Morton sneered. "No, they won't leave. Trust me, I know them." He lowered his revolver slowly as he watched his cousin. He spoke calmly, "Jesse, think about it. Right now, it's maybe two years in prison, if that. But if you pull that trigger, you won't ever see home again. You don't want your mother acting like mine, do you? Let her go and lay the gun down."

Matt's right eye remained aligned with the rifle's sights on Cass Traver's partially exposed head. Taking a shot was too risky due to the flailing little boy's terrified screaming and crying while struggling to get away. The young boy's twin brother kept coming back to help but was pushed away again and again. He came back while Cass' attention was on Morton and Jesse and bit Cass' arm. Cass jerked his arm out of the kid's mouth with a shout and then slammed the revolver against the side of the little boy's face with a hard impact that sent the boy to the ground holding his cheek, screaming and writhing in pain. It was followed immediately by fierce yelling from Lizzy.

"Cass..." Matt yelled angrily but was stopped by Davey, the oldest sibling quickly marched across the porch towards the boy. Cass turned slightly and raised his elbow to emphasize the gun pointed at the little boy's head. "Don't try it!"

Davey pointed at his little brother screaming in pain on the porch. The boy's head was cut open and bleeding profusely. "My brother is hurt. Can I get my little brother?" He shouted emotionally.

Cass nodded once while casting a glance at Matt.

"Just keep the little maggot away from me!"

Matt was infuriated by the kid being hurt and seeing a grown man pointing a gun at a child. He spoke evenly, "We're at a stalemate, Cass. How do you want to solve it? You don't want to hurt those kids, and I don't want to see them hurt."

"You and Morton leaving might do the trick," Cass replied.

"That's not an option. You just heard Morton, and he's right. Right now, there is no murder charge; you might face prison, but that's temporary. Don't make it permanent."

Cass pulled the revolver's hammer back until it clicked. "We'll do it my way. Your choice; you or the kid. Step away from your horse, Marshal. If you don't want this kid's blood on your hands, then you better step out in the open."

The sound of the hammer being cocked sent a chill down Matt's spine. In the past months, he had been in a similar situation where the Reverend Abraham Ash was being held hostage, and it did not end well. The vision of Reverend Ash's head splattering against the school's wall haunted him still to the very day. It scared him to think of seeing the little boy's head do the same. More frightening, with the hammer cocked and the jerking and struggling of the little boy or one of his siblings fighting to save him, could end with an accidental shooting which is what killed Abraham Ash. Matt silently pleaded with the Lord that no harm would come to the child being held by Cass.

Cass repeated, "Move away from your horse!"

Matt kept his aim as he spoke, "I will move away from the horse as soon as you lower that hammer. We don't want any accidents here. If you want to shoot me, at least make it fair by lowering the hammer and letting that boy go. That's the least you could do. If you do that, I'll step away from my horse and give you one shot free."

"Give me one free shot? Like I need charity to get the draw on you?" he chuckled as he lowered the hammer. He repositioned himself to be better equipped and ready to take a clear shot once Matt stepped into the open. "I'll release the boy when you step out with your rifle lowered. Agreed?"

"Yep… agreed," Matt said while simultaneously pulling the trigger. The bullet hit square in the center of Cass's forehead, blasting the bullet through his head and splattering blood and matter against the wall behind him. Cass fell back across the porch, dead, still holding the child.

The sound of Matt's rifle percussion and seeing Cass falling back on the porch, dead stunned Jesse. He spoke softly to Lizzy, "Go get your kid," and released his grip on her.

She immediately ran, bawling, to scoop Augustus up in her arms and hold him close to her heart. The boy was unharmed.

Matt turned his hardened eyes to Jesse. "Drop the gun, Jesse."

Jesse let the revolver fall from his fingers. "You lied to Cass."

"Yes, I did," Matt admitted simply. "And you're under arrest."

Chapter 34

Matt knew that if he locked Jesse overnight in the Hollister jail, there was the possibility of thirty or forty sheep shooters storming into the jail and hanging him. Matt and his deputies could stay in jail to protect him, but if the sheep shooters were so inclined, the three lawmen could not withstand that many men filled with wrath and intent on getting their vengeance upon a child rapist. To avoid any temptation of doing so, Matt and his deputies shackled Jesse's wrists and rode for home. It would be another long night where exhaustion would overtake them, but when they got back to Branson, they could sleep peacefully, knowing Jesse was locked safely in the secure jail of the marshal's office. They arrived in Branson long after midnight and locked Jesse in the jail before going home and collapsing on their beds to sleep.

Waking up, Matt sat on the edge of his bed not looking forward to the task of informing Holly

Fairchild of her husband's death and her home being a heap of ashes. There was absolutely no pleasure in notifying a family of a loved one's death.

He rubbed his face and yawned. He closed his eyes and prayed, "Good morning, Lord. I need to go speak with Holly, and I ask that you'll give me the strength to do so and be a light in the darkness that is about to surround her as she mourns. I know Holly says she is a Christian, and I pray she is because she will need you. I ask that you give her comfort during this terrible time and help her draw closer to you. I pray that she seeks you and finds her strength in you in the days and months ahead.

"Thank you, Jesus, for the blessings you have given me, watching out for my deputies, and keeping us safe this week. Lord, I know that I fail to be a good representation of you every day to the world around me. Could you help me to be a better representation of you today? In your name, I pray. Amen."

Matt looked at his Bible, it was left open on his bedstand. He was anxious to get the hardest part of his day over with so he could spend the remainder of the day with Christine. A buggy ride to their hilltop with a picnic basket was more appealing to him than anything else he could think of, except their wedding day. They had a month to go until August 31st, and then they could spend the rest of their lives together. Matt looked forward to it, and day by day, he grew more excited about it. He had much to be thankful for.

Matt picked up his Bible and began reading the

next chapter where he had left off a few days before. Being a Christian was more than saying the right words and playing the part. It is a daily walk where time alone with Jesus in prayer, silence, and reading God's word are vital to keep from straying like a child wandering in the woods that eventually gets lost in the wilderness. It is easy to close the Bible and not pick it up for a few days, and those days turn into weeks if not months. It may not seem evident at first; mere procrastination to read the Bible *later* becomes a layer of dust coating the Lord's Word, and time in prayer becomes a cold half-hearted prayer for forgiveness at night. In the morning, the thought of praying or reading God's Word might cross one's mind, but another day of procrastination to read it *later* eventually leads to a hardened heart that does not want to read the Bible at all. Falling away from an intimate relationship with Jesus can be too easy without a church to attend and time dedicated to drawing closer to Jesus through daily reading of the Bible.

Matt had a routine of reading two chapters of the Old Testament, two chapters of the New Testament, Five psalms, and a single chapter of Proverbs every day. Reading the Bible was like a fresh mountain spring to Matt's soul. It was constantly refreshing to be nourished in the spirit like water refreshes the dehydrated body. Strength, a sense of joy, and comfort from his anxieties and worries filled him as he read. The Bible has a power that no other book in the world contains the power of God's promises and love for everyone, no matter what they have done. A man could take everything from him, including Matt's life, but the God of the Bible would never leave him. There was not a person in the world that could take the promises of God away from him.

***

Matt knocked on Holly Fairchild's hotel room door, feeling the same sickening sensation in his stomach that he always felt when he had to notify someone of a loved one's death.

Holly opened the door and stared at him with moisture thickening in her big blue eyes. "Is it true?" she asked weakly. "Is Robert really dead?" A tear trickled slowly down her cheek.

Matt nodded sadly. "It is."

Her eyes closed, and she began to weep quietly as her arms came forward to hold him. He held her as she began to sob louder and grow weaker as more weight was leaned against him. Matt casually stepped inside her room, turned as if dancing a slow waltz, and closed the door for the privacy it allowed.

He wondered how she heard the news as the telegraph line had been cut outside Hollister and not repaired yet. He remained quiet and let her mourn on his shoulder. After a few moments, she pulled away and wiped her nose and tears with a cloth handkerchief that was already in her hand.

"Is it true that he was dragged like a common thief and hung?" she asked through her tears.

Matt answered softly, "It is. I am very sorry, Holly."

She gasped and sat weakly in a padded chair. "It's my fault. If I had stayed there, it wouldn't have happened."

"No. If you had stayed there, you would have been killed, too." He sat down near her on the end of the davenport and explained all that had happened since the day Matt brought her to Branson.

She wiped a fresh tear from her cheek. "I know Laura and her family. They are such good people. Will she be okay?"

Matt shook his head sadly. "Eventually, Lord willing. She was pretty traumatized."

Holly's eyes hardened. "And that's why the sheep shooters came?"

"Yes. There is nothing left, Holly. It's all burned."

"Where is Robert's body?"

"I am having it shipped here. It should arrive tomorrow, probably."

Tears slipped down her cheek quietly. "Kent told me about Robert this morning. He said he watched it happen and did nothing to stop it. He should have done something; it is what he was hired to do." She snapped bitterly.

Matt shook his head. "I am sorry, Holly. If there is anything I can do for you, let me know."

She gazed at him sorrowfully. "What about arresting the men that killed my husband?"

Matt had been agonizing over the answer to that question, as he knew it would be asked. "All of the men that attacked your home were wearing black dusters and hoods over their faces. I asked Kent if he could identify any of them, and he said no. You know as well as I do that if I arrested Gunther and the sheriff, thirty to forty, maybe fifty people would swear they were somewhere else. I found that out trying to find the man that killed Wes Wasson. I have no proof, evidence, or solid ground to make an arrest. It's very frustrating, but no one in Hollister will tell me anything, and I have nothing to go on. Probably every man in town is guilty, but until someone feels like they can talk to me, I can't do anything."

"So, they get away with it!" she snapped bitterly with hardened blue eyes.

Matt nodded. "Unfortunately, for now. I hope someone up there will be haunted by knowing the truth and come forward, and then I can make an arrest. But until then, I have no witnesses. Even your servants, who were allowed to leave, could not identify anyone. I asked about horses, boots, brands, anything that would help identify any of the men, but your servants were too scared to notice anything that would help."

"Where are the servants? Were any of them hurt?"

"No. None of them were hurt at all. They are coming here. I told them where you were and gave them money to buy passage on a stage."

"Thank you."

"You're welcome."

There was a knock on the door.

"I don't know who that would be. If it's William

and David, ask them to come back tomorrow. Today is not a good day," she said, not feeling like having company.

Matt opened the door expecting his cousin, but Kent Kruse stood at the door with a vase of wildflowers he had picked from the countryside.

"Matt?" Kent said with surprise. "I wasn't expecting you to be here until later. Well, I came to see Holly. I'm assuming she's here."

"She is."

Kent stepped in the door and approached Holly with the vase. "I picked you some flowers."

Holly's eyes burned into him sorely. She stood and shouted emotionally, "Take your flowers and go give them to a whore! You should have tried to protect Robert! Matt would have; he would have stood his ground and tried to save my husband. But you hid like a coward. I want you to leave and don't come back!" Her lips quivered with emotion.

Kent was taken aback by her anger. "Holly, I would have been killed too. Don't you understand? I had no chance; I didn't have a weapon. I fell asleep in the boat. What could I do?" Kent asked.

"Matt, make him leave. Leave now!" she shouted.

Kent set the vase on a table. "I didn't have a choice, Holly." He turned and asked Matt, "Did you find Jesse and Cass?"

Matt nodded. "Jesse is in my jail, and Cass is in a box."

Kent tapped Matt's arm approvingly. "Well, at least there is a bit of justice in there somewhere for someone."

When Kent left, Holly said, "I own that property up there now, and I'm going to rebuild it just like it was. If I must hire a thousand men, I will do it to make sure that the woolen mill is built and that valley becomes the sheep capital of Oregon. It's the least I could do for Robert and his legacy. He had one dream, Matt, to build the Fairchild Woolen Mill and have his name cemented in with bricks. I will see it gets done and Robert is never forgotten." She sniffled and wiped her nose. "I'd like to be alone for a while."

"You know where to find me if you need me," Matt said.

"Yes." She added quickly, "Matt, before you go, do you think Jesse Helms would feel anything if I asked him how he felt about my husband being killed because of him?"

Matt shook his head. "No. Jesse wouldn't feel a thing. He'd just make you feel worse."

"I'm sad enough already. I'm going to need a friend, Matt. I hope you and Christine are true."

Matt smiled empathetically. "We're here for you."

Chapter 35

A single gunshot sounded the alarm at the Big Z Ranch. Charlie Ziegler's stern green eyes shifted to the worried expression of Eli Barso, who stood with his father, Johnny, and the Willow Falls Sheriff, Tom Smith. Eli had informed Charlie two days before that Vince and Tad Sperry were getting a small gang together to round up a few head of Big Z stock from the western range and drive them to Branson to sell. Tad Sperry had recruited Eli to help, and Charlie encouraged Eli to play along and keep him informed.

Eli told Tad and Vince where the cattle were and when the ranch hands would be away from the grazing herd. It had been several hours since the inexperienced rustlers cut out six cows and pushed them west across the unsettled areas of the valley to avoid being seen from the roads and homesteads. Eli had informed Charlie and the others that Vince planned on taking the cattle before sunrise that morning. Eli had come to work expecting to find Vince and the other three fellas of his newly formed gang tied up and waiting for the law, but they were nowhere in sight, and he was told to get back to cleaning stalls like any other day.

Now, hours later, Adam Bannister and his ranch hands were returning with four young men with their hands tied uncomfortably to their saddle horns while being led into the heart of the Big Z Ranch to face Charlie Ziegler and the law after being caught rustling six head.

Vince Sperry, the overweight and oldest of the rustlers, put on a sour face, but his eyes could not hide the fear of being caught and taken to the Big Z homestead. Near him rode his teenage nephew, Tad Sperry, who appeared more angry than afraid. Behind them rode another teenager from Natoma named Booger Krebs. Booger's actual name was Caleb, but due to a dark mole at the edge of his right nostril, he had always been known as Booger. He was the nineteen-year-old stepson of Jerrick Helms, who managed the Helms Dairy for his father.

The fourth young man was a seventeen-year-old friend of Tad's named Scotty Dixon, the son of Walter Dixon, who worked for Crawford Farms. The teens all appeared nervous, but Scotty was already in tears, fearful of his father finding out about the crime he had foolishly partaken in. His father had warned him not to make friends with Tad and Booger, and now he was facing the consequences of not listening to his parents. He didn't know if the result would be being hung from a sturdy tree or sentenced to years in prison. The only thing Scotty did know was he was scared to death.

Behind the four rustlers rode Nathan Pierce and a pair of newly hired ranch hands named Jordie and Paul, who led two hearty beeves by lead ropes.

Charlie Ziegler stepped out of the barn to meet Adam at the corral of the old barn. His green eyes scanned the four young men severely. "What did you find, Adam?"

"A group of fools mostly." Adam was already standing beside his horse and untied a branding iron from behind the cantle. He handed it to Charlie. "They branded over two of our brands and had the third heifer ready to brand when we found them camped about five miles out on the flat and half a mile from the river. They took six; the other four are back with the herd."

Charlie looked at the branding iron and then at the burned flesh of the two heifers. The large half-inch breadth of the iron covered the thin Z brand very well. "Steven made this brander. I see his mark." He looked at Scotty Dixon weeping with a stern glare. He spoke coldly, "Tears, son, don't move me."

"I'm sorry," Scotty apologized with a high-pitched voice. "I never wanted to do this. Please believe me, Mister Ziegler. It was Tad's idea."

"Shut up, Scotty!" Tad shouted.

Charlie walked around the front of the four rustlers and raised the branding iron. "You won't do it again; I can promise you all that." He looked at Adam. "Tie them to the fence with their backs exposed. I'll grab my whip."

Overhearing Charlie, Sheriff Tom Smith said, "Charlie, I'll take them to the jail and file charges."

Vince Sperry's eyes widened at the sheriff's words. He knew the county judge gave harsh penalties for such thievery. Vince had seen what prison had done to his older brother Alan and knew Alan was much tougher than him. The idea of going to prison sent a chill up his spine; he nearly choked over Tom's words.

Charlie's tone was definite, "We're not filing any charges, Tom. We'll handle this ourselves. They were caught on my land stealing my cattle. I believe I have the right to punish them. And even if not, I'm still doing it." He pointed towards Adam and the others. "Tie them to the rails, knees and hands. I'll be back."

"Charlie, you know I have to arrest them," Tom argued. He and his deputy were not invited to be there by Charlie but were informed of the pending theft by Eli's father, deputy Johnny Barso.

"Tom, when we're done, you can arrest them if you think it's necessary. But I'm guessing they'll learn their lesson by then." Charlie walked purposely towards the original barn, where he kept his whip hanging in the tack room.

Adam spoke to his hired hands, "Well, you heard the big boss. Let's get these idiots tied to the rails. Tie them up tight." He began to free Vince's hands from the saddle horn and paused to grin at Vince. "I suppose this would be a good time for you to show me a thing or two about fighting. I know you mentioned that a few times in the past." He jerked Vince out of the saddle and let him fall to the ground. "Oops, I didn't see you falling, Vince." He chuckled as he pulled Vince to his feet and shoved him towards the corral.

"Sheriff," Scotty pleaded, "You can't let him whip us. Mister Ziegler's not serious, is he?" he asked as Marvin Aggler as Paul Hubb tied his wrists to the top rail of the corral. Paul knelt and tied the boy's knees against the bottom rail. The same was being done to Tad and Booger.

Tom shrugged his shoulders helplessly. "Charlie's right. You are on his property, rustling his cattle and branding his beeves. But I know your father, Scotty, and I don't think Charlie could whip you as hard as your father will when he finds out what you did."

Scotty began to bluster as the tears fell down his cheek.

"Eli!" Marvin shouted towards the old barn over the sniffling and blubbering of Scotty. "Grab me that spool of twine out of the tool room and bring it here."

Tad glared at Eli as he carried a spool of twine out to Marvin. Tad spoke bitterly, "You should be tied up too! You're the one that told us where the cows were and when to get them." He turned to Adam. "He should be whipped too, if not more so. It was his idea all along! Huh?" he asked Booger.

Marvin grabbed the back of Tad's blond hair and pulled it backward harshly. "Don't lie, son; it's unbecoming of a thief to lie. No, I guess they go together like pigs and dung. They're the same thing in my view."

"Don't call me *son*, you old goat's ass!" Tad shouted.

Marvin smiled a crooked smile. "You remember that when I get a crack of that whip on your soft skin." He chuckled. "Troublemakers like you are nothing more than a little extra boot grease to be wiped away."

"I'll polish your boots with your blood, old man!" Tad exclaimed with fierce determination in his eyes.

Marvin slammed Tad's face down against his tied hands effectively. "Keep talking. Here comes Charlie now. You'll be weeping like a baby before you know it, tough boy."

"Never!" Tad hissed with flaming eyes.

Marvin chuckled with his crooked grin. "You have spunk but no brains. Charlie, is it okay with you if I get the first crack at the tough boy here?"

Charlie tossed Marvin the leather bullwhip. "Have at it."

The four young men's shirts were ripped open, exposing the white flesh of their backs.

Marvin tested the bullwhip out in the air. The loud and intimidating sound of the whip's sharp crack made Scotty Dixon cry out with alarm. "Get ready to cry like a baby, tough boy," Marvin taunted.

The first strike of the ten-foot whip cracked with a loud snap leaving a long and thin red welt across the smooth skin of Tad's back. He flinched abruptly and arched his back as far as his tied arms and knees allowed him. He grunted painfully with a clenched jaw and tried to break the bonds that held him, but he refused to cry out.

Marvin swung the whip again, leaving an echo of the loud crack to flow across the ranch. Another stinging welt rose across Tad's pale white skin. Tad grunted with the agonizing pain. His eyes watered, and his breaths were short and labored, but he refused to open his mouth.

Scotty sobbed at the sound of the whip while Booger hyperventilated with the terror of expecting to be lashed soon. Vince breathed through his mouth as his chest rose and fell anxiously as he watched his nephew endure the tormenting pain.

Marvin struck again and again to a total of seven lashes, one for each cow they had taken and one extra strike of the whip for branding two of the cows. At the end of seven lashes, Tad's body quivered in pain as if it was cold. The whip left seven well-defined welts crisscrossing and broke the skin in a few places where the welts overlayed. Tad's eyes watered as tears flowed down his cheeks, but he turned his head back and glared at Marvin, his mouth clenched in a tight snarl. In his hate-filled eyes was the victory of refusing to give Marvin the satisfaction of crying out. He sneered as he said through a pain-induced quivering voice, "My grandma has beaten me worse than that, old man."

Marvin was impressed by the boy's grit and determination, despite the pain that he was clearly in. Marvin chuckled appreciatively and handed the whip to Adam to whip Vince next.

Adam practiced a swing with the whip a few times to get the sharp crack to sound just right. He didn't have the same experience working with a whip that Charlie and Marvin had over the years.

Charlie said, "Don't crack it like you would a towel. Don't pull your wrist back like that; twist your wrist like you're skipping a stone or throwing a rock. Point your wrist where you want it to go and let the whip do the work."

After a few more practice tries, Adam got the whip to snap with a loud crack that was nearly as loud as a gunshot. He tried it again with the same result. Scotty Dixon began to sob loudly with fear of being lashed.

Adam took his place behind Vince. "Vince, let's see if you're as tough as your nephew. I may hit harder than Marvin, though. Let's see." He swung the whip overhand, and to everyone's surprise, he directed the leather across Tad's punished back. The crack was sharper, louder, and harder than any Marvin had swung, and it brought forth a scream from Tad that could not be silenced as he broke into loud, uncontrollable sobs.

Adam nodded with satisfaction. "I guess he's not so tough."

Vince began to curse at Adam, but a crack of the whip on Vince's skin changed his bitter cursing to a loud cry of anguish. A touch of blood dotted the skin with the growing welt as the echoing crack faded in the distance.

"That's one," Adam said. "You only have seven more to go. I think you should get an extra lashing for leading these boys into trouble." Adam swung the whip as hard as he could. The sharp crack and bellowing cry made Tom Smith's ears ring. He turned away, not wanting to watch the punishing whip in Adam's quickly accomplished hand.

***

Mary Ziegler stayed in the house and cringed with every cry of Vince's pain and the anxious sobbing of the two younger teens. Annie Lenning also sat in the house with her children, not favorable of allowing them to watch the whippings. Annie could tolerate many things and believed in punishment for crimes but hearing the whip's high-pitched crack sent chills down her spine. She preferred not to watch.

Mary covered her ears to block Vince's screams. "I remember one other time that Charlie and Darius whipped a man for trying to steal a horse. It was horrible. Darius was much stronger then and much meaner than he is now; same with your uncle, though. They had no mercy on that man. Ten hard lashes they gave him."

Annie frowned. "I never heard a story like that."

"Oh yes. Coincidently, that horse thief was a Sperry too. It was their father, Albert Sperry. That was years ago, before you were ever born. Albert Sperry was a thief, a drunk, and a good friend of your father's. He either left or disappeared about fifteen years ago or so. Mattie Sperry and Gerry both say Albert ran away, but there are rumors that he disappeared at the hands of his brother-in-law, Gerry Helms. I don't know which is true."

"I knew my father was friends with theirs, but I didn't know they were good friends," Annie said. She cringed with another high-pitched crack of the whip and a scream from Vince. Adam seemed to be taking his time to finish the lashes. "I wonder how proud he would be of his children now?"

Mary exhaled heavily. "Those poor Sperry kids never had a chance in life. Annie, there was a time when I would have taken all of them kids in. Believe it or not, that Jannie Sperry was once a beautiful and sweet little girl. She was truly a beautiful girl, but her mother is a Helms, and they are a rough family. Mattie ruined all those kids, and now her grandkids."

Annie listened. "I've met Mattie. She's quite a woman," she said sarcastically. She closed her eyes and flinched as another loud crack of the whip brought a loud cry of pain.

"Oh! I hate listening to this!" Mary shouted and stood up to pace the floor. The deep bellowing of Vince Sperry made her cringe. She looked out the window and watched Adam move from Vince past Tad to stand behind Booger Krebs, who was already pleading with loud sobs not to be whipped.

Mary burst out the door and jogged towards the corral for the first time in years. She slowed to a stop after a short distance and lifted her hands to her mouth to yell, "Charlie!" She began jogging again, "Charles Ziegler!" she shouted.

Adam moved behind Booger and paused as he watched his aunt hurrying towards them.

"Charlie," Mary called again to get his attention as she got closer. "You need to stop whipping those kids! They are terrified enough; can't you see that?" The anger on her face was fierce.

"I'm not whipping them; Adam is," Charlie explained softly. "And you shouldn't be running. You could trip and hurt yourself."

"You know what I mean. Look at them! Those boys are terrified. They'll never do anything like this again. You've already terrified the beans out of them."

"Sweetheart, they need to be punished," Charlie explained.

"Terror is punishment enough!" Mary shouted. "Give them a little bit of mercy and take them to their fathers or hand them to Tom. But do not whip those two young boys! Adam, put that whip down!" she hollered.

Charlie gazed at his wife and relinquished to her wishes. "Adam, cut them loose."

Adam frowned. "How about just one crack at each of them to let them know what to expect the next time?"

"No!" Mary demanded. "Do as you're told, Adam. Tom, can you take those two boys to their fathers and tell them how lucky their sons are?"

Tom Smith was happy to oblige. The whippings had been brutal and made him cringe to have to watch. "Yes, I will gladly do that."

"Thank you." Mary walked behind Vince and gasped at the blood on his back trickling down his skin and the horrible welts on Tad's. She cast a stern glare at Adam. "When was enough, Adam?"

Adam coiled the whip. "Seven lashes each. One for each cow they stole and one for the branding iron. Big boy there got an extra lashing for leading the boys into a life of crime."

Mary's temper boiled. "Cut them loose right now!"

"Fine. Nathan cut their binds," Adam said as he took a position between Scotty and Booger. "You boys are lucky my aunt wanted to spare your backs. Don't ever step on our land again." When their hands were cut free, Adam grabbed both boys by the side of their heads and slammed them together with a quick flash of his hands. Both boys fell to the ground rubbing their heads.

"Adam!" Mary seethed.

"It was an accident, Aunt Mary. I saw a bee and didn't want them getting stung."

Marvin couldn't resist but chuckle. He turned his head to see Tad Sperry glaring at him with a devilish stare. Marvin nodded with a lopsided grin. "You might want to sleep on your belly tonight, kid."

Chapter 36

Matt adored his fiancé, and as he listened to Christine talk with excitement, he shifted in his seat to put his full attention on her. They were having dinner with Morton Sperry and Audrey Butler in a quiet corner of the Monarch Restaurant. Matt had bathed that morning, changed into some clean clothes, and was refreshed and ready for a few quiet days before being the Best Man at Morton and Audrey's wedding on Saturday. The business around Hollister wasn't finished; they would go back to Hollister in a week or so to investigate further the murder of Wes Wasson and the massacre at the Fairchild Estate. He thought it was best to let a few days pass to allow the tempers to settle and guilt to build on the consciences of at least one or two of the men involved. But for now, to be with Christine was all he wanted to do.

Christine had much to tell Matt as well. He loved the childlike expressions she would use when she was excited. He watched appreciatively as she said, "Remember how I used to get to sing at the dance hall last Fall? I get to do it again this Saturday night." She extended her flat palms towards Morton and Audrey. "I know you two are getting married on Saturday, but I have to sing on Saturday night. So, I've been practicing the pieces of music we'll be doing. Isaac, the new fiddle player in the dance hall band, tuned the piano, and it sounds even better than it did last year. Isaac will be playing the fiddle and banjo on a couple of songs. He's singing a couple of songs with me too. He's so talented. It will be so much fun."

Matt said with a sparkle in his eyes, "That's wonderful. I look forward to listening. I hope you sing that song that you wrote for me." He knew how much she enjoyed opportunities to play piano and sing.

"I will if you are there."

"Of course, I'll be there." Matt dipped his biscuit in the gravy of his mashed potatoes and took a bite.

Audrey asked, "They don't let you sing very often?"

Christine wiped her mouth with a cloth napkin. "The dance hall doesn't make money when I sing. It takes time away from the other girls and me dancing. Occasionally Bella asks if I could sing a song or two, but this is one full hour of singing. My grandmother taught me how to play the piano. She and I would sit on the piano bench and play while singing hymns to the audience of my grandfather. I sure miss singing with her and my grandfather's appreciation of it."

Audrey gazed at her with interest. "I love to play and sing too. That's our wedding night, but Morton and I can go there to listen and have our first dance to your singing."

Christine wrinkled her nose. "Women are not allowed into the dance hall unless you're a dancer. It's for men only. But if you were to come with Matt and Morton, no one would say anything. And I'll let Bella and Dave know in advance if you decide you want to come listen."

Morton offered a slight smile. "What if Audrey wants to become a dancer? Can you get her a job?"

Audrey slapped his arm playfully with a light laugh. "I'm not near pretty enough to be a dancer like Christine."

"Oh, yes, you are," Morton argued.

"You're very pretty," Christine stated.

"Thank you," Audrey said awkwardly. She didn't consider herself overly pretty, but the words were nice to hear. She told Matt, "I admitted to Christine that I originally didn't think too highly of her because she worked in a dance hall. You know, because dancers, hurdy-gurdies, and saloon girls don't have very wholesome reputations in some places, but I've never been exposed to it, so I only know what I've heard. I'm humbled to say my judgment was very wrong. Christine is a wonderful newly found friend. And I am so thankful for the life and friends that the Lord has led me to. I am so thankful."

Christine pointed at her with a nod of agreement. "Me too. I told you how I ended up working for Bella. I will always be thankful to Jesus for bringing Bella and Dave into my life. They gave me a life when mine seemed over and brought me here." She smiled at Matt. "Where I met the man who I'm going to spend the rest of my life with."

Audrey's sincerity showed in her eyes. "Amen! Praise the Lord for how he cared and blessed you when you needed him the most. It always amazes me to hear stories like yours and how God arranges the most unexpected blessings just when everything looks the bleakest. As I told you, my father is a preacher, so growing up, I heard many stories about God's timing and miraculous interventions to bless his children. And now, I have my own story to tell."

Christine nodded in agreement. "Yes, you do! The Lord is always faithful."

Audrey said with a laugh, "However, if it was me in your shoes, I'd be panhandling on a corner or digging out privy pits because I can't dance well at all. I'm as clumsy as a drunken horse, and you'll see that for yourself when Morton and I dance after our wedding. I'll probably break his toes right there while you're singing. If he starts hollering in pain on the dance floor, you'll know exactly why."

Morton chuckled. "I doubt that. I've had horses step on my toes and they aren't broken yet."

Matt was never comfortable sitting with his back to the door or with a window behind him, so he always sat facing the restaurant door. His interest rose when he watched his cousin William Fasana enter the restaurant, followed by Lee Bannister.

The expressions on their faces revealed there was something very wrong and concerning. A bad feeling swept up Matt's spine.

William handed a note out to Matt. "Read it now; it's urgent. It's the third wire today. This one was sent to me. I already replied for you."

Anxiety suddenly filled Matt's chest tenfold as he opened the telegraph and read the words. His breath escaped him, and he slumped forward in horror.

Lee spoke quickly, "I have arranged for you and William to take my coach and will have spare horses waiting at every stop along the way to get you there quicker."

"What is it?" Christine asked, taking the note from Matt's hand. "Oh no! Oh Lord, no."

Morton reached out his hand to take the note.

Matt spoke with a shaken voice, "Audrey, you're going to have to cancel your wedding this weekend because I need Truet here for Jesse Helms's court arraignment. I'm taking Morton with me." He looked at Lee. "When is the soonest we can leave?"

"First thing in the morning. Tonight, if you want."

Matt spoke to Morton. "Get a bag packed. We're leaving tonight. You too, William."

"What is it?" Audrey asked with concern. She took the note and read the words that came from Matt's father in Portland:

William,
Tell Matt,

Come quick
Gabriel and Evan are missing.

"Who are…" she began to ask.

"Gabriel is Matt's sixteen-year-old son," Christine replied before Audrey could finish. "He went to Portland to visit his grandfather and is apparently now missing. Let's pray," Christine said. "And then you need to go, Matt." Her beautiful brown eyes filled with frightened tears. "Bring your son home."

Acknowledgments

First and foremost, I must thank my wife, Cathy, for always being encouraging and supportive. Thank you for always listening. It means a lot. My son Keith is the first to read anything I write. I appreciate his honesty, criticism, and suggestions—a few of them I added to this story. His opinion and constant encouragement are greatly appreciated. I am blessed with a very supportive family—Jessica and Chris, Chevelle, Katie and Isaiah. Thank you.

I also want to thank Patience Bramlett and the folks at CKN Christian Publishing, who work hard to make the Matt Bannister Series not just available, but possible. They have my highest appreciation and respect.

A Look At:

When The Wolf Comes Knocking

Some wolves attack when their prey is at its weakest. Some charge fiercely. Others...knock softly.

When Greg Slater returned home from college for winter break, his whole world changed. After rescuing his high-school sweetheart, Tina Dibari, and helping sentence his best friend, Rene Dibari, to life in prison, Greg fell in love for the first time.

Fifteen years later, life isn't easy, but Greg and Tina are working on their marriage. But an old fear has come back to haunt them...

Rene has escaped prison, and he's thirsty for revenge.

As shocking truths unfold, Greg and Tina face a ripple in their faith and in their home. Tina starts doubting her faith and seeks comfort in a friend with lustful intentions. Meanwhile, Greg struggles to navigate this new unrest in their relationship.

Unfortunately, evil stops for no one, and three very different wolves are after the Slater family.

Will Greg and Tina's love be enough to keep them together, and—more importantly—will their faith hold true when the wolves come knocking?

AVAILABLE NOW ON AMAZON

About the Author

Ken Pratt and his wife, Cathy, have been married for 22 years and are blessed with five children and six grandchildren. They live on the Oregon Coast where they are raising the youngest of their children. Ken Pratt grew up in the small farming community of Dayton, Oregon. Ken worked to make a living, but his passion has always been writing. Having a busy family, the only "free" time he had to write was late at night getting no more than five hours of sleep a night. He has penned several novels that are being published along with several children's stories as well.

www.ingramcontent.com/pod-product-compliance
Lightning Source LLC
Chambersburg PA
CBHW011420010726
47494CB00011B/2435